Praise for Catherine Landi[s]

"A remarkable tale of a special f[...] refreshing new voice. . . . [Ruth] c[...] of Huck Finn, who went looking f[...]"
—*The Atlanta Journal-Constitution*

"Vivid . . . the author [has] an admirably individual style."
—*Dallas Morning News*

"The perfect beach read."
—*Marie Claire*

"*Some Days There's Pie* is a standout effort by an author to watch. It's the kind of novel that book clubs will devour, for it will definitely prompt provocative discussions. I advise reading it with pen in hand so you can mark the many meaty pundits the author has coined. Landis bowled me over with her marvelous book, and I can't wait for her next one."
—*Chattanooga Times Free Press*

"This is a lovely book. While it depicts the pettiness of small towns, it also illuminates the kindness of strangers to a strange girl who needs time to grow and become kind to herself."
—*The News & Record* [Greensboro, NC]

"Both Ruth and Rose are stunning characters, drawing on the traditions of genre mavens Lee Smith and Jill McCorkle. Landis's Rose brings dignity to a class of older Southern women usually depicted as porch-dwelling gossips . . . a treat. One can only hope that there's more of this talent waiting to be served."
—*Macon Telegraph*

"Chock full of colorful characters: boozing boarding-house neighbors, newspaper Lotharios, compromised politicians, and a burned-out poet who writes graffiti. But there is no more original character than Rose, an uncompromising but compassionate person. . . . This is an outstanding first novel, full of insight, pathos, and what Rose might call 'hard sayings.' Like her character, Rose, Landis is digging for the truth, and she nails it time and time again."
—*The Roanoke Times* [VA]

"Together, Ruth and Rose draw strengths from each other. Tennessee author Catherine Landis subtly develops the relationship between these women at different stages of life. Ruth and Rose do the best they can amid disappointment, failed dreams, and acts of forgiveness."

—Southern Living

"Ruth's endearing first-person narration captures the head-on realistic approach to life's disappointments with which many hard-knock Southerners confront adversity. . . . Landis has a keen eye for detail, a highly tuned ear for Southernisms, and a wry sense of humor."

— Metro Pulse [Knoxville]

"An unforgettable story that's about as Southern as one can get. An inspiring, heart-warming story that's filled with an engaging cast of characters. . . . Here's to Ruth and Rose, two women who dared enough to believe that by pursuing dreams, they could make them come true."

—The Sanford Herald [Sanford, NC]

"Alternately wise, poignant, droll, and sassy, this debut charts the life-changing friendship of two singular Southern women. . . . [Landis] could take off as a voice of the modern but eternally quirky South."

—Publishers Weekly

"Landis's debut novel reads like a tougher version of Fannie Flag; fans of Southern literature will surely appreciate this wry and clear-eyed tribute to the power of friendship."

—Booklist

"It's rare to find a narrator with a personality so vivid she might really have existed, but Catherine Landis offers one spirited and believable character after another in *Some Days There's Pie*. She has achieved what every fiction reader craves: emotional delicacy, sophistication, a powerful sense of place. This is a standout first novel."

—Arthur Golden, author of Memoirs of a Geisha

SOME
DAYS
THERE'S
PIE

SOME
DAYS
THERE'S
PIE

CATHERINE LANDIS

ST. MARTIN'S GRIFFIN
NEW YORK

To my mother,
Charlotte Walker Landis

www.stmartins.com

Library of Congress Cataloging-in-Publication Data

Landis, Catherine E.
     Some days there's pie / Catherine E. Landis.—1st ed.
          p. cm.
     ISBN 0-312-28384-9 (hc)
     ISBN 0-312-30929-5 (pbk)
     1. Women—North Carolina—Fiction. 2. Female friendship—Fiction. 3. Women journalists—Fiction. 4. North Carolina—Fiction. 5. Terminally ill—Fiction. 6. Young women—Fiction. 7. Aged women—Fiction. I. Title.

PS3612.A548 S66 2002
813'.6—dc21   2001058853

First St. Martin's Griffin Edition: May 2003

10   9   8   7   6   5   4   3   2   1

CONTENTS

ACKNOWLEDGMENTS

For this book, I wish to thank the following:

Alicia Brooks, my editor at St. Martin's Press, for her insight, honesty, and tireless stewardship.

George Witte, editor in chief of St. Martin's Press, for his gracious support.

My agent, Henry Dunow, for his constancy and confidence in me.

Cheryl Pientka, for her perserverance and humor.

SOME
DAYS
THERE'S
PIE

1 | ON MY WAY TO THE REST OF MY LIFE

Rose is dead. I am sorry for it but not surprised; she's been dying for years now. I found her lying on the roll-away in Room 12 of the Little Swiss Inn in Mount Claire, North Carolina. It's just like Rose to have left me the double bed. *I don't want to be any trouble,* was what she said all the time, but there's a lot of people who say that kind of thing who are loads of trouble. Rose never was.

We had been driving since that morning, starting in Lawson-ville, where it was hot. It was not hot in Mount Claire. It was chilly, and I had already started worrying that this damp air was not going to do a thing for her but make her sicker. We were on our way to Texas because Rose was born in Texas, in a little town on the Gulf of Mexico, to a mother who claimed to have a little Cajun in her and a daddy who ran a printing press, which was why Rose swore she had ink in her blood. Cajun or ink, either one could account for a lot. When I met her, she was seventy-nine years old but looked older, bent over like the letter C, which made it so she peered up at you when she talked, like a turtle out of its shell, craning its neck to see the sky. Her skin was wrinkled and pale, and her voice had gone rusty from too many cigarettes.

Rose claimed she had aged early, but her hair was still the color of mountain clay; she was named for it, red on the day she was born, the only one in the family, Red Rose.

The Little Swiss Inn had no restaurant, and I had gone looking for supper. "You want to come?" I had asked Rose.

"No, Ruthie," she said. "I think I'll just lie down for a minute."

"I'll bring you back something."

"I'm not all that hungry right now, thank you."

"What do you want?"

"Whatever you get, hon. You decide."

I let it go at that, because I knew she was telling the truth. Rose did not care about food. She said she never did, and I believed her, because food and clothes and houses and all those things that keep a body together were things Rose never thought about, which can be an admirable quality in a person, but sometimes I wondered if it didn't make her do dotty things, like when she left half-eaten sandwiches on other people's desks, or buttoned her shirts up crooked. Her house reminded me of Durwood's, the hardware store next door to where I grew up, which was a mess, partly because that's what happens when something gets old, when it moves through time holding on to things, not because some things are worth holding on to, but because it takes too long to sort through them. Durwood had boxes of Christmas ornaments older than me on the shelves, but he saw no reason to buy more until those were gone. Year by year they had dwindled until there came a time when nobody wanted to hang anything that old on their Christmas tree. So there they sat, next to the hammers, which were mixed in with screwdrivers, which were mixed in with drill bits, which were mixed in with extension cords. If you were wanting nails, you had to scoop them out of a wooden keg and weigh them on a rusting scale, and there were cats everywhere. I worked over there at Durwood's, selling his wife's home-made fried pies, something you might not expect to find in a hardware store. People would come in wanting plumbing fixtures and a pie; I never got over that.

What you expected to find in a place like Durwood's was a potbellied stove in the middle of the floor, where men and near-men gathered to commiserate over the state of the world or the state of their lives, sometimes without words, just a look between fellows who know you and know what you mean. I used to imag-ine my daddy in a place like that. I used to imagine he would wink at me from across the store as if right there in Durwood's was where we belonged. I had no way of knowing if he was that kind of man, but that's how I pictured him.

Now, I never saw evidence of any such a stove in Durwood's, which tells you to look out; I'm likely to blow things up bigger than they are, but this much is true: Durwood's was a place where people went for more than what they could buy. You can go down to Kmart for a box of nails if that's all you want.

As for Rose's house, if I had suggested we straighten it up, she would have looked at me as if I'd gone crazy. Most everything she owned was given to her anyway, which was one thing about Rose; if somebody gave her something, she did not throw it away, so there were odd things, like dead house plants, and seashells sitting in little piles of sand, and the two Chinese dolls on top of the refrigerator, one jade green, the other robin's-egg blue, whose heads bobbed up and down when you opened the door. Some-times I wanted to shake her. I did not care what she wore or how she kept her house, but I hated that other people did. They had made her into a town character, the eccentric old lady, "old" being the key word, as if there is a point you can cross and lose your place in the world. Everybody loved Rose, but no one paid any attention to her anymore. People talked to her the way you talk to a child. They acted as if she were already dead.

The Little Swiss Inn was surrounded by woods with no sign of a restaurant anywhere. The office was in a trailer next to the highway, the front stoop covered with bright green indoor/outdoor carpet. I had to pry open the metal screen door and, instead of a bell, a tinny music box played the first two lines of "On Top of Old Smoky." I found the manager in the office flipping through a model-rocket catalogue. He was a large man who wore glasses too tiny for his head, and he did not look up when I walked in.

"So," I said. "Where in the world is Big Swiss?"

He frowned, stuck a finger in his page to save his place, then looked up. He did not laugh.

"Any chance of getting something to eat around here?" I asked.

"Sam's Deli. About a quarter mile down the road. They got pizza, too." He said I could walk. "No problem."

A sidewalk followed the road through the woods, crossed a large creek, then led to the town of Mount Claire. I passed a couple of gas stations, a 7-Eleven, a bank, and a post office before reaching the main part of town, where crowds of people were dressed in shorts and golf shirts, their children wearing T-shirts that said *Hilton Head* and *Grand Caymen Island* and *Ski Aspen*. They were buying corncob pipes and bird feeders and wooden bear statuettes with *Mount Claire* burned into their sides. I passed by stores that sold shuck dolls made by mountain people, which was probably true, if you were talking about the mountains of China. There was a snack shop making out like there's something so special about ice cream you had to pay three dollars a scoop to find out what it was. I didn't linger. I found Sam's Deli and bought two turkey subs and chips then stopped by the 7-Eleven. I got us some Cokes and a couple of candy bars: Butterfinger for Rose, a Bit-O-Honey for myself.

I had not wanted to stop in Mount Claire. My idea was to keep going, drive on past sundown into the night, eating up the miles in darkness. I liked that vision of myself, tough night driver, cigarettes and coffee keeping me awake, a sad song on the radio. My car did not have a radio, but that's beside the point. What I wanted was to feel like an outlaw, which was not so far-fetched since me and Rose had snuck away from Lawsonville without telling anybody. I wanted it to be me and Rose and the truck drivers and their headlights and the night sky and the sound of my wheels going faster than the speed limit, but Rose insisted she had to rest, so we stopped. If we hadn't, Mount Claire, North Carolina, would have stayed forever a tourist town I passed through once, a dot on a map that meant nothing to me.

When I got back to the room, Rose was lying on her back as if she were sleeping, but dead people don't really look like they are sleeping. There's something wrong.

"Rose?"

The only light in the room came from what spilled through the blinds, throwing stripes across the floor. They fell across the rollaway and Rose. I sat down next to her and held her hand. It was still warm enough to make you think, for a minute anyway, that what was happening wasn't really happening.

"Oh, Rose."

I sat there for a long time.

I don't know how long, but the first thing I remember noticing was the sack from Sam's Deli. I was holding it without knowing

I was holding it, when all of a sudden I looked and remembered it was there. Then I understood; Rose was dead. More than the way her arm was stiff when I shook it, more than the pulse I could not find; this simple fact: Rose was never going to eat that sandwich.

I did not know a lot of dead people, unless you want to count my daddy, but I did not remember him. I knew Marianne Johnson, a girl from school who was killed in a head-on collision with a lumber truck when she was sixteen. She had a locker near mine and once had asked to borrow my hairbrush, and I had said no. Marianne had hair that fell down her back like black satin ribbons. The strange thing was, after she died I found myself thinking about her all the time. It came to me at odd moments, like a dream that lingers in the back of your mind long past the time it should have faded away. I see the man who drove the truck. He is standing at his kitchen counter, eating a honey bun. He burns his mouth on coffee, which he drinks from a plastic travel cup as he walks out the door. It is dark still. When he pulls onto the highway I see a single stream of light, heading east. Then I see Marianne. She gets out of bed, drops her nightgown on the floor, gets dressed, and combs her satin hair. She eats nothing before getting into her small, white car, the envy of those of us who did not get cars for our sixteenth birthday. I see a single stream of light heading west, and I wonder. Was there a line between them, drawn before they were born, a line they raced along until that morning, or was it, simply, that one of them looked down to change the radio?

The part that gets to me is the nightgown. Because there is something about dropping your nightgown on the floor that says, I'm coming back.

I'm coming back.

But she didn't. Marianne Johnson was never going to pick up her nightgown, and Rose. She was never going to eat that sandwich.

It was not fair that Rose had died, and not just to her but to me, too. I am not going to pretend otherwise, because it is the truth. No matter what happens to somebody else, you are still thinking about what's happening to you, and what had happened to me was that the first purely noble thing I had ever done in my life had just come to an end.

2 | THERE MUST BE FIFTY WAYS

I never would have met Rose if I had not run off and married Chuck Allen Pirkle. I came close to telling Rose I married Chuck Allen because he was the best-looking boy in Tennessee, but Rose had already told me she married the best-looking boy in Texas, and I did not want her to think I was a copycat, although in her case it may have been true. I'd seen pictures. But the truth was, I married Chuck because he was leaving Summerville, and leaving Summerville was the exact thing I had wanted to do all my life.

Summerville, Tennessee, is where I'm from, although that's not its real name, just what people call the west end of Beaver Ridge. Our house was the only one on the highway next to Lonnie's Kwik Pik, the Esso station, and Durwood's Hardware, where my daddy worked until he died. Mr. Durwood Jones lived in a big house on thirty acres of land where he kept horses. The story was, he used to pick Daddy up at the hardware store and take him over there to cut grass, paint walls, move furniture, build decks, or work in the barn, and he must have been good at such things, because Mr. Jones would sometimes point to a deck or the toolshed behind the hardware store and say, *Your daddy built that,* like he was wanting me to be proud of something. In exchange for this work, Mr. Jones gave us our house, a small frame house, painted green, with a black tar roof, next to the store. It had four rooms plus a bathroom, a narrow porch across the front, and a flat, shady yard that backed into several acres of woods. I loved this house a long time before I was ashamed of it. My mama did not tell me how we got our house; it was my sister Margaret who did, but I don't know how she knew.

Mr. Jones used to brag about how he had no use for rich people, even though he seemed rich enough to me, and he liked to call himself a country boy, even though he was a long way from being a boy. It had to be some kind of talent, too, to be able to lean against the counter and say to men in cashmere sweaters that, *What's wrong with this country is people like you,* and have them nodding and grinning just because part of what was so great about going to Durwood's was Durwood himself. He wore work pants and work boots and a work shirt all the same sort of tan color, which was no color, like horse feed or dirt. His wife, Mabel, worked with him behind the cash register when she was not making the fruit pies, which she shaped into half-moons and fried and dusted with powdered sugar. Among the regular customers, those pies were one more reason to go to Durwood's. She brought her mother, Ida, whose mind was gone. They tied her to a wheelchair with the sash of a velveteen bathrobe and set her in the corner, where she stared at people and drooled, and if anyone asked, that's what they said. *Her mind is gone.* I was scared of Ida, but not nearly so much as I was of Mabel, a sturdy, grim-faced woman who was hard to tease. She was a lot like my mama, only Mama did smile some.

Summerville started out as a place where people came to escape the summer heat, which was how it got its name, and most days you could count on it being cooler up there by about ten degrees. The summer people built their houses along the edge of the ridge overlooking the city, and on a good day the view stretched all the way to Georgia. They stayed away from the rest of Beaver Ridge, where quarry men and loggers and moonshiners had been living since their great-great-granddaddies had climbed up the mountain years before, but somebody along the way must have figured it out. You put heat in those summer houses, you can live there all year, and the town of Summerville grew from there. The bigger it grew, the more it shoved the quarry men and loggers and moonshiners to the back of the mountain to make room for subdivisions, grocery stores, drugstores, dry cleaners, schools, churches, restaurants, ball fields, swimming pools, and golf courses. It must have happened fast, because when Mama and Daddy first lived there, Durwood's was the only store for miles, the highway was a two-lane road, and there was still a community of people who had known my daddy when he was a boy. But I never saw that place. The Summerville that's there today is the only one I ever knew.

My mama ironed other people's clothes. I suspected that we had more in common with the people who lived on the back of Beaver Ridge, yet there we were, in the middle of Summerville, alongside people who looked down on us. So I looked down on us, too. I tried to figure out why Mama did this to us, why we did not simply pick up and move where we belonged, but when I asked her, she only snapped, "Whose clothes do you think I would iron then?" Mama would just as soon get snakebit as answer any one of my questions, but she was right. At least she had a job; we had a place to live, and there was Durwood, who was all the time saying he owed it to my daddy to make sure we were okay. If somebody were to hand you the kind of life my Mama had, you would find there are not so many choices. My sister would not have wanted to move anyway. Margaret liked living in Summerville.

Mama's people came from Alabama. Her father was a tenant farmer. Her mother died when she was a young girl, leaving her to grow up with eleven brothers and sisters in a three-room shack in the middle of a treeless yard of crabgrass and red clay and ants. I knew about the ants because I stepped in a nest of them the one time she took us there. We left Summerville before dawn and drove for four hours without hardly stopping except for my brother, William, who whimpered to go to the bathroom every twenty minutes. Mama would tighten her grip on the steering wheel and say, *We aren't stopping,* but that would only make him whimper louder.

Hush. You can hold it.

Then William would start bouncing up and down in the back-seat, and his whimpering would turn to crying. William was twelve years old at the time, but he had the mind of a three-year-old and always would. I was nine and took William's side. *He can't hold it, Mama.*

Hush, the both of you, she would say, but she'd be pulling over anyway. I would get out with William to make sure he did not run out in the road, while Mama and Margaret stayed in the front seat, staring straight out the windshield as if they were still driving in their minds. Mama would not turn off the engine in case it quit. We drove a sun-bleached tan Chevrolet Impala that we'd had when Daddy was still alive. Anytime it broke down, Durwood fixed it, but there wasn't any Durwood on the way to Alabama.

We were going there to get Mama's silver bracelet. We had

heard about this bracelet all our lives, about how her mother had given it to her before she died, and how stupid she had been to leave it behind the day she ran off with Daddy. *You ought to go get it, Mama*, Margaret would tell her. *It's yours by right.* Mama always claimed she couldn't set foot down there as long as her daddy was still alive, but now he was dead, and Margaret, at thirteen, was more insistent than ever.

"Just go down there and tell them it's yours."

"I ought to."

"Don't let them tell you, no. It's yours by right."

"Don't I know it!"

I didn't care about the bracelet. I could not picture it on Mama's arm, and even though she said we could all take turns wearing it, I could not see it on me either. Still, the excitement was catching, the closer we got, because I had always wanted to see what it was like down there in Alabama. I was also anxious to see what Mama would do. The Mama I was used to was a woman who took in ironing from people who never looked at her, who said, *Yes ma'am,* to women younger than she was, who chewed on her fingernails when somebody complained about their shirts being folded instead of on hangers. But here was somebody marching down to Alabama like you better clear the way or else. It was hard not to think something had changed.

We turned off the highway onto the driveway of an old farmhouse that looked like it could use some paint. I was disappointed. A chain was broken on the front porch swing and some of the latticework was chipped, but the house was bigger than I had imagined, and there were flowers in the front yard and white lace curtains in the windows.

"That's not it," Mama said, and she kept driving until the driveway turned into a narrow, deeply rutted, dirt road. After a particular nasty scrape against the bottom of the Impala, Mama said, "Forget it," and stopped the car and made us walk the rest of the way. It was so hot, I thought I was going to choke. William was crying; I stepped in a nest of ants, and we were all soaked through with sweat when finally we reached the rusting trailer that had replaced the house where Mama had grown up. She said it was an improvement. But when we found out there was no bathroom, only an outhouse baking in the sun, Margaret, who had been holding it so she would not have to go by the side of the road, started crying too.

The only one still living there was one of Mama's younger brothers, Ricky, who had been a little boy when Mama had last seen him. A woman, his wife we guessed, was the one who greeted us, arms crossed over pillow-sized bosoms. We never got her name. "It ain't here," she said, when Mama described the bracelet.

"Is Glen around?" Mama asked. Glen had been Mama's favorite brother, the only one we had ever heard her speak of by name.

"Glen's in Mobile. Or Houston." She shouted through the door to someone inside the house. "Where is it Glen went to?"

"How the hell should I know?" came a man's voice from the darkness. The faces of three children were pressed up against the screen of the trailer door.

"We don't know where Glen is."

Margaret stepped in front of Mama. "You sold it, didn't you?"

But the woman did not look at Margaret. She narrowed her eyes at Mama and said, "It weren't real silver."

It was like somebody socked her. Mama's shoulders collapsed, and she turned her face away and put a hand over her belly.

"Who do you reckon was the biggest liar, your mama? She tell you it was silver, or was she another one fooled by that stingy daddy of yours?"

Mama took a step backwards, nearly tripping over William, who had coaxed a dog out from under the trailer and was lying in the dirt, petting and talking to it.

"I knew it," Margaret said.

The woman spat, and a puddle of brown landed in the dirt. "If you wanted it so bad, you shouldn't have left, Miss Priss Pants, thinking you were too good for everybody."

"It wasn't like that," Mama whispered. I was standing right next to her, or I would not have heard her.

"Too big for your britches. If you'd heard your daddy talk, you wouldn't be back here asking for no silver."

Mama was shaking her head. "I wasn't . . ."

Ricky came out of the trailer door, carrying a sack. He was a stringy-looking man with light brown hair like Margaret's. It was the first time I'd seen another person in our family with that kind of hair, because me and William were dark-headed like Mama. He smelled like gasoline. He wore a green work shirt unbuttoned all the way down with a name sewed in script letters over the breast pocket. The name said, *Earl*, but we knew it was Ricky. "Hey, Maggie," he said.

"Ricky?"

"We got RC Cola," he said. "Y'all want one?"

He jerked his head toward the trailer, indicating his wife ought to go inside and get us some drinks, then he walked toward a truck that was parked next to the trailer. He put the sack in the back of the truck and got in and drove off. Mama said, "We shouldn't have come."

Margaret was saying, "You make them hand over the money if they really did sell it. That bracelet was yours by right, and so is the money," but Mama was picking at her jagged fingernails and not listening to her.

"Let's get out of here," I said.

Mama looked at me, and there were tears in her eyes. She was not an old woman, but she looked like one to me, with strands of gray already in her hair and deep grooves on either side of her mouth that gave her face a tired, sunken look. I used to try to smooth out the wrinkle lines that crossed her forehead with the idea that she might feel better if they were gone, but that day in Alabama I decided she deserved them. Nothing was ever going to change. I don't know who was more disappointed, Mama or me.

"What if they're lying? What if they're just hiding it," Margaret was saying when I spoke up again. "Forget the bracelet, Margaret."

"What'd we come down here for then?"

"Ask her," I said, pointing to Mama, who was already walking away. I went to get William away from that dog.

"What about my RC?" Margaret yelled.

"Let's go home," Mama said.

When we got back to the car, it was missing its hubcaps, but it started. We made it home after midnight. And though Margaret brought it up for years, I never heard Mama mention the bracelet again. But ever after, if either me or Margaret complained about anything, Mama would look at us and say, *You could be in Alabama.* It was like her main weapon.

Mama's daddy had not believed in school, as if school were something you could believe in or not, although he sent four of his children there, and these four he chose at random, like God pointing a finger. Mama was not one of the four. But her brother Glen was, and he had taught her to read, which changed her life.

It's not that you would call my mama an educated person. She was educated in spots. Math, for instance; Margaret and I had to go with her to the store to keep her from being cheated, but she liked to read, almost anything it seemed like, paperbacks dropped off by some of the women who brought clothes for her to iron, mysteries by Agatha Christie, histories of the Civil War, stories about Greek mythology, anything. There was one book, a thin paperback volume of poetry called *Verses for Daily Living*, which she rolled up like a newspaper and carried with her all the time so that when she set it down, it stayed curled up. I remember watching as she would put down her iron and take *Verses for Daily Living* from the pocket, or if there was no pocket, the waistband of her pants, and curl it back on itself to straighten it, and turn to a page, and read with more emotion on her face than she ever showed to me.

When I was little, I could not wait to read, because I thought it would get me closer to Mama's world. I even learned early, before I was old enough to go to school, but it did not work. I know because once I came upon *Verses for Daily Living* lying on her bed and picked it up and tried to read the first poem. I could make out the words, although I did not understand them, but before I could ask, Mama grabbed the book out of my hands. "That's mine."

You're going to think Mama was just mean, but it's not that simple. I could tell by the startled look she got in her eyes; sometimes even she could not believe the things she said. That night I found on my pillow another book, somebody's beat-up school copy of *The Adventures of Tom Sawyer*, but who cared. I was too young for that book anyway.

My daddy grew up outside of Summerville in a wild sort of growing up, he and his five brothers practically raising themselves. Their daddy was always running off for months at a time, and there was something wrong with their mother. She was sick or something, possibly a drunk, but I don't think that was all of it, and Mama was no help. She either did not know, or else she would not say.

The story goes that Daddy and one of his brothers went down to Alabama one fall to hunt quail. They camped by a small stream near Mama's farm, and when they ran out of money, they knocked on the door of the big farmhouse. There was a barn needed fixing; they said they'd do it for enough gas money to get back home, so that's how they met, my mama and my daddy. They eyed each other for about a week before he walked up to her and said, "You ought to marry me."

She looked him over and said, "I reckon you're right."

That's all she would tell me. I tried to get more of the story out of her, but she said there was no more. Nothing buttoned up my mama tighter than a question.

When Mama left Alabama, her daddy told her, don't ever come back, so she didn't, not until after he died. She would not have had much of a chance anyway. From all I could tell, Mama and Daddy loved each other, but life was hard for them. It always had been hard for them, but it got harder. Right away they had Margaret, then a year later came my brother, William. They did not know anything was wrong with William until he was about two. I think it about killed my daddy. It pretty much knocked the wind out of their wanting any more children. Three years later, I had to have been a surprise.

Then one cold day in March, a horse Daddy was leading back to Durwood's barn spooked and knocked him down. Durwood said he must have hit his head on a rock, but he died, however it happened. The horse did not run off, I was told, a kind of strange fact that stayed with me as if it were some consolation. I was two years old and not, I don't think, much comfort to my mother.

But growing up without your daddy was just the kind of thing people in Summerville expected from a person like me. At school I was the only one who did not get charged for milk. I paid anyway, or else I didn't drink it.

If you were to follow the highway out of Summerville to the back end of Beaver Ridge, that's where Chuck Allen Pirkle came from, only he had left some years before to join the Navy. He ended up near a military base in Huntington, North Carolina, where he sold stereos to Marines. His store was one in a chain called Wuffer Works, and it was, if you believed Chuck Allen, ahead of its time. *This is the way sound systems will be sold in the future,* he would tell me, *except I'm doing it now.* Chuck Allen said *sound system* instead of *stereo,* but *stereo* was better than *record player.* *Never say record player,* he told me, so I didn't. You learn that some things are not worth arguing about.

He also told me never call him Chuck Allen.

Wuffer Works used what Chuck described as the warehouse method of selling. The year was 1978, and this was something new, no fancy showroom, just the goods, stacked high to make you think there is no end. Marines were good at buying sound systems. Sound systems were like second only to food to them. (They said *sound system* too. I never once heard a Marine say *record player.*) Chuck came back to Tennessee only for a funeral, his brother's, who drove himself into a tree one night on his way to pick up my sister.

I did not pay any attention to my sister's boyfriends, because they all looked the same to me. I used to get off the school bus, and there'd be one, sitting on the hood of his car, watching me walk to my front door. Margaret was four years older than me, and most of her boyfriends were older than that and should have known better. They slipped me sips of beer and told me dirty jokes and taught me to cuss. One night, I could not have been more than twelve or thirteen, I was watching television when one of them reached over and took hold of my tiny breast. He didn't try to kiss me or nothing, did not even look at me. It was one breast, one hand, as if he thought I might not notice. Who knows where Margaret was, although if I had to guess I'd say she was doing her makeup. When they're handing out prizes, that's the one she's going to get. Makeup queen.

So I hardly knew this fellow who died. James was his name. I know because my sister screamed it at the top of her lungs for three days.

"JAMES!"

I stayed out of it. But I went with her to the funeral, and there was Chuck. He was good-looking, tall and muscular, with a round face and blue eyes, and long, blond lashes that gave him a boyish look. By then I was almost 19, and working every day at Durwood's, and still living at home just like Margaret, who worked at the Red Food Store and complained all the time but never did anything about it. Chuck wore gray dress pants and a blue sports coat, white shirt, red tie, and loafers, like somebody who's gone to college and learned how to dress. It set him apart from his family. His mama kept grabbing people by their shirts and swearing she was going to sue somebody, and his daddy, smelling like a still, stumbled into a back pew of the Wilson Road Freewill Baptist Church and could not get back up. People made room for him. But Chuck gave his daddy an arm to lean on and smiled as if he truly did not mind, and I think that's what caught my eye. You're just not going to find a smile as sweet and true as Chuck's, and I don't mind saying it, even now. His hair was blond and curly and circled his head like a halo, and though he was no angel, he had that sense about him, that he would try to do right in the world, and at that moment, it was good enough for me. Chuck said he loved me for the way I laughed, which was possibly not the best thing to show off at a funeral, but why not? Some people, my sister in particular, said it was awful for us to find happiness in the middle of so much sorrow, but she would have done the same thing. We got married in a courthouse in Florence, South Carolina, and didn't tell anybody.

Huntington is on the east coast of North Carolina, not far from the Atlantic Ocean, forty-five minutes if you drive the speed limit, which we never did. It was a hard, gritty town with more asphalt than trees. Chuck lived in a two-bedroom apartment on the second floor of a huge apartment complex. The second bedroom was a mess of tangled wires and gutted metal boxes where he fixed broken stereo equipment, but in the living room was a brown leather couch and a black leather chair and a glass coffee table which he wiped clean with Windex twice a day. The base was marble and shaped like a tiger. The carpet was green shag, vacuum-striped. On the walls were posters of rock bands except for one that showed a picture of a seagull flying over the ocean at sunset. Chuck owned a lot of stereo equipment, which I was not allowed to touch, and the biggest speakers I had ever seen. I asked him what would happen if you turned them up full blast, and he grinned like a kid.

But Chuck decided he loved Jesus more than me. Maybe there's women who can stand that, but I'm not one of them.

Mostly I blame Phil. Before Phil stuck himself into our lives, me and Chuck had been having a good time riding down to the beach whenever we wanted, listening to records in the listening room of Wuffer Works. Chuck knew of bars we could go to where the music was so loud, I felt it in my feet. Sometimes we stayed home and watched TV and ordered Chinese food to eat right there on the bed like we were having a slumber party. I had never before been to a slumber party. We would put a six-pack of beer on the floor beside the bed, and when we finished it, we would go to the refrigerator and get another one.

Phil had been a longtime Wuffer Works customer, mostly in car audio, then he moved in two buildings down from ours, and I don't know what happened, but after that it seemed like, where there was one, you'd find the other, kind of a two-for-the-price-of-one deal. If Phil had robbed a bank, Chuck would have been tagging along. But Phil went down the road of a rock-hard brand of Christianity, possibly because of his wife, Tonya. Maybe I should blame Tonya.

Phil was an ex-Marine, a short, brooding man with a slow, deep voice that made you think whatever he said had more authority than any whiny, whiffling thing you might say. He had a thick, black beard he liked to pinch between his fingers, which drove me crazy. He worked in security, whatever that means, which was the point. Ask, and he would not tell you. *Top secret,* was all he'd say, but I didn't believe him. I said this once to Chuck, who told me I had suspicion in my heart. That should have been my first clue something was up. Normal people do not talk like that.

Phil and Tonya spent more time in our apartment than in theirs. They never asked either; they just came on in, and Chuck was always glad to see them, and he would send me into the kitchen to fix us something to eat. My speciality was Ritz crackers. I served them with slices of cheese, but then I started trying other things like liverwurst, olives, sardines, horseradish, cucumber slices, tomatoes, pickles, ham, mustard, and onions. Not everything worked, but you would be surprised at what did. I set the crackers on a plate and served them with beer in chilled mugs. It made me feel like a grown-up to live in an apartment with shag carpet and fix Ritz crackers and chill those mugs. We drank only Budweiser because the man who owned the distributorship bought a stereo from Chuck. "Loyalty," Chuck would say. "It's my middle name." He and Phil usually wound up down in the parking lot to work on Chuck's black Thunderbird, which left me with Tonya.

Tonya and me were a pair. There I was, tall and skinny like Mama, while Tonya was short and chunky with muscular legs and big boobs, which I might have envied if I half cared about stuff like that. Tonya was more impressed with what I could do on a Ritz. She said I was a "wizard in the kitchen," and sometimes she cried because she was not a wizard in the kitchen like me. She was newly pregnant and wanted me to get pregnant, too. *Come on, Ruth*, she would say. *You'll have a girl, and I'll have a boy, and they can get married*, which was how Tonya thought; everything easy, all wrapped up. She was a stubborn, pouty girl who got her way by stomping her feet and saying things like, *If you don't, I'll scream.*

But I was not about to get pregnant, and here's how: I did not eat those Ritz crackers. I didn't eat much of anything, which was how I stayed too skinny to get pregnant. I stole my first cigarette from a pack in Margaret's purse when I was sixteen and after that I found it was better to smoke than eat anyway. I could go a whole day on Melba Toast and TAB if I wanted. Mama, who did not smoke but was not big on eating either, never said nothing, but Margaret, who had the ability to hold in what she thought for about thirty seconds, watched me get skinnier and skinnier and could not stand it. She was already on me for not going to football games and parties and because my only boyfriend so far had been that sorry Homer Birdsong. She wanted me to have a lot of boyfriends and join the pep club and wear makeup instead of hanging out in the woods, looking at stars, which was the kind of thing I liked to do. It was weird to want to be alone all the time, she said; bad enough that William was different, but he couldn't help it. I had no excuse. One night she stared at me poking at a mound of mashed potatoes on my plate until she could not take it anymore. "You're not eating supper," she said.

I rolled my eyes.

"You never eat supper anymore."

William covered his ears and groaned. "Hush," Mama told him.

Margaret said, "She's not eating, Mama; you tell her."

"I can't tell her anything," Mama had said, but that's what she always said.

Now Chuck started dropping hints that I ought to fatten up, which burned me. I didn't see how it was any of his business or Tonya's either. Ordinarily I would not have been able to put up with any of this for long, but the truth was, Tonya and I did not have anything to do. Chuck would not let me work. He said I did not need to, which to his way of thinking was a gift. It's not. I told him I would be happier mopping grease off the floor of a hamburger joint than sitting in an apartment with only Tonya to listen to, but I sometimes wondered if it made Chuck feel grown-up, having me home, chilling mugs.

Putting olives on a Ritz cracker will not make you a grown-up. All you're doing is playing make-believe the same as a little girl playing dress-up, just with different props, but it took Rose to show me that. She showed me that it's not the props that matter, which I guess I had known all along but had never found anyone to know it with me. I had grown up with my sister Margaret, who believed if she could wear Pappagallo shoes, she would be a different person; the shoes would make it so, but I saw people laughing at her behind her back. They knew it took more than shoes, but they weren't going to tell her. Mama should have. She knew better—at least I think she did, but that was the problem. With Mama, you could never tell.

Phil and Tonya got Chuck to go with them to a church they called the Little White Church, which they considered daring, and you should have heard them. They thought they were genuine daredevils all because The Little White Church was not like any other church. It made me think of a child's block toy where you try to put the hexagon in the square hole. It won't fit. "What about the Baptists?" I asked, and Tonya said, "Nope."

"Methodists?"

"Nope."

Not the Presbyterians, either, and I knew better than to mention Catholics. The followers of the Little White Church had dug themselves a new hole, which might have been okay except they were trying to push me in it, too. I told Chuck I had been to church already and wasn't going back, which was true.

Mama thought church was the place where you got morals. You got toothpaste from a drugstore, bread from a grocery store, morals from church. She did not need any morals for herself; she already had hers, and besides, with all that had happened in her life, Mama was pretty sure God did not like her, so she didn't like him back. But Margaret and me she sent to the Summerville Presbyterian Church. There wasn't anybody else like me at Summerville Presbyterian, which was fine with Mama, because the way she thought about things, they wouldn't be rich if they didn't have morals. Mama dropped us off in the parking lot and waited in the car with William, while Margaret and I went through the big white doors together, but very quickly, somewhere in the green carpeted hallways, Margaret would lose me. I usually wound up crying, and somebody would help me find my Sunday school class, where women in silk dresses served butter cookies and taught me how to pray. Like Mama, Margaret got all this mixed up in her mind, the link between rich people and religion. It made her into someone who wants something she can't have. But me, I turned out the kind of person who ends up saying, prove it. Every time.

The Little White Church was in the woods between Huntington and the beach, and though you could not see the building from the highway, you could not miss its sign. It was the sort of sign you might find in front of a gas station, plastic, with movable letters that spell out CIGARETTES, COLD BEER, LIVE BAIT.

COMMIT OR LIVE IN THE PIT!

We drove by the sign, and I laughed out loud, but Chuck did not laugh. He mumbled something I could not hear.

"What?"

"They don't mean nothing by it, Ruth." He mumbled again. I hated it when he mumbled.

"What?" I made him say it again.

"I said, they don't mean nothing."

We were on our way back from the beach, and I was wearing a white bikini that Chuck had bought me. It tied together with strings, or as Chuck liked to say, *Undo them strings and what have you got?* I had slipped on shorts for the ride home, but on top I was still only one string away from nothing. "They mean plenty," I said, but Chuck would not talk about it. Sometimes I drove by that way on purpose to see what else they might say. There was a new message every week.

IF YOU PLAN TO TURN TO GOD AT MIDNIGHT,
YOU MIGHT DIE AT 11:30

Here was another one:

IF YOU FEEL FAR FROM GOD, WHO MOVED?

I found they were partial to questions.

WHAT WOULD JESUS SAY TO CARL SAGAN?

"Who is Carl Sagan?" I asked.

By this time it was August and no-kidding hot, and we were cooking hamburgers on the grill. It was a tiny grill. Chuck called it a hibachi, but I called it an if-you-can-only-fit-two-burgers-on-it-what-are-we-doing-having-company grill. Chuck was starting to think I was not as funny as I used to be. Phil and Tonya had talked Chuck into giving up alcohol, so they were sipping on Pepsi, but I was drinking beer and in one of those moods where you can wear a tank top and no bra and everybody else can just drop dead for all you care. The patio was so small only Chuck and Phil could sit out there at one time, so Tonya and I scooted our chairs up to the sliding glass door and talked through the screen, which may have kept out bugs, but it let out the air-conditioning. Chuck started to say something about astronomy, but Phil cut him off.

"Carl Sagan does not believe in God," said Phil.

"You ought to come with us Sunday, Ruth," Tonya said, but it was Phil I was staring at when I answered, "Maybe I will."

To get there, we drove a half a mile down a gravel road, tires sputtering, dust clouding up so bad I was glad I had not dressed up, but I would not have dressed up for anything after Chuck informed me that only hypocrites dress up for church. I wore jeans, my black Jack Daniel's T-shirt, and flip-flops. We ended up in a muddy place near a shallow creek that smelled like rotten leaves and new paint. The church was propped up out of the mud on cinder blocks and was both little and white, although I don't know what else I had expected.

"We're only small to start with," Tonya was explaining to me. "But we aim to grow," and she stretched her arms out as if to show how big.

I said, "What are you going to do then, call it the Big White Church?"

Phil glared at me.

There were no pews, just metal chairs people scraped against the floor getting situated. There were about thirty of us, not counting the children who were shuffled off to a separate room by a woman named Miss Betty. The preacher was Mr. Henry Barlow from South Carolina. He was a short man with stiff, black hair and massive thighs that were crying to break free from the black polyester pants he had pinned them in. He looked like someone who has a hard time sitting still; you wanted to hand him a football and tell him to run on outside and throw it. Mr. Barlow urged everybody to hug each other. I hugged Chuck, but that was not good enough, because here came Phil and Tonya wanting hugs, then a lot of other people I didn't even know. Chuck got red in the face like he thought I might say something, and Phil, with his dark, ferret eyes, was watching me, too. I'd had about enough of those ferret eyes. I was grateful when we got to sit back down.

Tonya was right, this was not like any church I had ever seen, with hymns and Scripture and a sermon; at least with the Presbyterians, you knew what was coming next. This was a let's-sit-down-and-chat sort of church, and what they wanted to talk about on that day was the devil. Henry Barlow wanted to know where we could find him, and I thought, here we go, another question.

A woman sitting next to me thought she knew the answer and said, "In Hell," but most everyone else had more specific ideas, like certain rock bands and movie stars. There was some debate over Richard Nixon, but Tonya said the devil was a woman, and her name was Gloria Steinem. Chuck suggested the owner of Wuffer Works, who lived in Dallas, Texas, and did not share Chuck's ideas about employee benefits, but as soon as he said it, Phil corrected him. "Aren't you forgetting your father, Chuck?"

Chuck looked down at his feet. "Oh, yeah."

I looked back and forth at them. Since when did Phil know anything about Chuck's daddy, was what I wanted to know. I swear, if that Henry Barlow had asked me where the devil was, I was prepared to ask him right back.

"*Who?*"

But he did not ask me. He turned to Phil, and everybody else got quiet. "In me," Phil said, and Henry Barlow whispered, "Praise God." Then he grabbed Tonya by the arm, and she nodded and said, "Amen," and the woman next to me, the same thing, but when he got to me he stopped. "And who are you?"

Phil said, "Why don't you introduce your wife, Chuck?"

Everybody looked at me. Chuck blushed so bad his ears turned red. He put his hand out as if to introduce me but did not say anything, as if he had forgotten my name. Then he remembered. "This is Ruth," he stammered.

"And Ruth," Phil said, "wants to know what Jesus would say to Carl Sagan."

It was like somebody flipped on the lights all of a sudden, everybody shifting in their metal chairs, grinning and looking over at Henry Barlow, who looked up toward the ceiling and whispered, "What would Jesus say to Carl Sagan?"

A man shouted, "Tell it, Henry!"

"What would Jesus say to Carl Sagan?"

A woman started crying.

Henry whipped out his finger, pointed to me, and said, "Jesus would say, *It's not too late!*"

The whole room busted open. I looked over at Chuck, and it was like I had never seen him. He was cheering and clapping with the rest of them, but his sweet face was twisted, and he had a frightened look in his eyes as if he had lost faith in his own self to do right. I don't know. He might as well have told me the earth is flat; I was bound to look at him different; I couldn't help it.

For a week I pestered him. "What's for dinner?" Chuck would ask, and I would say, "Ask Jesus." He did not think I was at all funny anymore. When Sunday came around again, Chuck got up early and proceeded to take the loudest shower I had ever heard. He dropped the soap. He slammed the medicine cabinet shut and tapped his razor on the sink. Then went to the kitchen, where he jerked open drawers and dropped spatulas and whisked eggs in a metal bowl with a metal fork. I heard him ripping his rock 'n' roll posters off the walls, and I was sorry for that, especially for the one of Tom Petty and the Heartbreakers, which I had come to admire. Back in the bedroom, he cut on the overhead light and stood in front of his closet scraping coat hangers against the metal bar. I knew what this was. This was a test. This was a test to see if I would get on out of bed and go to church without him having to ask.

So I got on out of bed. I shuffled into the kitchen and got myself a bottle of beer and lay down on Chuck's brown leather sofa. I was wearing only one of his shirts, unbuttoned all the way down, and black lace underwear. My bare legs rested on a fringed pillow. Chuck stood in the doorway staring at me as I took my finger and traced a plump bead of water sliding slowly down the beer bottle. When it reached the bottom, I sucked it off.

He said, "Are you coming or not?"

I smiled at him. "No, hon. I think I'll stay here and drink this beer."

Ordinarily I did not drink in the morning, but this was war.

When he left, I marched around the apartment throwing things into a duffel bag and cursing. I mean, for a while there we were having a pretty good time, me and Chuck, but it turned out there were two Chucks, Mr. Rock 'n' Roll and the one with the line to Jesus, and this second one, it was like Chuck sprung him on me out of nowhere. It wasn't fair, and I aimed to tell him, but by the time he got home, I had decided I did not even want the old Chuck back. I was through with both of them. When he walked through the door, I was sitting in the middle of the floor with the duffel bag in my lap. "Don't say nothing."

He sat down on the couch. "I'll take you back home if you want."

"No."

"Then what are you going to do?"

I could have told him to ask Jesus, but all of a sudden I had grown tired of spite, so I asked him for some money and a car. "Then I'll be fine." And Chuck, who once told me he knew Marines who weren't as tough as me, was satisfied. He took me to a used car dealership on the highway and bought me a 1971 Datsun 210, yellow with a black-vinyl interior that looked like a dog had chewed it up. Electrical tape covered the biggest holes. No air-conditioning. No radio. I didn't care. He gave me all the money in his wallet. I left him standing beside his black Thunderbird looking like somebody who had gotten off easy, which I suppose he did, but I figured it was the price for freedom. I put five dollars' worth of gas in the tank, which left me with just under three hundred, not enough to squander. I bought a package of peanut butter nabs and a beer and headed north.

3 | STUFF OF DREAMS

Rose told me you can't run away from your problems, and I know she was right. Sometimes it sure seems like you can, though, and sometimes you don't know what else to do with them. Sometimes it works. When I ran away to Lawsonville, I found Rose.

Lawsonville, North Carolina, is a small town on the Chocowin River north of Huntington about two hours. It is an old town that once was an important British port and would have been more important if a certain Lawsonville gentleman named Reginald Humphries had not foolishly entangled himself with a governor's wife. That is the story, still told, as if the citizens of Lawsonville were still mad at him. They will show you where he lived, and for twelve dollars a ticket, you can tour the Humphries House and Gardens, and they will tell you all about it.

Lawnsonville was built at the point where a small river called the Pratt emptied into the larger Chocowin River, which flowed into the Atlantic Ocean. The Chocowin was as broad as a lake, and people came there from all over to sail. Across the Chocowin River from Lawsonville was Chocowin County, which bordered the river until it ran into the sound. Rose lived in Chocowin

County on Highway 53, three miles from the Lawson County line. To get there, you crossed an arched bridge tall enough for sailboats to pass under, but there was a second bridge that headed south out of Lawsonville and spanned the expanse of water where the rivers came together. It was a drawbridge, half a mile long and low on the water, so driving across it made you feel as if you were in the water, on a boat maybe, or somehow hovering. I liked it so much I turned around and drove across it twice.

I stopped in Lawsonville because of that bridge. Since leaving Chuck, I had been driving fast, tossing Bruce Springsteen–like songs around in my head, songs about highways and leaving things behind, trying to make a story out of my life. The bridge made it feel real, as if I really had left something behind, shoved away by the force of my own movement the way a raft will float away from you when you jump off. It was evening when I came across, the sky a summer gray, the water, already dark. Lights from the town glittered on it like stars. Ahead was a place I had never seen before, and for a minute it made me think of dreams.

I am not the kind of person who's going to dwell on dreams. That's Margaret who does that. She's lived for so many wish-it-were-so's it is a wonder she still knows her name. But not me. Where there's a tree, I see a tree; that's all. I'm like Mama that way. But when I drove over that bridge and landed in Lawsonville, I started to believe that here, finally, I was going to begin my life, the life I was meant to have, where I could say, *boo*, and it would mean something. I bought a Snickers bar and another beer and found a place near the river to park my car.

I tried to sleep, but there's not a lot of room in a Datsun 210, front seat or back, so I got out and sat on the hood. Lights from the bridge made wavy paths across the river like a watery constellation, but in the sky there were no stars. The city lights were too bright for stars, and I was sorry. Back home in my yard in Summerville, it was a streetlight in front of Durwood's that used to block out the night sky, although after I found the switch that turned off that streetlight, it was okay. I had this idea that if I stared at the stars long enough, I could seal them in my mind, keep them with me like you keep a souvenir, something to take out and hold in your hand to remember where you were, although it never worked that way. The next night they would look new all over again.

I remembered the first time I saw Jupiter and realized it was a planet. It looked like a star so big you could mistake it for an airplane, except it never came any closer, an airplane in perpetual flight, and I said to myself, *That's no star.* From then on, it became important for me to find Jupiter whenever it was up. I lost track of it when I ran off with Chuck, who thought the only lights worth looking at shone from a new stereo receiver in a pitch-black room. Maybe Jupiter was up there now, or maybe somewhere on the other side of the sun, and I didn't know what there was in the sky to see anymore.

It was a long night. I'll tell you what made it seem longer; there was not one single person in the entire world who knew where I was. I couldn't quit thinking about that. Of all the people who knew me, not one would have guessed the hood of a car in Lawsonville, North Carolina. I especially could not keep my mind off Mama, who thought she knew where I was, but was wrong. It was not like I wanted to be with her or anything like that, because I didn't.

Still, I'd think about her. I'd see her getting out of bed in the morning, pulling those pants on, the blue ones that she has to safety pin to keep them from falling off her hips. She'll button up a shirt, the white one with the strawberries if you're lucky, but probably not. Probably the faded green one that I just can't stand. It won't be ironed, and she won't care, even though Margaret is always begging her to fix herself up, to buy something new, to at least *try* not to embarrass us. Mama won't even brush her hair; she'll just pull it back with a rubber band and go to the kitchen to make William's breakfast. William will be up already, up at dawn most mornings to check his mousetraps, the special ones Durwood got for him that don't kill the mice. If there's a mouse in there, William will take it to the woods in back of our house and set it free, but first he will hold it for a while, petting and talking to it. He isn't afraid of the mice, and even though Mama has told him a hundred times they will bite him if he isn't careful, he has never been bitten. They are all he has for pets since Mama says she can't have cat hair all over the freshly ironed clothes, and every dog we ever owned got run over on the highway. When he's finished with the mice, William will watch cartoons. He's got his shows mapped out every day, and he laughs at them, a big, rowdy, grown-man laugh from his little-boy mind. People who do not know him are usually scared of him, because they do not understand why he acts so dumb. Mama will make him eggs and toast. She won't eat anything herself, just coffee, and Margaret will sleep as late as she can get away with. She'll claim she does not have time for breakfast, which means Mama will yell, "If you don't eat these eggs, I'm going to throw them to the dogs." And Margaret will yell, "The dogs thank you." Like I said, we don't have any dogs, but that's what they say to each other anyway. Then Margaret, she'll be sure to slam the door behind her on her way to the Red Food, where she thinks she's something because she's made cashier. Mama will pull out the ironing board and start working. She'll fold the clothes into bundles of pretty colors, stacked crisp and neat like presents I could never touch. "Don't touch them clothes, Ruth," Mama used to tell me, like she knew I wanted to even before I did.

I heard a noise. Behind me, the streets of Lawsonville were empty, but I held my breath and listened anyway. Nothing. Slowly and as quietly as possible, I climbed down off the hood and got inside the car and locked the doors. Still nothing. I had two thoughts: one, if I needed a cop, how would I find one, and two, if I found one, wouldn't he want to send me home? I drove down to a warehouse at the end of the street where half a dozen broken-down cars sat vacant. I slept some, and by morning I was back to seeing a tree for a tree, because when you sleep in a car you don't have dreams. You have a door handle in your back.

The biggest street in Lawsonville was called Battle Street. At one end were banks, three of them, and at the other, churches, four of them, and in between, a line of dusty stores. I was starving and went looking for something to eat when I wandered into a hardware store, thinking it might be like Durwood's, and maybe it had been at one time, but it wasn't anymore. Now it was a chain store, laid out neatly with all the aisles marked so you could find things. In the aisle marked SEASONAL, I spied a small, blue electric fan shaped like a bear. You pushed his nose to turn him on. It was so hot out, my thighs had stuck to the car seat at six o'clock that morning, so I got the idea I ought to have a fan and bought it. I wandered next door into Pearl's Dress Shoppe, where I admired a purple knit vest that looked like daisies strung together. Holding it to my chest, I knew that Margaret would die for such a thing. "Put it on layaway," a saleslady offered, so I did. Then I went to Lucinda's Five and Dime.

I walked back and forth down the aisles until I found myself in front of the shampoos, reading labels. I could not remember if I had packed shampoo and reached up to touch my hair. Back in Summerville, people called me Brillo Head behind my back because of my dark, curly hair, and it was the part about me that hurt the most even though my face, with its peculiar jutting-out of the chin and deep, narrow eyes, was not what anybody would call beautiful. *There's a girl who needs her teeth fixed* is what I imagined people thought when they met me, but I knew it was my hair that people associated with me the most. Mama told me I got it from Daddy's side of the family. *He always had a wave*, was what she would say. I ended up growing it long so people would stop thinking I looked like a soap pad, but I think it made me look dangerous. I made decent enough grades in school, but it seemed to surprise the teachers, because I did not look like somebody who would be good in school. I looked like somebody who would just as soon shoot you the bird.

If I did try to straighten my hair, which never worked, Mama would sigh and shake her head and say, *There's nothing you can do about it, Ruth. You're just like your daddy*. It didn't sound like a compliment, and I did not understand. She said it all the time, too, and not just about my hair. *And how is that, Mama?* I would ask, but that was another question she was never going to answer, so once I pressed her on it. "Do you mean I'm good for nothing?"

She was ironing at the time and watching Phil Donahue on the TV, and when I asked her, she stopped ironing. Her arm was crooked and ready to push; the iron was pouring out steam from its nose like a snorting bull, but she was not moving.

"Hard to handle?" I said. I knew I was getting to her, although I did not know why. The arm released, and now she was ironing double time, back and forth across somebody's pink linen shirt. William, who was sitting in his chair three feet from the TV, shot out a burst of laughter over something Phil Donahue said. It wan't funny, but William never waited for something funny to laugh.

"How about smarter than you?"

This time Mama looked straight at me for about a half a minute, a long time for Mama. I saw her jaw clench tight like she had to work to keep her mouth shut. She had stopped ironing again, and I watched as her hand released the handle and fell to her side. Then she turned suddenly and walked out of the room. I could hear her in the bathroom, but my attention was on the iron, smoking on the pink linen, and I rushed to snatch it upright. Again William laughed at the TV. I stared down at the shirt on the ironing board, remembering the times Mama had yelled at us for even getting near the clothes with dirty hands or sticky fingers, yet there, in the middle of all that pink, was an unmistakable ring of brown.

Not long after that was when I left for good; *Just like your daddy*, I suppose she could say.

The longer I stood there in Lucinda's Five and Dime looking at the different shampoo bottles, the more I realized I had no idea what kind I wanted. *Normal hair. Oily hair. Dry. Extra Dry. Damaged.* It bothered me that I did not know. How could I not know? Suddenly I noticed that the saleslady at the cash register was staring at me. She was a tall, white-haired woman with a pink apron over her dress, and she was standing on tiptoe to get a look at me over the shelves. She was memorizing my face. *In case I stole something.*

I froze.

It happened so fast. It was like one minute I was fine, and the next minute I was definitely not fine. The air around me seemed to heat up and fly away, and I was sweating, and wanted to throw up, and my head hurt. My head hurt so bad I couldn't hardly see and couldn't hardly breathe and all I could think about was that I had to lie down. Now. I was going to have to find some cool floor and fall on it.

Then there was Rose. She was a tiny, old woman with short, red hair that stuck up every which way except here and there where she had mashed it down with bobby pins. Her back was crooked, and her face crowded with wrinkles, but she had the kindest eyes I had ever seen. She wore black stretch pants, a blouse a color like Easter grass, and pink tennis shoes. I didn't even know they made tennis shoes in pink. Her earrings, Mexican colors of red and yellow and turquoise, spiraled to a point like tornadoes. She took me by the arm and pulled me outside.

She led me to a bench on the sidewalk in the shade of a green-striped awning. The bench was made of iron, and it was cool. I remember feeling the coolness of the metal on my legs, but Rose's lap was soft and warm, and that is where she put my head. I was still sweating, and I remember a soft morning breeze sweeping up under the awning and across my cheeks and knowing at that moment that I was breathing again. I took deep breaths, like waves rolling in, rolling out, my eyes closed tight; I did not want to move. And Rose, she did not make me. But you can't lie on a stranger's lap without there coming a time when you know you ought to get up.

"Thank you," I said.

"It could happen to anybody," she said.

She told me her name was Rose, and I said mine was Ruth, and we thought that was funny, both of us having "R" names like that, although I told her I sure would have rather been named for a flower.

"There's nothing special to it," she said.

I felt better. Rose noticed it first; she said, "Your color's back," and I could tell it was true when she said it. My stomach wasn't all the way right, but otherwise I was fine. She did not stop me when I said I had to go. I headed toward the river and my car but with no real purpose. I didn't have anywhere to go.

I walked down to a vacant lot near the Pratt River, where a few scattered people leaned on the railing, fishing for crabs. Some had climbed over the railing to the rocks on the other side. They used chicken necks tied to strings for bait. It seemed to me that these were people born knowing this was what to do with chicken necks, but it was strange to me. Lots of things can feel strange when you're all by yourself, and I know now, if not for Rose, I would have gone home to Summerville, even though I did not want to. Standing beside the river, watching the greasy necks of chickens bobbing up and down, I kept telling myself, *I can't go back. I'll never go back. Never.* But people who say never don't know what they're talking about.

I might have gone home because there was nothing else to do, but again, there was Rose. I heard the rustling of a paper sack before I saw her. She handed me my blue bear fan, which I had left on the floor of Lucinda's. Then she pulled a sandwich out of her purse and gave it to me. My hands shook. It was chicken salad, big squares of white meat, crisp celery, pecans. Tears rolled down my face, but Rose did not say anything. She acted as if it were the most normal thing in the world to cry over a chicken salad sandwich.

Suddenly she stood up. "I'll be back," she said. I watched her walk away, slowly, her hands out like someone who is afraid to fall, until she came to a man standing farther down the railing. Right off you would think something was wrong with him, because he was wearing maroon pants and a coat on this hot, August day, and he carried a giant tapestry bag like the kind an old woman might have. He and Rose talked for a minute, then I saw her slip him something. Another sandwich?

When she came back she told me his name. "Cecil Swann," she said. "He's a poet."

I considered that. I did not know what to say. I had grown up watching Mama read *Verses for Daily Living*, but I did not know any poets. So I lied. "My husband was a poet."

Rose studied me.

"That's why I left him," I said. "You know poets; you can admire them, but you can't live with them."

She nodded as if she knew what I was talking about. I didn't even know what I was talking about. Then she peered at me again. "You look awfully young. When were you married?"

I shrugged and told her I had dropped out of college to marry Chuck. "My parents were furious. They're doctors, see. Both of them. Anyway, they hated Chuck because he was poor, which is probably why I married him. I've always been sort of a rebel."

The lie slid out of me from nowhere. I never even guessed it was there. I sure never planned it, but once it started, it was easy. A part of me wanted to take it back because I had no reason to lie to Rose. But part of me didn't. It was such a wonderful lie. Such a wonderful, wonderful story.

4 | GOODNIGHT IRENE

When Rose was a little girl, Pancho Villa and his gang came riding toward her hometown of Agua Vista, Texas. The way Rose told it, this would be like watching a tornado coming at you across a prairie; you move out of the way or get plowed under. Rose hid under her father's printing press with her mother, her sister, and her two brothers, while her father lined up in the street with the other men, guns loaded, waiting.

Rose called Pancho Villa a bandit. She said it with the most amazing spirit, clipping the word off her teeth like snipping string. *Bandit.* The soul of evil. There's enough excitement in the mere idea to last one person a lifetime. I got the feeling that's how it was with Rose: Once you've hidden from a bandit, nothing else even comes close. As she told it, Pancho Villa and his men crossed over the border from Mexico into the small towns of south Texas. They shot the men. Women and children they threw into the desert to live with the coyotes.

"I bet they didn't," I said.

Rose looked surprised. "They did, too."

"I bet they raped them first," I said.

She thought about it. "I wouldn't know about that, Ruth. I was ten years old. My mother told us that if Pancho caught us, he would throw us to the coyotes, and I am thinking that was bad enough."

I let it go.

Me and Rose had been sitting on the bench by the river all morning. We had watched Cecil wander down the river then back through town until he was out of sight. We had watched the draw-bridge unhinge and creak its way sideways three times for three different sailboats, backing up traffic, the cars like angry bees forced to wait behind a gate. The sun was high over the river when Rose stood up. She seemed to consider me for a minute then cocked her head. "Come with me."

We walked back down Battle Street, turned a corner, then went another couple of blocks until we came to a new, one-story brick building with a sign over the door that read, *The Lawsonville Ledger.* I followed Rose up the steps and into the building, where she worked in the advertising department. She offered me a chair next to her desk and picked up the phone. "I'll just be a minute," she whispered.

The advertising department was a large, open room with four desks, two on one side, two on the other, and at the back, a small, glass-enclosed office. Everybody in the room was either on the phone or talking to someone, and no one looked up when we came in. It was a clean, uncluttered room, white walls, gray car-pet, except for Rose's desk, which was covered with layers of coffee-stained paper. It was freezing in there. I was wearing cutoffs and flip-flops, which had suited me fine outside on the street but not sitting in this fancy office, especially after I looked down and saw that my feet were dirty. I don't know what it is, but there's something about having dirty feet that feels like a smudge on your character, and I was in the process of sticking them under Rose's desk, when I saw the woman across the room staring at me. I figured it was my feet that caught her eye, but she just wanted to bring me a sweater.

"You'll catch your death," she said, handing me the sweater.

"Thank you," I said. The sweater was brown and shaped like the back of a chair, where I imagined it was kept for times like these when the air-conditioning won out.

"I'm Deborah," the woman said, and she reached out to shake my hand.

I told her I was Ruth, but that didn't seem to be enough to explain myself so I added, "Rose's friend," even though I didn't know if that was right either. I didn't know what I was.

"Would you like a Coke, Ruth?"

Deborah led me to a drink machine at the back of the building and bought me a Coke. She must have noticed me eyeing the snacks, because she handed me another sixty cents. I wanted Milk Duds but bought potato chips because I figured Deborah would want me to eat something hearty. She looked like the kind of woman who could be any age, old before she was old, sensible gray skirt, sensible black shoes. She told me she was married to a Marine and had three teenagers, all boys, and before I could stop her, I found myself in the middle of a rundown of each one. Before we started back to the front of the building, Deborah put her hand on my arm. "So, how long have you been Rose's friend?"

"I really just met her."

"You know she's got cancer, don't you?"

"No."

It startled me, or else I would have pretended to know just to keep Deborah from getting the smug look that came over her face, like she loved handing out bad news.

"Lungs," Deborah whispered. "She had that operation a couple of years ago, but you know how that goes." She shook her head. "With cancer, there's no telling."

"Is she going to die?"

"Oh, honey, only God knows that, but isn't it sweet how they keep her on here at the newspaper? No one would have the heart to tell her to go."

I wiped my hands on my shirt and followed Deborah back to the front of the building, where I managed to drop the crumpled potato chip bag on her desk while she wasn't looking. Rose was still on the phone. She did not look sick to me. A package of caramels was spilled across her desk. She had one stuffed in her cheek and was crinkling the empty cellophane between two fingers and, when she saw me, she handed me one, too.

I followed Rose home that afternoon in my car. She had to sit on a pillow to see over the dashboard, and with her little head barely poking up over the steering wheel, she reminded me of the *Kilroy Was Here* pictures I used to draw for William. I had gotten the idea from watching Lucy Applewhite, who happened to be one of the most popular girls in our class, draw a *Kilroy Was Here* picture on our history teacher's grade book when he wasn't looking, and I went home and tried it. I wasn't as good at drawing as Lucy Applewhite and probably would have thrown it away, but when William saw it, I had to draw about a hundred for him. As far as I know, he's still got them pinned to his wall.

We drove out of town across the Chocowin River over the bridge I had not yet crossed, the tall one that looked even higher from the top than it had from below. It made me dizzy, and I had a crazy urge to drive off into midair as if some unseen force were tugging at my car. I held on to the steering wheel with both hands and made myself look straight ahead until I reached the other side. Rose, I noticed, sped up. On the other side of the bridge was a sign turned upside down. **Welcome to Chocowin County, Population 1,036**. The speed-limit sign was shot through with bullet holes. We didn't pass anything after that but scrubby forests and farms.

Rose's house was about five miles down the highway, a bright yellow cottage between two huge soybean fields. We pulled into a gravel drive. She took me upstairs and gave me a choice of two bedrooms, one blue, the other yellow. The blue room had belonged to Rose's daughters, Carol and Alma, who had shared it as children. Carol lived in Lawsonville and worked as a nurse at the Lawson County Hospital. She had never been married and lived alone, and Rose seemed to think she might drop by anytime, but not Alma. She mentioned something about a husband and a child, but it was clear Rose did not want to talk about her, and it made me think there was something of a mystery about Alma. The yellow room had been Rose's until a few years back when Carol made her move downstairs, *in case you fall and break your hip and then, Mother, what would you do?*

"Carol is always looking after me, you see."

"I guess you're lucky then."

"I don't need looking after."

Rose picked up my duffel bag and carried it to the bed in the yellow room. She dusted off her hands. "I'll tell you what's funny; you spend years dreading the day your children are going to leave you, then they don't leave. What's worse you think?"

"Beats me."

"Carol is stubborn. She's one to hold on to things, but things change. What she really wants is what she can't have."

"And that would be?"

"She doesn't want me to die."

"It's not a bad thing to want, Rose."

"Everybody dies, Ruth."

On the wall of the yellow room were photographs of Carol and Alma looking nothing in the world like sisters. Carol was the fair one, on the heavy side, with an enthusiastic expression on her face as if she could not wait to tell you something, a front-row sort of girl who always had her hand up for the teacher. Alma was darker-skinned and prettier. Also secretive, like there was something about the way Alma did not look into the camera that made you think she might be hiding something. The largest picture on the wall showed neither Carol nor Alma. It was an old photograph that looked like a painting, faded and lined with spiderweb cracks and surrounded by an oval frame, of four children standing in a row from shortest to tallest. Rose saw me looking at it and pointed to the tallest, a boy. "My brother, Frank," she said. "He was an artist. Such a talented boy; you would have been amazed."

"What happened? Did he die?"

"Influenza." She whispered it as if it might creep from its dank cave and snatch us both. She pointed to the next boy. "Tommy," she said. "Drowned in the Gulf of Mexico when he was seventeen." She moved her finger down the picture. "Guess who this is."

"You?"

She nodded. "The baby was my sister Frances. She's dead now, too, but she lived a long, full life. Died only a few years ago from old age or meanness."

"So you're the only one left."

"It wasn't long after this picture was taken that we hid from Pancho Villa, and I'll tell you the truth; I should have been scared out of my wits, but I wasn't. My mother was, and I pretended I was, too, but I felt safe there under my father's big press. Deep down I believed that nothing bad could happen as long as we were together." I was thinking about how being in my family felt more like I was about to fall off a cliff, when she reached up to the picture and touched the glass above the tallest child and said. "I was wrong. Maybe we escaped Pancho Villa, but we were never safe. Frank died the next year, then my mother died a few months later of the same thing."

I asked Rose how she lived with so much sorrow, and she said it was because of it that she did. "I never thought life was going to be easy."

We went downstairs for supper. Rose made me a tomato sandwich, and it was the best tomato sandwich I had ever tasted. She told me it was nothing. You have to know your tomatoes, and you have to toast the bread, is all. That's the secret. You never, ever, want soggy bread. "How do you know your tomatoes?" I asked, and she had to think about that. Finally she decided it was the color. Dusty red is what you're going for, and there's no way to know what that is except, you bite into enough bad tomatoes and you know. I understood the part about the toasted bread. We took our sandwiches outside to eat on a small, brick patio stuck randomly among the weeds in the backyard as if whoever built it had closed his eyes and said here. There was room for three lawn chairs. Along one end was a low wall you could prop your feet on. If you kicked at it, slivers of loose mortar tumbled out. She made me spray for mosquitoes, which were bad this time of year in Chocowin County. "They weigh on your mind," she said, "but I'll take them any day over spiders. In Texas we had spiders big as your fist."

"Wolf spiders?"

"Tarantulas."

"Don't even tell me."

"We lived across the street from the beach, and we'd walk over there, my brothers and I; Frances was too little, and weren't we a sight! Mother made us wear our raincoats so the neighbors would not see us in our bathing suits, which tells you something about my mother. She would not have approved of what they're wearing today, no ma'am. She would have had a thing or two to say." Rose looked over to see me pulling my cutoffs a little farther down my thighs and shook her head. "Don't worry, hon. I'm not a thing like my mother. When we got back from the beach at the end of the day, Mother would make us hang our coats on the clothesline to dry. Now this one day, I put my arm through my coat sleeve like this"—and here she stood up and pretended to put her arm through a make-believe sleeve—"and a tarantula dropped out the other end." Here she pointed to an imaginary spider running across the ground.

I whistled. "I wouldn't live near no tarantula, Rose."

She grinned.

"I had to fight off a wolf spider one time back in Summerville. They'll jump at you if you don't watch it, and this one, he came at me, and I had to stand on a chair. My brother, William, he wouldn't hurt an animal for nothing, not even a spider, but I had him bring me the dictionary. The big one. Got him in one throw and told William it was an accident."

"Your brother, William? He's still living there in Tennessee, I suppose."

I didn't say anything at first, just looked down at my feet and let the moment pass. There wasn't any reason to go into all that. "I guess." I whispered and waited, but Rose did not ask any more questions. I said, "Wolf spiders are scary, but they're no tarantula."

She nodded. "It's all in what you get used to."

Rose from Texas. There ought to be a song, I said, which made her laugh, and for me there were few things in this world more satisfying than hearing Rose laugh. Rose ended up telling me a lot of stories that night. She seemed surprised at how eager I was for them, and once she stopped to ask, "Are you sure you want to hear this?"

"I'm hanging on every word."

She knew I really was.

That night I lay awake in the yellow room. I had never been one good for sleep anyway. I used to lie awake nights listening to Margaret sleeping in the next bed, wondering how she did it, night after night, so easy. I could turn on the radio, and it would not wake her up, but I didn't care about the radio. I would rather it had been Margaret up half the night with some old radio than me. Mama was the same way. Most nights she would be sitting at the kitchen table playing solitaire with a deck of cards so old they had turned sticky, their backs showing a picture of the Parthenon and a deep blue Athenian sky. I used to point to that picture and tell her I was going to take her there someday, the one thing I could say to make her smile. She played solitaire like there was a fire, whipping those cards out, *slap, slap, slap*, but when it was over she simply swept up the cards with one hand and started over, never seeming to care if she won or lost. When I wandered into the kitchen to be with her, she would give a weary sigh, as if she had certainly passed on this disease of not sleeping, but she did not know what to do about it.

I got out of bed and looked out the window. A half-moon lit the highway, a dark and silent road crossed with shadows, and as I watched it, I wondered if Mama might be looking out her window at another highway, also silent under the glare of Durwood's yellow streetlight. She did not know where I was, and I could not call her, because she did not have a phone. Durwood had one, and to Mama that was close enough; if you needed to call some-body, you could walk next door. If the hardware store were closed, she had a key, because it used to be her job to sweep up after hours, which she did every night after supper, taking Wil-liam with her so he could play with the cats. (Durwood preferred he did not go over there during business hours.) When Margaret got old enough, she took over the job, which she didn't mind to do, because after she finished, she would stay over there talking on the phone. When I was still at Chuck's, I had to wait for Mama to call me, which she hardly ever did. "It's long-distance, Ruth," was what she would say, as if that were a reason.

I pulled out of my duffel bag a bottle of Jack Daniel's, which I had taken from Chuck's. I forgot shampoo, but the Jack Daniel's made it; now what does that tell you? I poured the whiskey with a little water into a Dixie cup I found in the bathroom, then hunted for a pencil and piece of paper at the small desk in the corner of the room. I sat down and wrote.

Dear Mama,
   I am fine. I hope you are fine, too.
   Me and Chuck didn't work out, but that's a good thing, so don't worry. (Tell Margaret she was right!!!)
   I have moved to Lawsonville, which is still in North Car-olina, not far from Huntington. Look it up on a map if you want and show William.
   I have made a friend. Her name is Rose.
                                          Love, Ruth

The problem with a Dixie cup is the bottom gets soggy, and you end up thinking it's going to bust through any minute, so I took the bottle and sucked the whiskey through my teeth, filtered fire; it squeezed tears right out of my eyes. I reread my letter and decided to add one more thing.

P.S. Mama, I am not coming home, so don't look for me.

Then I picked up the bottle, tip-toed downstairs, and snuck outside to the patio. In the dark, the soybean fields seemed to spread out endlessly to the left and to the right, and the sky above looked huge. I spied what I hoped might be Jupiter a little above and to the left of the moon, and I turned a chair so it faced that way, and I sat down. It was loud out there, with the summer night sounds of tree frogs and crickets, just like home. I closed my eyes and listened, remembering the summer I was thirteen and decided to sleep outside every night. The first night, Mama had helped me drag blankets out to the yard, enough to make a pallet so I would not wake up sore. After that she would not help me, as if that might make me quit, but she should have known me better. I hauled them myself. I picked a spot of open sky framed with trees so the stars would be the last thing I saw before I went to sleep. I did not know their names yet, but I had no need to know names, and if anyone had tried to teach me, I would have covered my ears, because there's times when knowing too much can take the fun out of a thing. It was enough to look and see them there, to know I was not the kind of person who would miss half my life inside four walls and under a ceiling. Mornings, my blankets would be covered with slugs. Like friends, they came every night, more as summer turned to fall, and I started hearing Mama saying things to Margaret like, *I hope she's not planning to sleep out there in the cold,* as if the weather had anything to do with it. There were times I swore my own mama did not understand one single thing I did. I picked my slugs off one by one and put them in the grass, their slimy trails like memories on my blankets.

Mama would watch me and the slugs from behind the kitchen curtain as if I might not notice she was there.

By now the whiskey had settled in my belly and had found its way to my arms and my legs. I sat there listening to the frogs, sipping whiskey, and watching stars for I don't know how long when it came to me that "Goodnight Irene" was the best song ever written. I had been running through a bunch of songs in my mind anyway, because I did know a song about roses and Texas; I just could not remember how it went. I knew another Texas song called "El Paso," because William listened to it until the record got too scratched to hear anymore, and from there I remembered "I'm So Lonesome I Could Cry," but when I got to "Goodnight Irene," I stopped.

Sometimes I live in the country.
Sometimes I live in the town.
Sometimes I have a great notion,
to jump into the river and drown.

You find me truer words. To do it justice, you got to give it your all, so there I was, singing "Goodnight Irene" at the top of my lungs, every verse, some twice. I stood up and walked all over the yard singing it. I nearly reached the highway before Rose caught me and hauled me back to bed.

The next morning, I sat at Rose's kitchen table staring slit-eyed at a cup of coffee, the last from a pot Rose had already drunk. I balanced my elbows on the table and held my head in my hands in an effort to half manage the pain; otherwise, it was like my brains had come loose. Rose put two sausage patties and a piece of toast in front of me. I closed my eyes. "Mind if I smoke?"

"Go ahead," she said. I offered her one, but she waved it away.

"I'm supposed to be quitting," she said and walked to the sink to rinse dishes, humming a song that sounded a lot like "Goodnight Irene." I groaned.

"You liked it last night."

"Don't remind me."

In a minute she was singing another song.

"Shoo fly, don't bother me,
Shoo fly, don't bother me,
Shoo fly, don't bother me,
For I belong to . . . what?" She turned around to ask me.

"How would I know?"

"I thought everybody knew 'Shoo fly.' "

"I don't."

"It's *somebody*. For I belong to *somebody*."

She carried my untouched plate to the sink. I could see above her slippers, her legs were papery white, smooth, and shiny. I could make out bones along her crooked spine under the faded pink seersucker bathrobe. She left the room to get dressed, and I went to the sink and splashed cold water on my face, then I sat back down and put my head on the table and closed my eyes.

When she came back, she sat down next to me and picked up the newspaper and began reading it. I waited. My head on the table, my arms over my head, I waited for the lecture about my unruly behavior last night, but there was none of that. It was just me and Rose at the table, and she was reading the newspaper. When she put it down, she said, "One of my favorite songs is one my mother used to sing about a little boy who is dying, but I can't remember all the words. I can't remember half the songs she used to sing. She sang all the time, in the house, in the yard. My brothers and I used to get her to go to the beach with us, and she would sing there, too. She had a beautiful voice. I suppose all children think their mothers' voices are beautiful, though; isn't that right? By the time I got old enough to think any different, she wasn't around to sing anymore, now was she?" Rose smiled as if she saw some humor in this. "That one song, though, I wish I could remember it. It makes me mad, see, that I can't."

I lifted my head. "What was he dying of?"

"Who?"

"The little boy in the song. You said it was a song about a little boy dying."

"I don't know. I seem to remember he asks his mother to wipe his brow, so my guess would be he had a fever. But in the song, he is such a brave little boy, lying there in the bed, telling his mother to give his toys to his friends, telling her to put his little shoes away after he dies. He's so good-hearted, see, so generous, even in death. That was the part that broke us up, him being brave like that, while all his poor mother could do was wipe the sweat off his face. My brother, Frank, and I about collapsed into tears every time we heard it. My father wouldn't even stay in the same room. I sure wish I could remember those words."

"What if I got sick, Rose? What if I got cancer or something like that?"

She studied me for a minute. "Then you would live with cancer."

"No I would not. I would die."

"So, you would live until you died."

"But I'm too young to die. It's different when you're old, isn't it, Rose?"

"Are you asking me?"

"Do you have cancer, Rose?"

"No."

"Good," I said. "Okay then, forget cancer. Let's say I'm hit by a car."

"Do you die?"

"Hell yes, I die. I'm hit by a car."

"Then the world will go on without you."

"Great."

"It really will."

5 | MESSING WITH THE WRONG DOG

Rose once stood on a dead man. She didn't know it was a dead man. She thought it was a log, which was the joke, the part of the story that was so Rose-like, the reason people still told it after all these years. It happened when Rose was much younger and worked for a weekly newspaper in Chocowin County called the *Chocowin County Crier*, which was never taken seriously because of its size. The whole of Chocowin County was kind of like that, not taken seriously because of its size. When something happened in Chocowin County, it wasn't exactly news; it was more like *what-those-people-do-down-there*. At least that was the feeling you got up in Lawsonville, where people knocked themselves out trying to make their city important, as if the memory of past glory rode them, and they were bound to make it that way again. Chocowin County didn't have any past glory. Just swamps.

The *Chocowin County Crier* had belonged to Rose's second husband, Raymond, and they had worked on it together until he was hit by a train. Carol was six years old at the time, Alma on the way, and Rose felt like she had no choice but to take the whole thing over. She wrote the articles, took the pictures, sold the ads, typed it up, laid it out, took it to the printer, and sometimes even delivered it. What made her famous was not so much the articles she wrote about county news, what the county commissioners did, for instance, or the school board, or wrecks on the highway, but stories she wrote about everyday people, and not only from Chocowin County. She went all over. She'd take a person you wouldn't think anything about and make them sound like somebody, and here's why. Everybody's got a story. She believed it the way you're going to believe the sun comes up every morning.

"I wish I had as many stories as you, Rose."

"You do, hon. Your whole life is a story."

"Not mine."

She looked at me. "Last I heard, you ran away from home with a poet. If that isn't the start of a good story, I don't know what is."

I shrugged.

"What about your parents?" she asked.

"There's nothing much to say."

"I suppose you've told them where you are?"

"Sure."

"Because they might worry."

"You don't need to worry about me, Rose."

"I never worry," she said. "It's a waste of time."

Because of the *Chocowin County Crier*, it seemed like everybody knew Rose. We could not walk down a street without people calling out, *Hey there, Rose*. The newspaper lady. If you asked her, she would tell you it was what she did best, although her daughter, Carol, would argue this was not such a great thing. Carol would tell me another story, a story of forgotten dinners and missed school plays, the story of a childhood interrupted by phone calls and sudden dashings-out-the-doors. When their mother left like that, Carol and Alma stayed with Rose's friends, Mrs. Pickle and Mrs. Ellis, two widowed sisters who were not unkind, just not their mother. They lived in Lawsonville, and sometimes Rose took them there to play in their big house with the secret attic and the big back porch that overlooked the river, but most of the time, the sisters would come out to Chocowin County, and they would bring games and crayons and peppermints. Alma did not mind it so much. When she got older, Mrs. Ellis taught her how to cook and, when Rose got home, they presented her with a plateful of cookies or an apple cake. Carol would not help. She sat backwards on the sofa staring out the window, watching for her mother.

The worst was when Rose was called out in the middle of the night. Carol says she always woke up; something was wrong; she could feel it. The stairwell ran down the middle of their house, landing in a hallway in front of the back door right outside the kitchen, so Carol would go, *creak, creak*, down the stairs, following the light from the kitchen, where she would find Mrs. Pickle sitting at the table with a cup of hot chocolate, a sketchbook, and a box of pencils. Mrs. Pickle was a freakishly tall woman with long hair that was forever spewing out of the bun she tried to put it in. She was the only woman Carol knew besides her mother who never wore a dress. "Join the party, fellow night owl," was the kind of thing Mrs. Pickle would say to Carol, as if this was fun.

"Fun it was most certainly not," Carol told me. "It was certainly not how normal people lived."

One night there was a murder. The sheriff of Chocowin County appreciated newspaper reporters the way you would gnats in your eyes, so he was not one to call Rose, but one of his deputies, a man named Bud Snow, liked her. You are going to want to know what I mean by "like." I have no idea. For all of

Rose's stories, there was an awful lot she kept quiet about, but I found out it was Deputy Snow who gave Rose the Chinese dolls on her refrigerator. He got them in Florida, but it wasn't Rose who told me. It was Carol, who also said she remembers standing at the bottom of the stairs in her pajamas the night of the murder, begging her mother not to go, but would she listen?

The sheriff already had his murderer, a man named Felix McCarthy, who had woken him up hollering over it. The problem was, Felix was drunk and could not remember where the body was, which was why he and the sheriff and two deputies and Rose ended up plowing through the woods with flashlights on a moonless night.

Rose didn't have a flashlight.

The story goes that she stood for a good ten minutes before figuring out that the log she was on was not a log, but the corpse.

"It was more like ten seconds," Rose said.

But that's how stories grow, like legends, passed around until they are as good as town currency. Things happened to Rose. People said she was a tough bird, but they also said she was crazy. People felt obliged to fill me in. They told me Rose stories, although I didn't believe all of them.

Rose got me a job answering phones at the *Lawsonville Ledger*. The reception area where I worked was enclosed by glass, although there were windows you could slide open if you wanted to talk to somebody. I sat in a gray swivel chair on a clear plastic mat. I had my own metal filing cabinet, a white plastic in and out box, and a drawer full of pencils, pens, paper clips, and note pads. A list of extensions was plastered to my desk with yellowing tape that you could peel off in tiny threads with your fingernails. People who came in off the street passed through me first. *You got to see the business manager,* I would say. *Down the hall and to your left.* Or, *You're going to have to talk to our editor about that. Let me see if he's in.* Regulars got to where they were calling me by name. *How's it going, Ruth?* I was pretty good at this part of my job, which surprised me, because I had never been good with people.

To my left was the advertising department, headed by a man named Purdy Hughes. Purdy was nervous and tended to make people who worked for him nervous, so it was generally quiet to my left, although to look at him, you would not think he was someone to fear. He had a tiny face, round belly, and stiff, tufty hair the color of sand. There was a running joke about what he kept in the bottom drawer of his desk as if you could not smell it, plus he had an odd habit of wearing cloth belts with pictures of animals sewn on them. I never got over those belts. Rose and I slipped each other notes depending on the day:

Purdy would have been an office joke if he had not had so much power over the lives of the people who worked for him, but he was a petty, spiteful man who liked to catch people breaking his rules. If you crossed him, he would get you back. I owed my job to so many receptionists before me who had quit or been fired because of Purdy, although I had no faith I would end up any different.

To my right was the newsroom, run by a colorful man named Ed Stivers, who tended to shout. Most of the reporters were young and excitable, too, so as a rule it was rowdy to my right. I kept my windows closed to keep down the noise, most of which came from a reporter named Jackson Price, whose desk was just on the other side of the glass from me. Jackson did not call himself a reporter. He called himself an investigative journalist, as in, *Hello, I'm Jackson Price, an investigative journalist with the* Lawsonville Ledger, which made the guys back in layout practically fall all over themselves making fun. But Rose said it was not his fault and, instead, blamed Watergate in which the hard work of two reporters had brought down a president. "Anymore you have to be an investigative journalist to feel like you're doing your job," she had said.

Jackson was handsome. He had black, wavy hair and dark eyes, and women back in the business office made a point of bringing memos into the newsroom just to peek at him, but he didn't do a thing for me. The editor, though, Ed Stivers, he was another story, although you might not think it. He was a short, scrawny sort of man who was losing his hair, but there was something about him you couldn't put on paper. When Ed Stivers walked into a room, he filled the room, and whatever it is that gives a man that kind of power; I don't know. Rose told me to look out for him, which shows you how smart Rose turned out to be, but I couldn't help it. All he had to do was look at me, and I'd get the creepy crawlies up my arm as if my arm were something to stare at, as if there was nothing in this world more naked than my wrist.

Rose waited until after I got my first paycheck from the *Ledger* before suggesting that I move to my own place. She had a friend, Victor, who rented rooms in his house. It was an old house across from the Pratt River, with a magnificent green porch circling it like a skirt. Victor was waiting for us on the porch in a large, wicker chair, a fragile-looking man with long, graying hair he had pulled back in a ponytail. He was the organist for St. Paul's Episcopal Church, Lawsonville's oldest, a fact which had led him to write a booklet on the history of St. Paul's. He had six hundred copies printed, then placed in the Chamber of Commerce for tourists, only no one at the Chamber of Commerce cared, and often he would go in there and find them buried under pamphlets for Dragon City, a miniature golf course and go-kart track. The few wandering tourists who did make their way into the church had no one to greet them. No tour, not even a plaque to read. Victor was by himself on this mission. He also taught music appreciation at the community college, a job he suggested was trying.

Victor lived on what I would have called the second floor of the house because it was up one story from the street, but houses here were built this way to protect them from floods. There were two floors above Victor's, but you did not reach them by going through his apartment; in fact, you did not go into Victor's apartment, hardly ever. Victor was a collector of antique chairs, and he did not want people sitting on them, so when you knocked on his door, he always came outside, pulled the door closed behind him, and talked to you on the porch. I saw the chairs once. They were grouped together in small clusters as if they were having conversations.

To get to the third and fourth floors, you went through a door on the side of the porch to a back flight of stairs. Rose said she believed she'd stay on the porch on account of bad knees, so I followed Victor by myself, and when he reached the third-floor landing, he stopped. "A young man lives here," he said and winked at me, but just then the door opened, and out he stepped.

He was a little older than me but not by much, skinny, with dark, straight hair that hung down in his face. Michael was his name. He looked startled to see us standing outside his door, and he put up a hand as if to shield himself. "Victor, I've got to run."

"Don't you want to meet your new neighbor?"

"Hi," he said to me. "Now, I swear I've got to go."

Then he turned and started down the stairs. Why he stopped, I can only guess; he heard the voice of his mother, or somebody, in the back of his mind saying, *Be polite,* so he came back up the stairs and held out his hand. I shook it. "Well," he said. "I guess I'll see you around then."

"I guess."

When he left for good this time, Victor turned to me. "You'll love Michael when you get to know him. You won't be able to help yourself."

We walked up the next flight of stairs to a door, which opened onto still another set of stairs that took you to the fourth floor, which looked to me like the attic, jury-rigged into an apartment. I didn't mind. It would be like camping out. Near the top of the stairs were three small rooms, a kitchen, a bathroom, and a bedroom, connected by a long, narrow hallway to a large living area that stretched across the front of the house. The living room had dormer windows on three sides that looked out over the river.

Victor ran around opening windows. "There's always a breeze off the river," he said, which was not usually true, but true that day. Because the side windows faced each other they pulled air in through one side, straight out through the other side, strong enough to knock over a lamp. We sat on a nubby, green couch in the center of the room, and Victor told me about the history of the house, which was built in 1756 by a sea captain for his bride. "Soon after he moved her in," Victor said, "the captain prepared to set sail, but during the weeks of preparation, his wife was besieged by dreams in which he drowned under a raging sea. She pleaded for him not to go, but he was a sea captain, for heaven's sake. He was also a man of reason who put little stock in the mysteries of dreams and superstition, but to calm his wife, he told her that in his dream he had been an old man, dying in her arms. You know, of course, what happened next."

"What?"

"He sailed away and, just as his wife had feared, was swept overboard in a storm and drowned."

"No."

"I swear. But when the news came ashore, she would not believe it and lived the rest of her life locked inside this very house vowing never to come out until he returned. It is said she died three years later of a broken heart, although I'm never clear on the mechanics of that. Do you know, Ruth? Does the heart just stop working or what do you think happens?"

"I sure don't know."

I walked over to a window and looked out at the river and the vacant lot beside it. The only building on that side of the street was a bar called Jack's by the River. To the left I could see the South Lawson drawbridge and the wide Chocowin River. I watched cars drive across the bridge. The water underneath was churning in ribbons of white foam.

"Tell me, Ruth," Victor said. "Do you believe in ghosts?"

"No."

He nodded, but I got the feeling he did not believe me. "You?" I asked. "Have you ever seen a ghost?"

"No. But I feel certain they are here, at least our sea captain's wife, but I don't think she wants to talk to me."

"Well, she better not talk to me."

"I thought you didn't believe in ghosts."

"I don't. But just in case."

As we went back downstairs, Victor said, "You ought to get yourself a fan. It's unbearable up here when the wind dies down."

I could see that. Even with the breeze, I was sweating, although I don't mind to sweat. Rose and I got to talking about it one day, and she admitted the same. As long as you don't have too many clothes on, that's the trick. If you can sweat free, skin to air, air to skin, then sweating can make you feel like you're ready for anything, good for something in this world. I did not mention this to Rose, but it helps also to have a can of cold beer to press against your face every now and again.

When we left Victor's, we headed back into town and met Carol at Dickie's Diner for pie, except I would not eat the pie. Carol nudged it closer to me, like maybe if I noticed it, I might eat it, but I didn't want pie. I told her that when we sat down. "I'll just have a Coke," was what I said, but she ordered it anyway. Blueberry. Carol got stains on her teeth from hers.

Carol looked just like Rose only younger and bigger, all-over bigger, like if Rose was a car, Carol would be a tank, but she had Rose's same red hair and same pasty skin that would not age well, and I often wondered if Carol ever looked at Rose and saw her own future. We sat in a green booth, the same one Carol always sat in when she ate at Dickie's, which turned out to be almost every day, usually meat loaf, mashed potatoes, and lima beans unless it was breakfast; then it was hot cakes and sausage links. The sign out front read Virginia's Diner, but Virginia's nickname was Dickie, so that's what people called it. Virginia "Dickie" Beaumont was Carol's best friend.

We always had to meet Carol at Dickie's because she would

not set foot in Rose's office on account of the recent newspaper articles criticizing the Lawson County Hospital, where she worked as a nurse. Carol did not call them articles. She called them *a rampage*, but she was not alone, because people all over town were saying the same thing. *Stivers is on a rampage against that hospital*, you would hear them say, because Stivers's style was to focus a lot of attention on a single story, *to go after it*, as he put it, for days or sometimes weeks at a time. Rose did not call it a rampage. She preferred bee in the bonnet.

Carol had her own theory. The articles had started when the reporter, Jackson Price, caught eighteen members of the Hospital Board of Directors coming out of a meeting in the back room of Allen's Surf and Turf. The next day's headline read: **Hospital Holds Illegal Meeting,** illegal because of the "sunshine law," which required public board meetings to include the press, and there was no law the newspaper knew more about. Stivers taught his reporters always to be on the lookout for illegal meetings, and they had been extremely successful at this, catching the Lawson County Commissioners several times, the Lawsonville Planning Commission, and the Chocowin County School Board.

To me, the meeting seemed a little thing, even a silly thing, but, Rose explained, to Stivers, it was everything. If people could meet in secret, she said, they could do anything, and it was precisely because Stivers took the public meeting law so seriously, that people assumed his campaign against the hospital began with that meeting at Allen's Surf and Turf, but Carol said no. She claimed the whole thing started because of a dog.

Stivers's dog was big and black and, it was said, more big than pretty. I never saw it. Ed Stivers lived in a house outside Lawsonville on a road that ran alongside the Pratt River. People said it was a strange house for Lawson County, shaped like a circle, modern and off to itself in the woods. There were other houses on the street but not enough to make Stivers think he could not let his dog roam. It roamed all over the place, too, boundless, like it sighted its territory from the air, even crossing the Pratt into the River Woods Subdivision, where it roamed, big and wet, among the brick and stucco houses and well-tended yards of people like Sam Waters. Who knows what happened? Carol said she didn't. Maybe the dog bit somebody. Maybe it tore up somebody's flower garden. Or maybe Mr. Waters just didn't like dogs, but for whatever reason, he did not try to find out whose dog it was. He should have. But he didn't. He called the pound.

Mr. Waters owned a tractor dealership in Lawsonville. He was also chairman of the Lawson County Hospital Board of Directors. "And if you don't think that has anything to do with all this," Carol said, "you can call me a fool."

On the day we met Carol at Dickie's, the newspaper had run a front-page article going over, item by item, a hospital bill sent to a Mrs. Eloise Snell for gallbladder surgery, and hinting that certain charges were not on the up-and-up. Carol handed Rose the newspaper and said, "This has gone too far."

"I know," Rose said.

"You ought to quit," she told Rose.

"I'm not going to quit."

"You ought to quit anyway."

I took the last sip from my Coke and said, "Did you ever think, Carol, that somebody had to give Stivers a copy of that bill? I mean, it's not like there aren't people in this town on his side."

Carol sighed and looked down at the slice of pie in front of me. She never looked at me. It was like she thought if she ignored me, I might go away. Dickie stopped by to bring Carol another glass of iced tea and Rose a fresh cup of coffee. "Would you like another Coke, honey?" she asked me.

"No, ma'am," I said.

"She's not eating that pie," Carol told her.

Dickie sat down beside Carol and smiled at me. She was a small, angled sort of woman, the kind you'd look at and say, *Now there's a woman with elbows.* She had wispy blond hair that tended to fall in her face unless she pulled it back, which she often did with pink or yellow bow-shaped barrettes, as if she still thought of herself as a little girl, except here came out of her mouth a deep voice, soothing and gentle like somebody's mama ought to sound singing a lullaby. I loved to hear Dickie talk, like when she said *oysters*, it was as if the first syllable were padded just like real oysters feel padded, soft and yummy to the ears.

Carol reached over and took a bite of my pie. "Mind?" she asked.

"Go ahead," I said.

"I've been thinking, Mother."

"Not again," Rose said.

"That it's time you quit your job and moved in with me. Dickie and I were saying the other day how nice it would be if you came to live with me, weren't we, Dickie? Then I wouldn't have to worry so much about you anymore."

"You don't have to worry about me now. Worry makes a bad thing worse and a good thing foolish, so stop it."

"I know that's what you always say, but listen. I could get somebody to build a second bathroom next to the spare room. That way you'd have some privacy, if you needed it. I could call Clark; he would build it for us. If you moved in with me, you wouldn't need to work anymore."

"Don't be ridiculous," Rose said.

Carol and Dickie gave each other a look, then Dickie turned to me, "Where in the world did you get such nice hair?"

"It's not so great."

"You should let me fix it up sometime."

Carol took another bite of my pie, leaned back, and sipped her tea. "So, Mother. What did Dr. Henry say?"

"I have no idea," Rose said.

Carol put the glass down. Dickie put her hand on Carol's arm. "I thought you had an appointment this morning."

"I did, but I canceled it."

"What did you do that for?"

"Because," Rose said. "I'm not sick, and Dr. Henry's an idiot."

Dickie gave Carol's hand a little pat then stood up. "I'll be right back, y'all," she whispered.

Carol turned suddenly to me. "I wish you'd eat some of this pie."

"She doesn't want pie, Carol," Rose said.

"Thank you anyway," I said, smiling. I wanted Carol to like me. I should have eaten that pie.

| MALLING

The phone rang about a week after I'd moved into the apartment while I was sitting in the dark, watching the traffic light on the bridge below turn from red to green to yellow then back to red, the colors like streamers waving on the water. I had the radio tuned to a station out of Raleigh that played thirty minutes of nonstop music after midnight. It was Rose on the phone. "Cecil's in jail."

Cecil Swann went to jail several times a year for writing on walls, but it was not going to do any good because Cecil was never going to quit. It was his job to write on walls. He was, as he put it himself, a public poet. This time it was the new mall. Cecil hated the mall, but he was the only one, because the rest of Lawsonville could not wait to finally get it. *We'll be just like Raleigh*, people said. Nobody seemed to care that the mall had destroyed an entire swamp, although Cecil said plenty of people were going to care, the next time it rained hard, and all that water had nowhere to drain. He wrote in huge, black letters across the side of JC Penney:

IN THE MALL
YOU ARE MALLING
THE MALL IS YOU AND YOU ARE THE MALL
BEWARE OR BE-MALLED

"It's graffiti," I told Rose.

"It's not hurting anybody."

"It's still illegal, Rose."

She was coughing all of a sudden and could not answer me. "Rose?" She had set down the receiver, but I could hear her in the background, and in a minute she came back.

"I'm going to get him," she said.

"Are you all right?"

"I'm fine."

"How about I meet you there."

City Hall was only three blocks away from my apartment, and I had planned to walk, but on my way down the stairs, I ran into Michael, who was coming up. He looked at his watch then at me. "Going out?"

"Yeah."

He shrugged and put his hands in his pockets. "Where are you going?"

"To meet Rose."

"Rose?"

"My friend . . ."

"I know." He looked at his watch again. "It's late to be going out."

"Yes, it is."

"You shouldn't be walking around town this late at night."

"Why, isn't it safe?"

"You should just be careful."

I nodded and was headed down the stairs when he spoke up again. "Did you know, I hear you at night sometimes. Through the floor. The radio and . . ." Then he pretended to pop the top off an invisible beer can and drink.

"What are you saying; I should be quieter?"

"No, no. It's nice to have company." He smiled.

"Right. Well. See ya."

I got to City Hall before Rose and waited for her on the wide, stone steps, still warm from the heat of the day. Rose drove a noisy, pale blue Buick, the sort of car you heard before you saw. I heard her turn off Elm onto Battle Street, then watched as she slowed and parked under a streetlight. She could have seen me had she looked, but she did not look, and for a minute I could not swear it was Rose. In the half-light she looked like a much younger woman, somehow straighter, thinner, taller, a Rose that used to be, and I was suddenly sad that I had not known her then, when she was young. I would have liked to have been young with Rose. She closed the car door and headed across the street, muttering to herself. She was wearing white knit pants, a red blouse, and baby blue house slippers. As she got closer, she barely looked up. "How about we don't tell Carol about this," she said as she marched up the steps to meet me.

The police station was on the second floor, up a wide, wooden staircase. It made me nervous. I had an uneasy feeling about the law, which was something I learned from Mama. She avoided the police because, although she had never done anything wrong in her life, in her mind there was no way the law could be on her side. I remember watching her drive the Impala; if a cop was around, she'd white-knuckle the steering wheel and hold her breath until he passed; you'd think she was hiding a dead person in the trunk. She especially worried about William getting in trouble, and she did not trust herself to explain how it was with him, that he could not have meant whatever he might have done. The way I saw it, she spent most of her life keeping out of the way: *If they don't see you, they can't crush you*—one way to live. Rose wasn't one bit scared.

There were three officers in the police station, and they all seemed to know her. "Howdy, Miss Rose," one said. He was a skinny man with a funny way of walking, as if one leg were shorter than the other. "Can I get you some coffee, Miss Rose?"

No one seemed surprised to see her. A large, silver-haired officer teased, "You sure you want him, Miss Rose?" He handed her something to sign. "You ought to buy that boy some paper to write on, Miss Rose," he said. "It'd be cheaper than bail."

"Y'all ought to leave him alone," she said.

The police station smelled like somebody had left their lunch out too long. It was lit with flittering fluorescent lights, and the green-speckled linoleum on the floor was peeling. Rose sat down, filled out the form, then stood back up. "And you'll drop the charges if he cleans it up?"

The officers looked at each other, then the skinny one spoke. "We're not going to be able to keep doing this forever, Rose."

"I know," she said.

"I'm just telling you," he said.

A young policeman with tight lips and buzzed hair brought Cecil out. Cecil would not look at anybody, not even Rose. He was dressed in exactly the same clothes he had been wearing the first time I had seen him standing by the rail next to the river, maroon pants, navy coat, but this time he had a black knit hat, which he squeezed between his hands. He stared at the floor with eyes that looked like he had forgotten how to sleep. You could smell him from across the room.

"You okay, Cecil?" Rose asked.

He shrugged.

"They treat you right?" she asked, pointing to the policemen who stood now in a sort of line, grinning. The silver-haired one offered Cecil a doughnut. Cecil did not take it, but when the skinny one held up the tapestry bag, Cecil lunged for it. The officer then yanked it back, while at the same time, the young policeman held Cecil so he could not reach it. Two inches, maybe, separated Cecil's fingers from his bag. The policemen were all laughing now. "You steal this from your Mama, eh, Cecil?" the skinny one said, and they laughed harder.

"Maybe he stole it from Rose," the silver-haired one said.

"What else you think he gets from ole Rose?"

Then the officer stopped laughing and said, "If I ever read anything else you write on a wall, I'm locking you back up and throwing away the damn key."

Rose walked over to him, saying, "Why, Earl, I didn't even know you could read," and she took the bag right out of his hands.

Rose held Cecil's hand as they walked down the courthouse steps. She led him to her car, opened the door, and helped him inside. I watched them from the top of the steps, and when she closed the door, she turned and looked up at me. "You can come, too."

I followed them to Rose's house, stopping off to get beer, and when I got there, she and Cecil were already in the living room, sitting in the dark with cups of instant coffee in their hands. Cecil was stretched out on Rose's gold, velveteen sofa. Rose was next to him in a big, red chair, which was next to two dead plants and a stack of old newspapers. There were other stacks of newspapers along the wall next to the door, and hanging above them were two pictures; one, a blown-up photograph of Rose in a flight suit, and the other, a watercolor beach scene. In the center of the room was a coffee table that looked like an old wagon wheel covered with glass, and on it were two ashtrays shaped like dogs with red plaid beanbag bodies and little brass bowls on their backs for ashes. Those ashtrays were my favorite part of the room. Rose didn't mind if you put your feet on the table.

Nobody knew how old Cecil was. People claimed he and Rose had once been lovers, and maybe they still were, although Rose never said, and I figured it was nobody's business. Sixty-six was what Rose guessed, although even she did not know for sure. "I can't tell you he knows," she said. They met each other when Rose wrote a story about him for the *Chocowin Crier*. At the time, he was writing poetry and living under the porch of a restaurant in Sutter's Cove, which now was a tourist town on the river, but then it was just a place where local people ate. It wasn't really even a restaurant, just a bar that served oysters and sometimes clams with saltine crackers. Cecil wrote poems on the walls, both inside and out, and people used to sail in off the river to drink beer and read the stuff he wrote. Rose said he would be there still, probably getting into a lot less trouble, if the restaurant had not been sold, but it was, and the new people did not want Cecil hanging around. They nailed up cedar shingles on the outside. Inside they painted the walls. A thousand poems buried under salmon-colored paint.

Rose wanted me to hear one of Cecil's poems, and as she rummaged through his old bag, she told us that her father back in Texas had filled notebooks with poems that no one ever knew about. "My sister, Frances, found them after he died. I'm no judge, but I thought they were pretty good. They were hidden in the back of a file cabinet in the print shop, more than twenty-five notebooks full. Frances never did get over it. I have one of the notebooks; Cecil's seen it, you remember, Cecil? Frances always said she would send me the others, but she never did, and now I don't even know where they are." She started coughing again and stood up and walked to the kitchen, where she got a drink of water. I looked at Cecil, and he looked back at me. When Rose came back, she continued looking through Cecil's bag. "Ruth was married to a poet," she said. "Why don't you tell Cecil about him, Ruth."

I had my feet propped up on the wagon-wheel table, a beanbag ashtray balanced on my stomach, and with that, it was my turn to cough. "What's there to say?"

"Well, what kind of poetry did he write?"

"Bad." I took my feet off the table and lit a cigarette.

Rose said, "Everybody has to start somewhere."

All I could think of was the last sign I'd seen in front of the Little White Church in Huntington: WAL-MART IS NOT THE ONLY SAVING PLACE, so quickly I added, "Religious."

Rose nodded. "I'm sure he was sincere."

"And that was only half his problem."

Rose turned to Cecil. "Tell me which poem you'd like to read to Ruth."

"None of them."

"Here," she said, handing him an old, stained envelope scribbled with words. "Read this one."

He looked from me to Rose then back to me again.

"You want a beer?" I asked him, and he nodded. "I'll get you one." He drank it down like water. Then he pulled his black knit hat low over his head and began to read.

Hear them gathering,
the ducks of autumn.
Squadrons advancing

from one pond to the next.
One pond,
one lake,
one river to the next.
Counting survivors.
Tedious this, dodging bullets.

I remember summer, along a country road.
Papa,
alert, as Papas are,
prepared to engage on sturdy feet
and whatever you can do with a strong bill.
Mama and ducklings in the morning glories.
I surrendered,
crossed the road,
wished him silent luck for all that lay ahead.

Rose and I clapped, and Cecil drank the rest of my beer. Then Rose handed him another poem to read, saying something about this one being her favorite, saying how Ruth ought to hear this one. It was about a river, except he could not get through it. His voice softened down like a balloon losing air and, before we knew what was happening, he was taking long pauses between words which, at first, I took to be part of the poem, like it was supposed to be that way. Then the pauses got longer. Finally I figured out he was crying.

Rose stood up and placed her hand on his shoulder. He handed her the poem and put his face in his hands, his shoulders moving with silent sobbing. Rose stroked his back. I went to the kitchen and got him a Little Debbie Oatmeal Cream Pie and another beer, which settled him down. He lay back on the sofa and closed his eyes.

It was hard not to like Cecil after that. Not that I had ever disliked him, but Cecil was not the kind of person you're going to want to go out of your way to meet. But when you see the sadness in a person's life, somehow you have to like them, and it came to me that it was these sad parts of a person that Rose always managed to see.

Cecil fell asleep on the couch, and Rose covered him with a blanket. "He really hates that mall," Rose said.

"He ought not to write on walls, Rose."

"How're you going to stop him?"

"I don't know, Rose. I don't know."

I drove home near sunrise following a half-moon like a streetlight over the highway, thinking about all the things in this world I did not know.

Cecil had holed up on the velveteen sofa in Rose's living room where he slept, scribbled on a yellow legal pad, and smoked. I told Rose, "Why pay for cigarettes? Just go inside and breathe."

I went out there one Saturday and found Rose sitting outside on her patio, drinking coffee and reading the newspaper. She read every word of the newspaper every day, starting with the comics, a habit she said she got from her father, who had let her and her sister proofread his paper as soon as they could read. I walked down to a small creek that ran through the woods behind her house, and when I got back, I asked her what it was called. "Sinking Creek," she said. "My younger daughter, Alma, used to go back there, too. She liked to catch bugs."

"Why do they call it that?"

"I don't know."

Sinking Creek was now a trickle of water in a muddy ditch, but Rose said that by spring, the water would be over the banks, covering the roots of trees now sticking out of the mud like bones. "That's why the mosquitoes are so bad in my yard," she said. "Anytime you get water rising and falling like this, it's heaven for mosquitoes."

"Where does it go?"

She folded the newspaper. "Want me to show you?"

But to my disappointment, she did not follow me to the creek but started back toward the house. "You're going to get Cecil, I guess?"

She turned around to look at me. "I'm going to get snacks. How about we make it just the two of us today?"

We took along a couple of cold sausage patties wrapped in a paper towel plus a bag of potato chips and two Cokes in a plastic bag and started into the woods. The trees here were tall, straight pines that you'd swear were planted in rows, and maybe they were, by paper companies. Their branches started more than halfway up their trunks, so the effect was of walking through a tidy grove of poles, pine needles under our feet. I led the way along the creek bank with Rose picking along behind me. We walked without talking except when I stopped and waited for her to catch up. "You want to turn back now? I don't want to get so far we can't get back."

"No, no, we've come this far. There's something up here I want to show you."

Which was fine with me. I had spent half of my childhood in the woods behind my house in Summerville. It was where I went to get away from home. To tell the truth, there was nothing truly horrible there, but William was all the time pestering me to play with him or draw him pictures or something, which I didn't mind to do, but you can't keep it up all the time without going crazy. If Margaret was home, she and Mama would likely be yelling at each other, and if she wasn't home, Mama was the loneliest person to be around I know. I had no friends. It was one of those things that only hurt in waves, because there were times I would tell myself, *Who needs them,* the kind of thing you say with your head held high, but other times, it felt like somebody had bored

a hole right through me, I was that lonely. I never felt lonely in
the woods.

The woods behind my house stretched all the way to the edge
of the ridge. They were thick and brambled, but there were paths
cleared by boys I did not know, although I liked to pretend they
were cleared by Indians. These paths would take you almost anywhere, the fastest way from a hundred tamed lawns to Lonnie's
Kwik Pik, where you could buy bubble gum or cigarettes. I stayed
clear of the subdivisions, keeping to the least-worn trails, the ones
that plunged deep enough into the woods to lose the sounds of
car engines, barking dogs, and children. I came out along a narrow road that wound along the edge of the ridge where some of
Summerville's original vacation homes stood, large, rambly
houses with huge yards, some set so far back from the road you
could not see them except in the winter, when the leaves were
gone off the trees. In spring, I wriggled onions up out of the
ground on the side of the road to eat along the way. There was
an art to it. You had to hold the stems close to the ground and
pull without jerking, then they would pop out of the ground,
whole and covered with dirt. I cleaned them by peeling off the
outer skins, exposing the pure white bulbs. They tasted hot and
crisp.

About a half a mile down the road on the ridge side, past where
the last house was built, was a large rock overlooking the valley.
Umbrella Rock, because that's what it looked like, an opened
umbrella, a half a toadstool gripping the cliff. I would lie up there
in the sun like a snake on a warm rock, watching hawks or listening to the wind, but this was not the best place. The best was
under the rock, where you could go if you shinnied down the side
of it. The rock jutted out past the edge of the slope, so to get all
the way under you had to hold on to a skinny dogwood and swing

out, then around, which made it seem dangerous, like there was a price for entry. It felt like being in a cave, my own private hideaway, although I knew other kids went there, too. There was a burnt-out place where a campfire had been, and on the rock walls, names written with charred sticks or chipped out of the limestone, names and dirty words. I pretended the campfire was evidence of former Indian dwellers, the dirty words, messages written in a mystic, long-forgotten language. I sat in the dirt, looking at the valley through a wall of trees, a quiet wind, a snap of limbs, an occasional hawk, and the twittering of smaller birds alarmed by me.

Rose and I followed Sinking Creek through the woods for about an hour before stopping to rest beside a large pool. The Cokes were warm. We drank them anyway and ate potato chip crumbs, licking our fingers and sticking them into the bag, then licking the crumbs off. I leaned against a tree and asked Rose, "Is Cecil your boyfriend?"

"He would like to think so."

"Are you going to marry him?"

"Good grief, no. You know the only reason I got married the first time was because Larry DuPres threw a ball through a hole in a barn door."

"How would I know?"

"Fourth of July, 1928. I knew better than to marry him, so I made him a deal."

"That if he hit that hole . . ."

"I never thought he'd do it. He had a good arm, but he was fifty feet away, for heaven's sake. My sister was furious. She never did like Larry. *He is not,* she would say, *a man of his word,* which may have been true, but I don't know how she knew so quick. She was a born fuddy-duddy, trying to fill our mama's shoes is what I think, but I was always and forever my father's daughter. He looked at life like you might an ice-cream store; you can choose vanilla if you want. You know you're going to like it, and there's always enough, but you can try different flavors."

"So what was Larry, Rose? Chocolate?"

She thought for a minute. Then she said, "Pistachio Almond."

Larry DuPres worked for the Texas Oil Company selling lube oil to businesses in southeast Texas, and one of them was the printing shop owned by Rose's daddy, Frank Smith. The family no longer lived in Agua Vista. After her mother and brother died, her father moved them to a small town called Bland between Port Arthur and Galveston. He knew people there, some uncles on his mother's side, and there were cousins who helped him run the presses. Rose told me that her mother had wanted to move there all along to get away from Pancho Villa, and had her father listened, they might have escaped the influenza, a regret he carried with him for the rest of his life, although Rose pointed out that, had they stayed put, her other brother, Tommy, would have avoided the fishing crew that went down in a late autumn storm.

When Larry showed up, Rose was already near 30, past the age when people spent time wondering who she might marry. Larry was tall and dark-haired and different from the boys Rose had known all her life, who thought the best life offered was drinking bootlegged beer behind Forrest Winfrey's feed store. "He'd come to town in a company car wearing a beige Palm Beach suit, pressed white shirt, blue print tie, and cream-colored fedora with a baby blue band above the brim," Rose said. "Took my breath away. He was a ballplayer, and when he showed up, somebody would always be scrambling to get up a game. They would head to the field behind the Church of Christ, and those who did not join in would stop what they were doing to watch a few innings. Me too. He claimed to be part French and could trace his heritage all the way back to the pirate, Sir Francis Drake."

Sir Francis Drake was an Englishman. It was Frances who pointed this out to Rose. "She was not as pretty as I was," she said. "If she had been the one with my red hair, she would have been singing a different tune."

Rose explained she wasn't so interested in the French part of his story as she was the pirate part, because it was no feat to imagine Larry on a pirate ship, leaping about on the rigging, waving a sword in the air, and the reason had everything to do with the way he threw a ball. Everybody in town liked to see it, but for Rose it was especially thrilling because right before every pitch, he would search the crowd for her, and when he found her, he would smile. *Watch this*, he seemed to say. Then he would start. He would stand perfectly still with the ball hidden in his glove, and those that had seen what came next would hold their breath. Even those who had never seen it would hold their breath, because there was something explosive underneath all that stillness, like watching a rocket right before it takes off. Larry was not a huge man, but he was muscular; you could see it when he rolled up his sleeves. Rose said muscles like that, you can't hide in clothes. He would stand still for longer than you'd think necessary, then, slowly, he would begin to raise his arms. Everything after that happened so fast you couldn't see it until the ball was zooming straight into the catcher's glove. He never threw high or low. Nothing inside or outside. He pitched a fastball straight down the middle every single time, which may not have been enough for the major leagues, but it was a rare local boy who could catch up to it. After each pitch, he would seek out Rose with his eyes once more. *See that?*

"Sometimes I didn't stick around for the whole game," Rose said. "I guess he had to look up and find me gone."

"Sounds like it might have done him good."

"I was no dummy. Besides, I didn't know; maybe he had a girl like me in every little town."

"There couldn't have been another girl like you, Rose."

The Fourth of July picnic was next to the ball field between the church and Colin Walker's old barn. It got up to 102 degrees that day, and, Rose told me, anything I knew about humid I could put in a box and throw away, because there was no humid to beat southeast Texas in July. In the air was the smell of sulfur from the oil refineries, of fried chicken and peach pie and cow manure. Rose was wearing a yellow dress, she said, "to set off my hair." Some of the men were tossing balls to each other when somebody pointed to a hole in the barn door and dared Larry to throw one through it.

"Larry didn't have it in him to turn down a dare, but it was while everyone was gathering to watch when he leaned down, and whispered, 'If I make it, will you marry me?' "

"I still can't believe you did it, Rose."

She smiled. "He had the bluest eyes I'd ever seen."

As I sat there in the woods by Sinking Creek listening to Rose with her wrinkled face and crooked back, I tried to imagine the young Rose in the yellow dress. I swear I could almost do it.

Rose and Larry moved up to Port Arthur, where everything was going along fine until the Depression, then the halls of the Texas Oil Company were suddenly lined with men with nothing to do. All those men stood around not hardly talking to each other, waiting to see who would lose his job. One day, word came down that the district manager was in from New Orleans, and everybody panicked, but the boss, a man named Henry Fletcher, threw Larry a broom. "Act busy," he said. So he did. Larry swept the floor as if the very existence of the company depended on the condition of that floor, and when the district manager passed by, Larry looked him right in the eye.

"People who told the story later said it was just the kind of thing Larry would do," Rose said. "To look a man in the eye like a dare, because, that Larry DuPres, if he was going to be fired, it was going to be his way or no way, but I knew they were wrong. Larry needed that job. That's all he was trying to tell the man, and I imagine when the district manager closed his eyes that night, he went to sleep with the face of Larry DuPres staring at him out of the darkness, a face in a thousand that meant something." Thirty-one people lost their jobs that day, but Larry wasn't one of them.

"He never forgot it either," Rose said. "But it changed him. It was like there was life before the broom and life after, but life after belonged to the company. I think it took all the joy right out of him."

They began to move around. Jackson, Mississippi; Johnson City, Tennessee; Little Rock, Arkansas; Wilmington, North Carolina. Wherever the Texas Oil Company sent them, they would go, leaving friends, leaving routines, packing up boxes that never got unpacked. Rose said it was lucky they did not have children then. But wherever they went, Larry always managed to make new friends, bringing with him his good looks, his good arm, and his reputation for being a "wise-cracker." (Rose meant wiseass, but her mother had taught her not to curse.) Larry pulled pranks. His favorite was to take people on drives in the company car, stopping halfway across a railroad track and pretending the car would not start. He would keep trying to start it, and keep failing, until they heard the train whistle, and only after his passengers scrambled out of the car would he start it for sure, easy as pie, and drive to safety. He took apart one fellow's car and reassembled it on his roof, and he herded another friend's milk cow into his bedroom while no one was home. "The darnedest thing," said Rose, "was people loved him anyway. Maybe it's rarer than you think to find somebody who makes you laugh."

And who will do anything for you. For as mischievous as Larry was, Rose said he was also generous, the first one in line when somebody needed help, moving furniture, fixing cars, even lending money, and more than that; he was successful. Even during the Depression, Larry managed to sell more oil for the Texas Oil Company than any other salesman, which was one of the reasons they kept moving him. Once he shored up one place, they would send him to another. But the more they moved, Rose said, the more there seemed to be an edge to his pranks. Like the time in Little Rock he took a live tarantula to the office and set it loose.

"I can't believe you would tell another tarantula story, Rose."

"I can't help it if it's true."

"I don't care if it's true. A person ought not to have but one big spider story in their life. That's enough."

"I've got more."

"Don't even tell me."

"The thing to understand, Ruth, is that Larry went too far."

"Too far? Are you kidding? I would have killed the son of a bitch, and that, Rose, is the truth. I suppose that's why you left him?"

"No, hon. It took a lot more than that for me to leave." She raised her eyebrows, narrowed her eyes, and lowered her voice like somebody who's watched way too many spy movies. "Her name," she whispered, "was Eleanor."

She discovered Eleanor in a letter at the bottom of a suitcase.

"I wasn't trying to snoop, either; I would not have noticed had it been white. A folded piece of white paper? Could be anything, only it wasn't white. It was lavender. *Little Larry is getting bigger, and I need more money.* You know what I said to him? I said, that baby doesn't need any more money; what that baby needs is his daddy. Straight to his face, I said it."

"What'd you do that for, Rose?"

"It's what I believed."

"I think you let him off too easy."

"You think?"

"I would have strangled him."

"Larry would not have lived long around you."

"No kidding."

That's how Rose found herself in a bus station in Wilmington, North Carolina. She had planned to buy a ticket to Texas. By then Frances, who never did get married, was working full-time in the printing business with their father, and there were inklings in his letters that she had more ambition than he thought necessary. Already she was selling pens, pencils, staplers, paper clips, art supplies, and all kinds of fancy paper, and she was talking about expanding to a second store down the road, all of which were good for business. Rose understood this. She knew if the business did not grow, it might die, but she sympathized with her father, whose heart was in his printing shop and the small newspaper that came out of it. Some things are better off dead than altered out of recognition, so there was a place for Rose, a role to play, to rein her sister in, but . . .

There was always this *but,* and every time she got to this part of the story, I waited for it. I suppose Rose could not help feeling a little bit like a failure, to have come so far and now to be going back.

While Rose was waiting in the ticket line, there was some commotion, and she looked up to see an old black man running, although to see Rose imitate him through the trees next to Sinking Creek, it was less like running than hobbling fast. A policeman was right behind him, shooing him out of what was then considered the "white" section of the bus terminal, when the man tripped and fell, hitting his head on the edge of a bench. Nobody around him moved. Nobody spoke. It was a sort of rip in time like you might see between scenes in a play when the actors stop, and everything waits for the scenery to change. Then from somewhere inside the bus station, a woman in pin-striped pants came striding toward the man. She helped him up and sat him back down on the bench. There was a cut on his forehead. She took him by the hand and led him to a water fountain, the Whites Only water fountain, where she took a tissue from her bag and helped him wipe the blood off his face. The policeman approached her, but she glared at him and said, "Shame on you."

"It was something to see a woman traveling in pants like that," Rose said. "You just didn't see it in those days, plus this woman was six feet tall if she was an inch, but more than anything, if there was a rule, she was breaking it."

Only after the woman had helped him buy his ticket and situated him safely back on a bench did she retrieve her bags and board her own bus.

"When I got to the ticket window," Rose said, "I pointed to the woman in pin-striped pants, and asked the man, 'Where's that bus going?'

" 'Lawsonville,' he said.

"And I said, 'One way to Lawsonville then.' "

By now Rose had sat back down on the ground next to me. We leaned against the same pine tree, our four knees bent in a row, two tall, two short. I wadded up the potato-chip bag and took a last swallow of Coke and thought about all she had told me. "I guess it's lucky for me you did not go back to Texas," I said.

"You betcha," she said.

By the sound of passing cars, I could tell that Sinking Creek had followed the highway for some distance, but then it had cut right, deeper into the woods. It was about five feet wide now and deep enough so I could no longer see through it. The water moved slowly; I could hardly tell it moved at all. From where we sat, I could see where the woods stopped abruptly in the distance. I helped Rose up, and we continued following the creek in that direction until it emptied into a gigantic marsh. It was like an explosion of sky, coming out of the woods like that, marsh grass rolling to the horizon, broken only by the snaking of a small river.

I dropped the sack and ran toward it. "Let's go, Rose, let's go," I yelled, and behind me I could hear her yelling something back at me, but I did not understand what she was saying. I ran until the mud under my feet grabbed hold of my shoes, pulling me down. "Help!" I called to Rose, but by then she was laughing.

"You better help, or I'm going to be sucked under. The alligators will eat me."

"There aren't any alligators."

"How do you know?"

"I don't." She was still laughing; she could not help herself.

But there were no alligators, only mud. Up to my knees there was mud. Rose held out a fallen tree limb and braced herself, and I held on to it and slowly walked myself out, my legs covered with slime of a sort of greenish brown color. Rose pulled one of the empty Coke bottles out of the bag. "Fill this up with water and pour it over yourself."

"You do it. I'm not going near that water."

"Follow me."

We circled the edge of the marsh until we came to a road. The road crossed over the marsh on a low, narrow bridge, and when we reached it, we sat down, dangling our feet above the tiny, frantic crabs in the mud below us. From the bridge it was easy to scoop water into the bottle to pour over my legs, streams of dirty water running down my skin. We took off our shoes and lay back on the road with our arms tucked under our heads, feeling the sun on our faces. The air smelled salty, and from the sky came the cries of seagulls.

"You know what this is like, Rose?"

"What, hon."

"Like driving a car barefoot, sand between your toes, radio blaring, you singing along." I was remembering how I used to drive back from the beach with Chuck, a beer between my legs, my brown arms streaked with sea salt, my hair sticky and windblown. Chuck usually let me drive. He liked to pretend he was playing a guitar.

Rose was nodding. She said, "I remember the time Iris Witherspoon and I snuck out of the house in the middle of the night and ran to the beach in our nightgowns."

"How old were you?"

"Sixteen."

"That's pretty shocking, Rose."

"If anyone had found out, it sure would have been. We never told anyone."

"And Iris? Whatever came of her?"

She shrugged. "Probably dead by now."

It was while we were lying there on the bridge, I asked Rose about the woman in pinstripes at the bus station. "That was your friend, Mrs. Pickle, right?"

"Georgia Pickle, yes. A widow already when I met her. She ran a boardinghouse, and by the time I got off the bus in Lawsonville, I had a room. She was an artist, you know, like my brother, Frank. I told her about Frank there on the bus, and she agreed; it's one thing to die, but to take all that talent with you . . ." She sighed and shook her head. "Georgia Pickle pried it out of me that I liked to write, and we used to camp out on her big back porch among the African violets and pink sultana, where she would paint her landscapes, and I would write stories at a small wicker table she set up especially for me. I sent them to my father, who got a kick out of publishing them in his newspaper. I've still got copies somewhere around the house."

Mrs. Pickle's sister, Mrs. Caroline Ellis, also a widow, lived in the house, too, and while Mrs. Pickle painted, Mrs. Ellis cooked, and her cooking, Rose said, was famous. Often people who did not live in the boardinghouse ate there, and one of these was Raymond Lee, who owned a small newspaper down the road in Chocowin County. Raymond was a large man, well over six feet tall when he stood up straight, which he hardly ever did, slumping instead as if trying to fit into a shorter world. He was an awkward sort of man who talked to himself and bumped into things. "He might have told you his body refused to cooperate with him," Rose said, "but that would imply a sense of humor, and Raymond did not have one. Not even a trace. He wanted one, all right. He laughed at jokes other people told, but I could tell he didn't always get them."

Raymond was happy for Rose to work with him on the *Chocowin County Crier*. The problem for Raymond was, he was not at heart a newspaperman, having inherited the *Crier* from his father, who, along with his mother, had died in a house fire while Raymond was away at school. With Rose working, Raymond was free to concentrate on the business side of the newspaper, leaving the writing and layout to Rose, and in time, they got married.

"What do you mean, you got married? What happened before then? Wasn't there more to it? I mean, were you in love?"

"Were you in love with your poet?"

"Who, Chuck?"

"How many were there?"

"He wasn't really a poet, Rose."

"Oh."

I let this sink in for a minute. "And no," I said. "I wasn't in love."

Rose did not look surprised, and I was thankful for it. She nodded and, in a minute, laid a hand on my knee.

I said, "I don't know, Rose. Raymond still doesn't sound like your type."

She didn't say anything, as if the answer were something she used to know. She inspected her arms, which were turning bright pink between the brown spots. Then she said, "I'll tell you the truth, Ruthie. There was something that made me think it would not last. Nothing I could swear to, it's just looking back, it seems like somewhere in the back of my mind I knew something was going to happen, although I sure never thought it would be a train."

Later Rose would show me the place. There is a cross gate now where there was not one then, but you can still tell by the way the road curves how you might not see a train until it was on top of you. Rose said she imagined Raymond talking to himself, looking up, and, as if it were a joke, not getting it until it was too late.

Rose gave me a pat on my leg then, without warning, she started to sing.

"Old Dan Tucker was a mean old man
Whipped his wife with a frying pan
Combed his hair with a wagon wheel
And died with a toothache in his heel.

You know that one, Ruth?"

"No, Rose, I don't."

"I'll teach you." So she did, and we sang it at the top of our lungs. I am thinking if anyone had come up on us that day, they would have sworn we were crazy, me and Rose, but I am telling you this: I had never felt less crazy in all my life. We found a place to sit in the shade of a live oak near the bridge. Rose leaned against it, and the next thing I knew, she was asleep.

The wind was rustling through the sea grass. I heard a bird cry out and searched the trees until I found it on a distant limb. I watched until it flew away, and when it was gone, all I could think about was Homer Birdsong. I had known Homer for a long time, from when he would come into Durwood's. By then I was working regular, summers and after school, at the hardware store selling Mabel Jones's fried pies. She made the pies in a small kitchen behind the store, but she had me wrap them and set them out on the counter. Her two sisters also brought things for me to sell, like jam and fudge and coconut cakes, also hand-sewn dolls and dish towels and aprons. Mabel Jones called her part of the store the Corner Cupboard, and she fixed it up nice so it hardly looked like part of a hardware store, but it was those pies of hers that were the main draw. Personally I could have lived without them because they were so sweet they made your teeth hurt; but I must have been the only person in town who thought this way. There was blueberry and apple, raspberry, strawberry, and rhubarb; whatever she took a mind to, that's what she would make, except there were days she did not feel like making pies, and those were sad days. People left with their heads hanging low, and I was the one who had to break it to them. But it's like everything else; some days there's pie, some days there's not.

Homer Birdsong and his brother, Joey, were carpenters, which is why they were always coming in to Durwood's. They owned their own framing business, and they were so good that when they finished one house, they would move on to another unless they didn't feel like it. There would be work when the money ran out; there always was, because around Summerville it was said you wanted a house framed up by those Birdsong brothers if you wanted a house to last.

It was Joey Birdsong who got Margaret to run away with him. Joey was the talkative one, the one who joked around with Durwood in the store, who liked to drive people out to the construction sites and show them what he could build. Joey was the one who made the deals and shook the hands while Homer stood behind him, grunting and chewing a piece of grass. Joey also happened to play lead guitar in a band that frequented beer joints around town, and that's probably what got to Margaret, that guitar. I never saw it, but she told me it was black with a silver lightning bolt painted on the front. He got an offer from a cousin up in Michigan to join a better band, and when he left, Margaret went with him. The problem was, Margaret did not want to live way up in Michigan. She never would admit she got homesick, but that's what happened, so she came back.

But it was while she was still in Michigan that Homer started coming around. I would look out the window and find him in my backyard for no good reason, sitting under a tree fooling with the bark or messing in the dirt with a stick. If I went out there, he'd say, *Hello, Ruth*. That's all, really. Nothing mean or ugly, nothing you could swear was one thing or another, but I knew there was a world of meaning in those two words.

Hello, Ruth.

It felt risky just to say hello back.

Homer said he had some Indian blood in him, and it was easy to believe because he had a hawk-shaped nose, and his hair was black as night or, as he liked to say, black as an Apache tear, and he had one to show me, a black and glassy stone he carried around with him in his pocket.

One day, I was sitting in the little cave underneath Umbrella Rock watching a hawk. I will tell you how a hawk flies. Like it doesn't care, like you would do if you could close your eyes and float around without worrying what you might bump into. It's what soaring is, except if you could soar it might mean you would be happy, and a hawk does not look happy. He does not look unhappy either; he soars because he can. I used to wish I could do that. I watched as the hawk dove down into the valley and disappeared, but then it pulled back up, and the strangest thing happened. It began flying in a circle in front of me. At first I did not believe what I was seeing; the bird was confused or else it did not see me, but it flew closer and closer with every turn until I would have been blind not to notice. Not to believe that bird was somehow talking to me.

Hello.

That's when I heard footsteps, and there was Homer Birdsong. He was standing in the cave in front of me like there was some magic to it; one minute, nothing, then poof, there he is. He tucked his hair behind his ears, put his thumbs in the pockets of his pants. This is all he said, and I will never forget it:

"I just thought . . . now that we're relatives . . ."

It was not like he grabbed me and threw me down; it wasn't anything like that at all. The way he started, it was nothing, just his fingers running up and down my arm while he told me everything he knew about hawks, which was a lot. I still don't know how he knew so much. He was on the part about how a hawk will eat the bones of his prey then throw them up later when he got around to the buttons of my shirt. I could have stopped him any time, if I had wanted.

I was fifteen years old. Homer was almost twice that, although I had to make him tell me his age. He was my first boyfriend, so I figured that meant I got to know everything about him, like when his birthday was, his favorite color, his favorite food, everything. I bought him presents. I saved him out the best fried pies. He already had a girlfriend, but I didn't care. People said they were going to get married, but I still didn't care. Her name was Stacy, and she worked as a waitress at a restaurant where she wore a red-striped uniform that came only halfway down her thighs. I figured Homer liked Stacy because of her looks, but I was the one he talked to. I was the only one in the world who understood Homer, and that's what counted. That's what I believed. I even told Homer one night; I said, "No one else understands you the way I do," and he did not deny it, although now I am sure it was not true. I did not understand Homer Birdsong one bit.

We would meet under Umbrella Rock, but after a while Homer got to where he didn't like to get out of the car. He would just pull up beside the road in front of Umbrella Rock, and I would get in, and he would take me as far as some dead-end dirt road on the back side of Beaver Ridge, where I might tell him about the kids at my school, or about Mama watching out the window for Margaret to come home, or about that mean Mabel Jones, who would not pay me extra for cleaning up the kitchen after she got through making all those pies. Those were the kinds of things on my mind back then. Or I might ask him one of my about ten thousand questions, because Homer Birdsong did not just know about hawks. He was practically an expert on a lot of things. So I would ask things like, how far away is the sun, or, what's it like to ride a horse, or, do you like scary movies, or, do you believe in God. And he would answer, *(93 million miles; it kills your butt; yes; and you've got to be kidding)*, while fumbling in his pocket for a rubber, which he would bring out and hand to me and point to the backseat of the car. This was not my favorite part. That first time under Umbrella Rock when it had hurt so bad, he told me, "It gets better." He was wrong. I was just lucky it never lasted long.

Afterward, we would lie on the hood of his car looking at stars. It was Homer Birdsong who taught me the names. I could pick out the Big Dipper already, but when I said, "There's the Big Dipper," he looked at me as if I had just correctly identified a dog. *So what?* One night he handed me a pair of binoculars, and said, "Look there." He was pointing to a starless patch of sky, but through the binoculars, I could see it was not starless at all. It was full of stars, and so it went, without binoculars, blackness; with them, more stars than I could count, a door to a secret world. Over the next few months he taught me Cetus and Sirius, and Betelgeuse, Orion, and the Pleiades, and he told me, no matter where you are in this world, you can always look up at night, and there will be the stars, the same stars, everywhere.

"What do you mean? I'm never going to be anywhere but here."

"Maybe not always," he said.

Homer didn't understand much about me, but he had been right about that.

My favorite were the Pleiades, a group of stars that looked like a smudge in the sky until you looked through the binoculars. Homer thought the only thing worth talking about was Orion, but I got tired of Orion, with its fierce straight lines, and would turn the binoculars toward the Pleiades. Homer called them the Seven Sisters and said, "Isn't that just like a bunch of women to tease you like that." I said no. They weren't teasing, just hiding. "From somebody like you."

Homer never did think I was funny.

Then he disappeared. Days went by, weeks, and I could not find him anywhere, but I could not cry over it. If you're going to be heartbroken over something you shouldn't be doing in the first place, you got to do it alone. Mama did not know about Homer Birdsong. I didn't want anybody, ever, to know, and in some ways it was a relief that he was gone. It meant no more sneaking, no more wondering what I could do to make him stay.

Then one day, Homer walked into Durwood's for a fried pie. He leaned across the counter. "You still love them stars?"

And maybe for a minute I was glad to see him, but over his shoulder I caught sight of Mabel Jones staring at me, and all of a sudden I knew she knew. She knew about me and Homer, was about worn-out from knowing. It made her sick to look at me; you could see it plain on her face; she could not have spit and made it worse.

Maybe everybody knew.

I turned so red I could feel the heat. I looked down at my feet and told Homer, "There isn't any pie today."

"Yes there is," he said, pointing to a strawberry. "There's one right there."

"I said there isn't any pie."

He stared at me. Then he looked at Mabel Jones. She didn't say a word, but he got the message and left. He never came back, but I stopped going to Umbrella Rock. I never went there again.

I was crying when Rose woke up. She stared at me, and I braced myself. I knew I was in for questions, starting with the obvious, *What's wrong*, but she did not ask. Maybe she thought about it. But I think it was right then, the moment Rose decided, if I wanted to tell her, I would, so I did the same for her. If Rose wanted to talk to me about cancer, she knew where I was.

"Help me up," was all she said. I did, and she walked back to the bridge and peered up and down the road. "You reckon this is the back road to Sutter's Cove?"

"You don't know?"

She shrugged. "It's where the tourists go now, Sutter's Cove. I never would. But it's good for oysters; maybe I should take you there sometime."

I motioned toward the water under the bridge. "So you think that's where this creek goes, Rose?"

"This is no creek."

"I mean river."

"Mosquito control ditch. It stays full, see, not like a creek. The idea is, if you keep it flooded, mosquitoes can't lay their eggs."

"Does it work?"

"You seen any mosquitoes?"

"Yes," I said.

She nodded. "So, Ruth, what's the difference between a mosquito control ditch and a boat canal?"

"Is this a riddle, Rose?"

"None," she said. "And I'll tell you why. Let's say you own a boat, and you want to be able to drive it from the dock in your backyard to the ocean. You could build a boat canal, if you could get a permit, which is not easy. But let's say the county comes along and digs a mosquito control ditch right past your house."

"You'd be a lucky dog," I said.

"You'd be luckier than that unless there aren't any plans for a mosquito control ditch to be built near your house."

"Then you'd be back out of luck."

"Not if you could pay somebody to build it anyway, build your boat canal but call it a mosquito control ditch."

"A boat canal in disguise."

She sighed. "If Ed Stivers really wanted a story, here's his story. He's never going to find anything on that hospital."

"So why doesn't he?"

"He doesn't know." I must have looked surprised because she shrugged then added, "I don't see why I should give away the best stories."

It was getting late, and I was worried about getting home. The sun had slipped behind a wall of purple clouds, fanning out rays like streaks of silver. Soon it would be dark. If we were lucky, we would be able to see our way back by moonlight, but I didn't know if there would even be a moon. "What are we going to do, Rose?"

She looked surprised that I had asked. "Hitchhike."

I had not spied one car the whole day, and I pointed this out, but Rose just said, "One will come," with that certainty of hers that could be calming. It could also be irritating.

"How far is it to the highway, you suppose?"

She peered down the road. "About two miles."

It felt more like ten. I ran it anyway. There weren't what you'd call reams of traffic on the highway either, but finally I stopped a man in an old green pickup. Turned out he knew Rose, no surprise. He went back and picked her up and had us home in time for supper, which we ate in the mall without telling Cecil.

"How about we don't mention this day to Carol," Rose said, as we sat in the food court eating our Chick-fil-A sandwiches. "Especially the part about the hitchhiking. Carol would have no appreciation for hitchhiking. She'd kill us both for sure."

8 | HOT PEPPERS

Cecil stayed with Rose until he finished cleaning the graffiti off the side of JC Penney, which was not as hard as you'd think, since Rose had made him switch to washable paint. He worked nights. It was faster that way, working all night, sleeping most of the day. People left him alone except for Sid, the *Lawsonville Ledger* photographer, who took pictures of him. Sid had taken a picture of the graffiti when it first went up, and now he had a picture of Cecil washing it off in the glow of parking-lot lights, and he was arguing that the pictures could be used in the paper as stand-alones, pictures that did not need a story to accompany them, just a cutline. Sid, who had little use for reporters anyway, was always wanting his pictures used as stand-alones; as he liked to say, "My pictures speak for themselves." He was arguing this with Ed Stivers, who would have been happy to use Sid's pictures if it weren't for Purdy, who claimed JC Penney would pull its account if the newspaper ran those pictures.

Stivers was not usually one to care. Purdy stormed into the newsroom several times a week demanding a halt to this story or that without getting a rise out of Stivers, who often looked amused, putting his arm across the shoulders of jumpy little Purdy, saying out loud so everybody could hear, "You know we can't mix advertising and news, now can we, Purdy?" But that wasn't the reason. The real reason was Stivers's philosophy, which was, *I'll print whatever I want.*

Which now had gotten him in trouble. At the Lawson County Hospital, seven teenagers had come in with a toxic strain of *E. coli,* two had died, and the whole town was turned upside down over it. Doctors from the Center for Disease Control in Atlanta were staying at the Holiday Inn on River Street while they figured it out. Stivers had suggested in an editorial that the hospital might be responsible, the message being that maybe, just maybe, those kids did not have to die, but it was not going to work. You're not going to be able to use the deaths of children that way, or, as Carol put it, "They died from a disease, not a hospital."

People were mad. All over Lawson County they were mad, and letters were coming in, so many they pulled a woman out of the business office to help open them, and the phone lines were busy all day long. I know; I answered those phones. I could tell which ones were calling about the hospital stories by the way they jumped right into yelling before saying hello. It was the advertisers, though, that mattered to Purdy, and they were telling him that, this time, the *Lawsonville Ledger* had gone too far.

"Gone too far," Purdy screamed in Stivers's face. "You're not going to have newsprint to spit on if you don't quit."

So if canning a picture of the graffiti on JC Penney would make Purdy happy, Stivers would do it. He did do it. "Stuff it, Sid," was what he said to end that argument. I told Cecil it was a victory for him that JC Penney cared so much, but Cecil was not one to put stock in small victories.

When he finished cleaning Penney's, he painted Rose's house, which was something he did for her every few years, and it was not hard to see how nice Rose's house looked compared to others up and down the highway, which were dull and weatherworn. Rose's house was canary yellow and always had been; you could give directions by the color of that house. Then Cecil left. Even Rose did not know where he had gone. "He'll be back though," she told me. "He always comes back."

"At least this time he didn't try to make you pay for getting his teeth fixed," Carol said.

The newsroom got a break from controversy the week the Blue Angels came to town. It was Jackson's turn to fly with them this year, which got his mind off the hospital, and I suspected even he was glad for that. It had become a tradition for the Navy to take a reporter for a ride in Blue Angel Number Seven, the only two-seater, the day before a big air show, because there was no better publicity. You give somebody the ride of his life, he's going to write you a good story. Even Rose got to do it once, the year she complained they ought to give reporters from the *Crier* a chance for once. Of course, she happened to be the only reporter from the *Crier*. She was sixty-five years old at the time, and that was how she came to have a photograph of herself in a flight suit on her living-room wall. "I did somersaults in the air right over the ocean in that plane," Rose had told me. "It was the best thing I ever did."

The day of the air show, Carol picked me up and we drove to Rose's house. Carol owned a straight-shift Mercury that she drove like a bumper car, gunning it, then shifting, then gunning it again. I held on to the dash as she threw the car in fourth gear and lurched over the bridge toward Chocowin County.

"You might help me keep an eye on Mother," she said. "She's come close to being arrested twice for sneaking into restricted areas, and today might be worse because it's her birthday. I swear, she's as bad as Cecil, who is the bane of my existence. Rules are rules, but try telling that to the two of them."

"It's her birthday?"

"Eighty years old today."

"I wish somebody had told me."

"Mother hates it when we make a fuss. It's best to ignore it."

We pulled into Rose's driveway. Carol honked the horn, and we waited. I took out a cigarette. "You're not going to smoke in my car, are you?"

"I guess not." I got out and stood in the driveway.

Carol called out to me, "Maybe you should go get her," but then the back door opened and out she came. I climbed into the backseat to let Rose have the front.

"Sorry," she said. "That was Alma on the phone wanting to come over today. I told her to come next week, but she was not happy about it. She said she had already made us a cake."

"Tell her she can make another one."

"I did."

"Where'd you get that shirt?"

It was, I'll admit, an amazing shirt, bright yellow with red toucans and giant, green ferns plastered across it. "Cecil found it for me."

"Of course he did," Carol said. "Did you know you're wearing it inside out?"

Rose stretched out the hem and peered down at the shirt which was, as Carol said, inside out, although no less bright for it. "I don't care," she said.

"I know you don't," Carol said.

Rose leaned over the seat and winked at me. "You are in for a treat. I flew with the Blue Angels, you know."

"She knows, Mother."

"With Captain Jack Evans. We might see him today."

"No, we won't," Carol said. "He retired a long time ago, don't you remember?" Carol looked at me in the rearview mirror then repeated herself as if, with Rose around, it was necessary to carry on two levels of conversation. "He retired a long time ago."

The Marine base where the Blue Angels put on their air show each year was a twenty-minute drive south of Lawsonville. It seemed a desolate place to me. The buildings looked small and plain against the barren landscape. Lone trees stood stranded like bulldozer survivors. A Marine directing traffic signaled for us to park in a field. Then we headed for a large parking lot next to one of the runways where already a huge crowd had gathered. Carol was telling us, "First we'll see the show, then get hot dogs so we can sit down and rest our feet, then we'll see some of the exhibits, although I don't want to stay all day, and Mother, promise me you won't go where you're not allowed. This is a military base; no fooling around."

Just then we heard the roar of engines, and here they came, six sleek fighter jets doing all kinds of tricks in the air, with Rose beside me whispering nonstop commentary: "All they have to do is move their hands a hundredth of an inch and blam, midair collision . . . that's how steady you have to be . . . nerves of steel . . . Captain Jack Evans let me have the controls, you know, and that's all it took, a tiny shift to the left, and we flipped around 360 degrees . . . they're drenched in sweat when they finish, that's what Captain Jack Evans told me . . . just dripping with sweat . . . Now when it was just the two of us up there over the ocean . . ."
I didn't know what to say.

"Did you really fly in one of those planes, Rose?"

"You betcha."

When it was over, Rose tugged on my sleeve and whispered, "I'll be back."

Carol was having what looked like a serious discussion about heartburn with the man standing next to her. By the time she turned around, Rose was gone.

"Where is she?"

"Probably just getting a Coke. Don't worry, Carol, she isn't a child, you know."

"Tell her that. I swear she wouldn't pull these stunts if Daddy were still alive. Let me give you some free advice, Ruth. No matter what else is wrong with you, just be thankful you had two parents."

I didn't say anything. I followed her through the crowd. There were concession stands and displays of military hardware and planes of all sizes: transport planes, fighters, bombers. Some were roped off so people could not get inside, but others you could climb in and sit in the cockpit. There were long lines of people waiting to get into those planes. Carol was headed toward a glass building at the edge of the runway with a giant RESTRICTED sign across the door when I looked across a wide, sandy field and spied Rose. "There she is."

She was being helped out of a helicopter by a young, uniformed man. The helicopter had just landed on a runway on the far side of the field so I could not swear right away it was Rose, but it was. She and the man got into a jeep, and he drove her along a bumpy path back across the field to where Carol and I were waiting.

"How about a hot dog?" Rose said.

"You are going to give me a heart attack," Carol muttered.

We found out that the young man was an officer, a fact that Rose kept bringing up as if to justify herself, and, more importantly, that he was the son of one of Raymond's cousins who had not grown up around there, but in Jackson, Mississippi. When the young man was sent to the base near Lawsonville, Rose had promised his mother to look after him, and apparently she did, although Carol swore later she had never heard of him. The young man took Carol aside and assured her it had been "no problem" to take Rose up in the helicopter. It was, after all, her birthday, and the least he could do for all the kindness she had shown him.

"What kindness?" Carol demanded when he drove away, but as soon as the words left her mouth, she held up her hands in surrender position, "Forget it. I don't want to know."

We got in line for the hot dogs, but Carol would not speak to Rose. She stood with her arms crossed and her back turned as if to let people know she was not with us. She kept it up all the way until Rose ordered two hot dogs, then she could not stand it anymore. "You can't eat *two*."

"I certainly can."

"You do this all the time, order more than you can eat, then I have to finish it." She turned to me. "She does this all the time." Then she stepped up to the window and directed the woman in the concession stand. "Please. Just one hot dog."

So I ordered two and gave one to Rose.

We found a bench and sat down, me in the middle between Rose and Carol. Carol turned to me. "She still thinks she's twenty and can do whatever she wants."

"She worries too much. You know what I say; there's nothing eats up a life quicker than worry," Rose said.

They weren't talking to each other. I had to turn, first to one, then the other, to keep up.

"She won't even try to take care of herself," Carol said.

"I say, people ought to mind their own business," Rose said.

"She may think this is funny, but she's not well."

"There's nothing in the world wrong with me," said Rose.

"Yea?" By this time, Carol was leaning over me. "How about lung cancer, for starters, or maybe you just forgot."

Rose bit into the second hot dog and chewed on it for a while. Then she turned to me, ignoring Carol completely. "There's a fellow I once knew; his name was Bert, sold me insurance, me and Raymond. Anyway, he got cancer. It was colon cancer, so bad they opened him up, closed him back, and sent him home to die. His wife was a friend of mine, Louise. She took good care of him, but at the same time she got herself ready, you know, to be a widow. She learned how to fill out a tax form, change filters, find the circuit breaker, take care of the car. She was proud of herself; I know she was because she told me, and though she knew it would be hard to live without Bert, she would be okay when the time came. Are you getting the picture here? Everything was ready for the day Bert died, except it turned out Louise died first. Slipped in the bathtub and drowned. Bath-oil beads."

"So what?" Carol said.

"So you never know, that's what." Rose said. She stuffed the last of the second hot dog into her mouth, dusted off her hands, and stood up. "Let's go home."

By the time we stopped at the Jewelry Bug on the way home, Carol had quit being mad. I watched them hold earrings up to each other and make comments. *I don't like the pumpkin ones near as well as the cats, Mother,* and, *I never thought orange did a thing for you.* Rose bought the cats, and she bought Carol a nice pair of pearls. I hung back, but as we were leaving, I picked up a necklace. It was a tiny gold dolphin on the end of a thin gold chain. "I can get that for you if you want," Rose said.

"Nah." I put it back.

The next week as promised, Alma did come over, and when I met her, she had her hands in a bowl of pie crust. Like Rose, she was a small woman but otherwise did not look a thing like her mother. She had dark skin the color of toast and straight, black hair which she nudged away from her face with her shoulder when I walked into the kitchen. She smiled at me. She had the bluest eyes I had ever seen. She tipped the bowl, and a pile of dough tumbled onto a sheet of waxed paper.

"Don't beat it to death," she said. "Some people do." Then she slid a rolling pin through a floured hand and with a few strong strokes, flattened the dough.

Carol sighed and looked at Rose. "That's not what Dickie says."

"Carol," Rose said, "hush."

Carol and Rose were at the kitchen table peeling apples, both of them frowning, and like children made to do chores, they were using more effort than necessary to do a simple thing. You'd have thought they were peeling trees. I picked up some of the peelings they had flung to the floor. Alma placed a glass pie plate upside down on the dough, flipped it, peeled off the waxed paper and, like magic, there was crust. With quick, tiny fingers, she pinched the sides and pricked it in the center with a fork. "You ever make pie?" she asked me.

"No, ma'am."

"I'll teach you," she whispered and winked at me.

Alma had piled Rose's kitchen counters with things you did not ordinarily find there, like jars of picked watermelon rind, pickled okra, apple butter, and chunky loaves of bread. Mostly, though, it was vegetables like yellow squash and long, green zucchini, fat, purple eggplants, cucumbers and peppers and heavy red tomatoes, sacks of green beans and sugar snap peas, bunches of lettuce, sweet corn and carrots and round, ruddy potatoes. Rose's idea of a vegetable was frozen peas or the celery you get in a can of soup, so this was something new. These were not your ordinary vegetables either. These were special because they did not have anything on them, like chemicals. No chemicals. Alma must have pointed this out to me ten times. If there's anything else people are wanting to put on a vegetable, Alma's vegetables did not have any of that either. God pretty much grew these vegetables, which was another thing that drove Carol crazy.

Alma lived with her husband, Dean, and their son, Jacob, on a farm about an hour out of Lawsonville, except it was not just a farm. It wasn't as simple as that. Carol called it a cult but not around Rose because, she said, Rose did not like to hear that kind of word. Carol had told me that Alma had always been a different sort of person, daydreamy, shy, and artistic, a person who did not necessarily see the world the same way other people did. For one thing, she mostly saw the good; as Carol put it, "She was incredibly naive that way." Like me, she spent a lot of her child-hood in the woods behind Rose's house, but unlike me, she collected things, pinecones and rocks and sections of moss and leaves and cicada husks and sticks and feathers, which she arranged on her dresser just so. Carol said that, when they were young girls, the one sure thing she could do to flip Alma out was to move a pinecone out of its place; otherwise, there wasn't much that upset her. Alma was not particularly good at things like keeping track of her purse, or remembering names, or being on time. You could count on her to be late, so much so that Rose and Carol knew, if you wanted her to be someplace at noon, you'd better tell her eleven o'clock to be safe. She went up to Greenville to study art in college, where she met Dean, a professor in the Religion Department, and they ran away together, ending up in California, where Dean got involved with a group of people who, years later, would call themselves Libertarians, although at the time they were simply people who seemed to find fault with everything. That led him, also for reasons Carol did not understand, back to religion, or at least a certain fringe kind of religion, and when they came back to North Carolina, a whole group of them came with them, and they bought something like twelve hundred acres of land and started the farm.

I asked Carol, "So what do they believe in?"

"I have no idea. God tells them what to do, and they claim to have a direct link, so I don't mess with them."

"I've known people like that."

I was, of course, thinking of Phil and Tonya and the Little White Church and wondered if I ought to steel myself against another onslaught of people trying to get me to think their way, but Carol said, "Don't worry, they keep to themselves," as if she guessed what I was thinking.

Jacob was nine years old now, but before Jacob there had been another son whom they had called Isaac, which was too much irony for Carol, who shook her head when she said the name as if the littlest things could made a difference in this world. He was just two years old when he died. As Carol told it, one minute he was playing, the next minute he was lying on the floor, still as dirt, with a fever of a hundred and four.

"Meningitis," Carol said. "You know what I'd have done. I'd have gotten that child to a hospital quick as fire, but that was not the first thing Alma and Dean thought of. They went and laid hands on him. The whole bunch of them, as if there weren't a lick of sense between them. Twenty, thirty people with their hands all over him for who knows how long before somebody got the bright idea that what that baby needed was a doctor. By then it was too late. He died in the car." From what I could tell, Carol would never forgive them.

Carol put down her apple peeler and stood up. The problem was, there wasn't anywhere to go. Dean was in the living room reading and, if you went in there, he would act as if you weren't there. A person like that can take up a whole room. Even Jacob would not go in there. He was on the floor under the kitchen table moving a group of colored stones into patterns, then writing something in a small notebook, a make-believe game, his own. Carol went to the window and looked out. Alma started a second crust for the top of the pie. She measured flour and salt then worked in the Crisco. Before adding water, she picked up a raw green bean and ate it. She handed me one. "Go ahead, Ruth, it's sweet."

So I did, and she was right. Alma smiled. "You can go ahead and eat that corn, too. It's as sweet as candy."

I took a bite of corn and another bean. "Maybe we ought not to even cook them," I said.

"Well, cook mine," said Carol.

Just then a car pulled into the driveway, and Carol announced, "Dickie's here," then went outside to help bring in a sweet potato casserole, a tub of slaw, and a lemon pound cake. Dickie was dressed up in a powder blue jumper and crisp white blouse. Her hair seemed to float around her head, and she smelled like flowers. She kissed everybody in the room, including me.

"Okay, Dickie," Carol said, pointing to Alma. "Tell her how you make a piecrust flaky."

Dickie looked at Carol, then at Alma.

"It's the Crisco, isn't it? It doesn't have a thing to do with how much you handle the dough; tell her."

"Oh, Carol, stop it," Dickie said. Then she reached out to

touch my hair. "Doesn't she have pretty hair? I wish you'd let me fix it sometime."

I flinched. People seemed to have an idea that curly hair was put there for people to touch, like public property, and I hated it, but Dickie did not notice. She put two bottles of ginger ale on the table and winked at Carol, who produced a bottle of bourbon, and the two of them poured themselves drinks that crackled over fat cubes of ice. They did not offer it around.

Dickie sat down at the kitchen table. "Did y'all hear what happened to Bitsy Caldwell's dog? You know, the poodle?"

"I always hated that dog," Carol said, and she sat down, too.

"Isn't Bitsy the one who had the raccoon loose in her house?" Rose asked. "I recall the last time you were here, you told us something about Bitsy and a raccoon."

"Yes, ma'am," Dickie answered. "It was a big raccoon, too. Crawled in through the pet door and got in the pantry, and poor Bitsy nearly had a heart attack. I doubt she'll ever get over it. They had to call animal control, but that is an old story, Rose. This is a different story altogether, and it doesn't have a thing to do with raccoons, so don't confuse me." She turned to me. "Tell me again where you're from."

"Tennessee."

"I know that, but where?"

"Summerville."

"It wasn't Summerville. But somewhere in Tennessee where there's a lot of hills. Are there many hills in Summerville?"

"Yes, ma'am," I said.

"But it wasn't Summerville. Anyway, Bitsy and her dog were visiting relatives over there in Tennessee where they got, what Ruth?"

"Hills?"

"Hills," Dickie exclaimed, clapping her hands. Dickie liked for people to help out when she told a story. "They were standing in the yard minding their own business when a man mowing his lawn up the street decided to stop mowing and go inside to check the score of a ball game. Does everyone see where this is headed? There was the lawn mower parked in his yard, which happened to be at the top of a very steep hill, and in a few minutes, here it came, down the hill and out of control, picking up speed as it hit the road. Bitsy said she kept expecting to see someone running after it, but no. This was a lawn mower with a mind of its own, and when it reached the bottom of the street, it jumped the curb and slammed into her poor dog."

Jacob poked his head out from under the table. "Is he okay?"

"Broke his leg," Dickie said.

"It just shows you how stupid that dog is."

Rose spoke up again. "Isn't Bitsy Caldwell somehow kin to Purdy Hughes?

"His ex-wife's sister," Dickie said. "You wouldn't find her in the same room with him now, though, I can promise you that. She's married to a heart doctor now, and after all that newspaper's done to the hospital?"

"That's what I thought," Rose said.

Alma was mixing cinnamon and sugar in the apples, tossing them in a glass bowl with a wooden spoon until they glistened and, while the others talked, she snuck me one. It was delicious, and I ate it slowly, licking off my fingers, thinking about how Dickie's stories were never as good as Rose's. Half the time you couldn't tell them from gossip. On the counter I spied a pepper and, without thinking, reached for it. It was a beautiful red, the color of Christmas, like when you come out of autumn, out of yellows and oranges and reds that fade into a brown and gray world growing colder; then all of a sudden there's red. A Christmas bow, a holly berry, a candy cane, RED, like you've never seen red before, and all of a sudden you're glad for the cold, and you would not skip winter for anything. I will be truthful about this. I had never seen a pepper any color but green. And to be absolutely truthful, I could not have told you for certain that what I had in my hand was a pepper at all. It looked pretty, that's all. Pretty and sweet, so I bit in. And tasted fire.

I came up screaming. Just like that, no waiting around to see what had happened, and it was an awful scream, too, as if my voice were a crippled thing. Rose and Dickie and Alma passed me glasses of water like firefighters passing buckets. I emptied one after the other, but it didn't help. Carol handed me an ice cube. "Suck on this," she said. I knocked it out of her hand and ran outside.

This wasn't any kind of pain I could share anyway. You stub your toe and it hurts until you think you can't stand it, but there's a crest to it, and when you reach it you know the pain's going to fall off, just give it time. This was not like that. This was pain that kept on rising. I remembered a funny thing Rose had told me once, after I had watched her grab her back getting up from a chair. When I asked if it hurt, she nodded, but then she told me she did not mind. "Pain makes you more human," was what she said. I told her she was crazy. "Who wants to be *more* human? I want to live forever." Rose did not say anything then, so different from Mama, who'd cut you off at the knee with some remark. *Well, you can't, so hush.* Or Margaret, who always had to finish a thing. If I had told Margaret I wanted to live forever, she would beat it to death until I finally backed down, until I begged to die, right then, to keep from hearing her prove me wrong. Rose, she kept quiet like she knew I was right and wrong at the same time, knew I knew it, too, so there was no need to waste words.

I ran to the woods behind Rose's house all the way to the creek where I splashed across to the other side and sat down on the mossy root of an old tree and cried deep tears for as long as I could, until they were gone, which was not long enough. Crows had converged on the trees near me, piercing the air with their cries. A lone pine creaked back and forth in the wind.

I remembered the Christmas I was ten, the year I was chosen to play Mary in the Summerville Presbyterian Church Christmas Pageant, even though everybody knew it should have been Sarah Lynn Moore. Sarah Lynn was the prettiest girl in our class, not a disputable fact either, but something that had been discussed and decided since second grade, although apparently no one told our Sunday School teacher, Miss Aileen Potts, who had her own ideas. This was one: No one was to get worked up over the costumes for the Christmas pageant. *Don't any of you go to any trouble,* she told us about a hundred times, but she had reason because there were fifth-grade Sunday school teachers in years past who had outdone themselves with real baby Jesuses, live sheep, and angels that rose into the air. Not Miss Potts. She let the angels have paper halos but everybody else, she directed, "Wear your father's bathrobe, cinch it in the middle, and put a dish towel on your head." Then she picked me to be Mary.

In the first place I did not have a father. In the second place, in my family you were going to need a whole lot in this world before you were going to need a bathrobe. We didn't have any bathrobes. I figured Mama would mumble something like, *Forget it,* and I would not get to be Mary, and that would be the end of it, but she didn't. She surprised me. She went downtown to Miller's Department Store and bought, with money we did not have, a baby blue satin bathrobe with white lace trim. It was the prettiest thing I had ever seen. I did not want to touch it; it was that pretty. Mama either. The two of us spent actual time looking at it as if it were something to watch. Like TV.

Margaret was furious. Margaret was saving pennies in a jar to buy a white Ladybug shirt with red trim. WHY? she screamed at Mama, and Mama said, "Because nobody in our family has ever been Mary."

"Nobody's ever been Margaret either," she yelled back, but that was just Margaret, and we didn't pay any attention. We didn't know what we had done.

Though we found out soon enough. The minute Miss Aileen Potts laid eyes on my baby blue satin bathrobe with white lace trim we knew. I watched Mama sink into a pool of knowing as Miss Potts shook her head back and forth saying, "I'm sorry. I'm so sorry," because, as it turned out, the reason Miss Potts had made the costume rule in the first place was so my mama would not have to spend money on the Christmas pageant.

What did she know about my mama?

She offered to pay for the robe, but Mama refused. I would not put it on. Sarah Lynn Moore, in her father's bathrobe cinched in the middle, got to be Mary that year after all.

But it was not the memory of the bathrobe that got to me anymore. Or Miss Potts. Or even Mama. It was this not knowing what everyone else seems to know that kept cropping up on me, all my life, the same thing, like I was absent the day of the lessons. Like bright, red peppers. Who knew they were hot?

The crows in the trees above me suddenly flew off, a wall of noise, moving out. I looked up, and there was Rose.

"You shouldn't be by yourself," she said.

"Yea, well, there's a lot of things I do, I shouldn't. What was that thing, Rose?"

"A chili pepper."

"It hurts, Rose."

"I know, honey."

She had brought me a slice of Alma's thick bread, which I ate, and a glass of water. Neither helped, but I didn't tell her.

"You know, Rose, sometimes I want to reach up, yank the curtain open, and scream, *Is this your idea of a joke?*"

"You'd almost have to believe in God to do that."

"Well, don't worry."

We stayed down there a long time in that strange silence of hers that was a comfort. I left before Alma's pie was done. I would not have been able to taste it anyway.

When I got home that night, I ran into Michael. He was slumped down in one of Victor's chairs on the big green porch, where he often sat in the evenings, sometimes with Victor, sometimes alone. Most nights we did no more than exchange a quick wave of the hand in passing, but on this night, he sat up and asked, "What's wrong?"

"Nothing."

"Your face is red," he said.

"So what."

I didn't stop. I marched right up the stairs as if he were not there, except he was. He followed me all the way up to my apartment then came on inside. I sat down, tucked my knees up under my chin, and covered my face with my hands. Now I am thinking that if somebody made a move like that in front of me, I'd back on out of the room, but not Michael. He stood in the middle of the floor like somebody who's forgotten how to walk. So I told him what happened. It didn't help. He stood there still, a tall, spindly person clearly confused about what to do for me. His straight, black hair hung down to his shoulders and was parted in the middle. He wore glasses which, in his case, helped; they made him look older. Finally he said, "Can I make you some soup?"

I took my hands away from my face. "Are you crazy?"

"I just thought, when somebody's sick you make them soup."

"I am not sick; my mouth is on fire."

He appeared unable to leave or to stay. I saw him looking around the room as if to stumble across the answer, so I said, "You can get me a beer."

He did. Then he said, "Stay right here."

He came back with a carton of vanilla ice cream. He scooped me out a bowlful and sat on the floor in front of me, watching me eat.

"You want some?" I asked.

"Sure," he said, kind of like a kid. He had that quality about him, and that was okay.

9 | SMOKE

Rose could not get it straight about me and Michael. "He is not my boyfriend," I told her.

"I'm happy you found yourself a nice young man then."

"Why?"

"Because," she said, "you're young. It's what you do when you're young."

"Not me." But still she would not believe me, so I had to tell her, "He already has a girlfriend."

"How do you know?"

"I've seen her."

Which was true. Madeline was her name, which fit her. Madeline. Say it over and over and it sounds luxurious in your mouth. It sounds willowy and breathless, which was what Madeline was like, wearing clothes nobody else would think of like slinky, black tank tops and these leopard-printed skirt things that wrapped around and tied at her waist. There are just so many women in the world who can get away with that kind of thing, and Madeline was one of them. She would insist, however, that she was not Michael's girlfriend.

"Michael and I are not involved," she told me.

Involved. I did not know what she was talking about. They used to be, she added. Involved that is. Now they were *just friends.* "The best," she said.

"Great," I said.

I met Madeline at Michael's one night when he invited me and Victor over for dinner. I did not want to go, but Rose said I had to. "I can't go, Rose. I'm no good with people."

"That's why you have to go."

"I don't *have to,* Rose."

"Do it anyway," she said.

When I got downstairs, Victor was trying to buy one of Michael's chairs. "He practically stole it," he explained to me, "from a woman down in south Lawson County. It was outside on her porch, for Christ's sake, with a bucket of corn set right on it, so truly it's a wonder it's not ruined. Michael offered her fifty dollars for it, which she snapped up, thinking she had a sucker on her hands; don't you think, Michael? You feel like a sucker?"

Michael grinned.

"She made him come inside and see if there wasn't anything else he wanted," Victor continued, "but it was all junk except for that chair. I told him I'd give him five hundred, but he won't sell. Not that I blame him."

I looked at the chair but could not see what was so great about it. It was crooked, and not just slightly either, as if maybe in the right light you wouldn't notice? It leaned sideways, and I could not imagine it would not fall over if you sat in it. Michael asked us if we shouldn't wait for Madeline to get there before we started eating. "She ought to be here any minute," he said. He placed little plates of cheese and crackers in front of us and poured us glasses of white wine.

Michael worked for the state as a historian. His job was to find historical structures, houses mainly, but businesses counted, too, and so did churches, which is how he and Victor had met. Michael shared Victor's opinion that St. Paul's Episcopal Church deserved a place on the tour of historic Lawsonville.

"St. Paul's makes the Humphries House look like a mobile home," Victor declared, carefully stacking a cracker with alternating slices of yellow and white cheese.

"It's not that bad," Michael said.

Michael's research was going to end up in a book, the idea being that if an old building were in this book, it would be harder to tear it down. Nobody was going to tear down St. Paul's, but, as Victor put it, "Michael's work is validating everything I've been saying for the past ten years."

"It's nothing," Michael said.

"You have no idea," Victor said.

"I wonder where Madeline is?" Michael said. He refilled our wineglasses and went to the kitchen to call her. When he returned, he and Victor resumed a discussion that, clearly, they had been having before I got down there, about the fact that somebody was planning to build a gas station in the front yard of one of their favorite old houses. The house itself would be spared, but as Victor said, having a gas station in the front yard would destroy its character. I was happy to let them talk while I listened. I enjoyed drinking the wine and looking out the window at the river.

Several times during the conversation I heard them bring up a Lawson County commissioner named Fingers, who was somehow involved in the plans for the gas station. They did not approve of Fingers; you could tell by the exasperated way they said his name. I knew a little about this Fingers and had seen him once when he had come into Dickie's Diner. His real name was Carl

Hines, except everybody called him Fingers because on one hand he had only three. He had slicked-down gray hair the color of some machine part, a long, red face, and stooped shoulders. The day I saw him, he was wearing a yellow bow tie and thin white shirt. Everybody in the diner seemed to know him. He stopped to talk at each table on his way to his booth in the back of the room, where Dickie met him, sweet tea in hand. I was making myself a cheese tower like Victor's when I heard him say, "Ruth here ought to be able to tell us more. She probably sees him in the newsroom all the time."

I shook my head. "I've never seen him there."

"Never?" Victor said. "That's funny."

"It's not so funny," Michael said.

"Then how do you explain the fact that Fingers and the *Lawsonville Ledger* always appear to be on the same side? You watch and tell me if I'm wrong. I can't remember one single time that Fingers hasn't wanted something that the newspaper hasn't been right behind him. Remember when Fingers wanted money for the marina? The *Ledger* came out in favor of it, and the billboard ordinance? Fingers was against that, and so was the paper. And how about that close vote on teacher salaries? The paper took his side then, too. He's got to have pull, that's all I can figure, am I right, Ruth?"

"I just answer the phones."

"It's that young guy, the reporter, Jackson Price," Michael said. "He's the one who talks to Fingers, but it's not likely Ruth would have ever seen him. Fingers is not going to do anything so stupid as to hang around the newspaper. He fancies himself Deep Throat to Jackson's Woodward and Bernstein." He turned to me and filled my empty wineglass. "Which one do you think, Ruth, Woodward or Bernstein?"

"I swear, all I do is answer the phone."

"How do you know all this?" Victor asked.

"Madeline," Michael said. "She says she knows Jackson."

"Isn't he that young man with the black hair?" Victor asked. "Handsome. Wears jeans and a tie? I hate to see a man do that. It's so tacky."

"I do that, Victor," Michael said.

"I have never once seen you in a tie. The thing that makes me furious is how Fingers is so sneaky. I ran into him last week and tried to explain the historical significance of the Parker House, and what it means to Lawsonville to preserve our historic buildings, and not just the buildings but the *integrity* of the buildings, and do you know what he did? He agreed with everything I said. We stood on the sidewalk for twenty minutes talking about how it was crime to put a gas station in the front yard of the Parker House, and by the way, did you hear about the tree?"

"What about the tree?" Michael said.

"The big oak in the front yard? They're going to take it down."

"I don't want to hear this, Victor."

"It's true. The contractor told me yesterday. Anyway, Fingers took me by the shoulders, looked me straight in the eye, and said, 'Victor, you're absolutely right.' Then the very next day he voted to approve the construction permit. I don't see how the man sleeps with himself."

Michael lifted a cookie tin from under the couch. It was covered with huge painted flowers of red and purple and gold on a black background, and inside it were three baggies of pot. He opened one, separated out the seeds, then packed it into a blue pipe and passed it to Victor. "No, thanks," I said, when Victor passed it to me.

"Which one did Dustin Hoffman play?" Victor asked.

"What?" Michael said, sucking on the pipe.

"Woodward or Bernstein, which one?"

"Bernstein," Michael said.

"Then that's Jackson."

"It doesn't matter, Victor, I was just trying to make a point . . ."

"And it was a good one," said Victor.

". . . that Fingers feeds Jackson information, and maybe that works for him. Jackson's an ambitious guy and, I would be willing to bet, not all that patient, so it must come in handy to pick up the phone and have Fingers tell you secrets. The catch is, he's got to turn around and write what Fingers wants. The editor, what's his name?"

"Ed Stivers," I said.

"He must be in on it, too."

"Right," said Victor. "Which is why the newspaper ran an editorial on how this town needs another Shell station on the corner of Battle and Oak, even if it means destroying the value of Parker House, which dates back to, help me out, Michael."

"Eighteen twenty-one."

"It's a crime," Victor said. "Did you see that editorial, Ruth?"

"I've never been a political person," I said.

Michael peered out the window. "There was no answer at Madeline's," he said. "She must be on her way. I'm going to start the shrimp."

Still Madeline did not come. We sat down to eat without her, shrimp, corn on the cob, salad, and bread, which Michael had cut into slices and put in a basket just like in a restaurant. He opened another bottle of wine. Halfway through dinner, the front door burst open, and in came Madeline.

"Sorry I'm late," she said. "I've just got a minute anyway.

Michael! No, sweetie, how could I eat? I couldn't possibly eat. You won't believe what happened."

She would not sit down. She had long, straight, dark hair and a habit of pulling it back with her hands, twisting it into a ponytail, then letting it fall to her shoulders, again and again, arching her thin, tanned arms in impossible angles. It wore me out. Madeline was executive director of the Lawson County Arts Commission, and she was complaining to Michael that one of her art exhibits, which she had scheduled for the lobby of the Lawson County Hospital, had been canceled at the last minute by the board of directors because of naked pictures. Madeline did not actually say, naked pictures. She called them her nudes, over and over, *my nudes*, so many times I was about ready to puke. There were really just two of them anyway, which she had already offered to take out of the exhibit.

"But they're backing out anyway, those chicken shits," she said, giving her hair a particularly violent toss. "They say they can't afford anything even faintly controversial as long as they're under daily attack by a certain newspaper."

"I just answer the phones," I muttered.

Michael started to introduce me, but Madeline interrupted. "Michael, sweetie! I have to run," and she was gone.

For a long time, Michael stared at the door. Victor stirred his ice water with his finger then vigorously dried his hand on a napkin as if he was sorry to have gotten it wet after all. "Well, I for one would like to tell her where she can put those nudes," he said.

"Shhhh," I said, putting my finger to my lips.

But it did not matter. Michael eventually came back to the table but he would not talk, and though he had not finished his supper, he would not eat anything else. Victor left. I was on my way out when I heard Michael say, "Please stay."

Please stay. You take a man like Homer Birdsong saying words like that and you've got trouble. Homer Birdsong might have looked like dirt, but looks don't matter when you've got a man who can make you blush just by saying hello. Men like that put a catch in your throat, make you go into some kind of brain blackout so you're doing or saying things you can't believe your own self. Not Michael. He said, *Please stay,* then went to wash the dishes, but that was Michael. He was the kind of person who could not carry on a conversation with dirty dishes in his sink.

He set me up with my own bottle of wine and a clean glass in a chair beside a large bay window at the front of the house overlooking the street and the river beyond. With its high ceilings and polished floors, Michael's apartment looked very different from mine, partly because mine had once been the attic, but also it was nicer. The walls were painted a light tan and were hung with black-and-white photographs he had taken himself. His furniture matched, all black and white and tan. The room was dark. I sipped my wine and watched the water bob up and down under the bridge lights.

When Michael finished the dishes, he took up his blue pipe and sat down on the couch across from me. "You like jazz?" he asked.

I sighed. "I have no idea."

He had arranged his records in alphabetical order on a shelf that lined an entire wall. He flipped through them until he found the one he wanted, then slipped it out of its cover so it landed edge to edge against his palms. He cleaned it with velvet and blew dust off the needle. I lit a cigarette.

"You're going to kill yourself that way," he said.

I pointed to his cookie tin full of pot and said, "There's a lot of ways."

He sighed. "Madeline smokes, too."

He handed me an ashtray made of tiny tiles, aqua and peach, too pretty to put ashes in, then curled up in a corner of the couch and closed his eyes. He looked more like a boy sulking than a historian, because to my thinking, historians were grown-up people who did not smoke pot and did not mope about girls they had no business with anyway. Because it was as clear as a cold night in December that he and Madeline were no better matched than, for instance, him and me. I found myself wondering what kind of girl he ought to like.

And me? What kind of boy? Not Homer, and not Chuck; that's two off the list right there, but there was no guarantee there would be others. Margaret had sure not found anybody, despite years and years of trying, and Mama never showed even the remotest interest. I watched the smoke from my cigarette snake upward in the dark. For a long time I watched it because the more I watched, the more it seemed that the smoke was following the music. Dancing smoke. It stayed with the beat of the music exactly, slowing at the slow parts, speeding up at the fast parts, zigzagging like crazy when the music got really fast. I looked over at Michael to see if he noticed, but he was still sunk in the sofa. I said, "My smoke is dancing."

He opened his eyes.

"Look at it," I said.

"Could be sound waves from the record player."

"What did you call it?"

"What, sound waves?"

"No, the other."

"Record player?"

I smiled. "I knew somebody once who would not let me call it a record player. I had to say stereo instead."

"That's stupid."

"Yeah, well . . ."

When the record was over, Michael put on another and sat back down on the couch. We waited; here it came, the dancing smoke, and we watched it together because this time he saw it, too, then after a while he said, "You'd like her if you got to know her."

"Maybe."

"Madeline, I mean."

"I know." We watched the smoke slow down when the music slowed. "It could be magic," I said. "Magic smoke."

"Could be. Or maybe we're both just drunk."

10 | THEN THERE'D BE SNAKES

People would tell you there wasn't much in Chocowin County, although you could see it for yourself looking at a map. It was mostly marshland spreading inland like a fungus, and even though you could tell it was pretty in its own lonesome way, most of it you could not reach. The marsh gave way to forest, wide swatches of tall, straight pines owned by paper companies, which meant that on any day you could drive by and see part of them gone, whacked down like summer grass. But to most of Chocowin County, the forests did not mean paper or even long walks in the woods; they meant deer, and when hunting season started, the county pretty much shut down. The rest of the year people either fished or farmed; that was about it for career choices. The farms were small, a little tobacco, a little soybeans, and some corn, but mostly potatoes on their way to being potato chips, which seemed funny to me. I would ride down the road picturing rows and rows of cheery potato chip bags stacked on grocery store shelves across America and think, *This is where it all begins*. This was end-of-the-world-looking country, sticking out into the Chocowin Sound like a forgotten land, like if you chopped it off, it would float away and nobody would notice.

Michael took me all the way to the end of it one day, past the last farm, past the last forest, past the last crab house to the tiny fishing community of Scoot. Nobody knew why it was called Scoot, but around Chocowin County if you wanted to say something was far-fetched, you'd say, *You're talking past Scoot now*, and everyone would know what you meant.

Michael's job required him to look at houses all over eastern North Carolina, but his favorite was one just past Scoot. It was his dream to buy it, fix it up a little bit at a time, then live there. He did not say, but you knew he wanted to live there with Madeline, which shows you how far off Michael was when it came to dreams. A woman like Madeline was never going to live in a house past Scoot.

You could not see the house from the road. Michael pulled over at a place that looked like nothing to me, no landmark or anything, just a side of the road that looked like any other side of the road. We had to push through tall brush that was windblown and brittle and snapped off easily, scratching my face and arms. I stepped in a mud puddle that sucked at my shoes. "Wait up," I called to Michael, who knew the way and seemed anxious to get there.

Halfway through the brush, we came upon a rickety wooden walkway that led to the house, which stood all by itself in a barren mud field. Short stalks of a strawlike weed poked through the mud like bristles on an old comb. The house was gray, not because it had been painted gray, but because it had been stripped of any color that once might have been there. It was so beat up by weather and neglect that from a distance it looked like all it would take was one more breeze and over it would go, but Michael did not care. He had seen worse, he said. Beyond the house was a huge marsh, also surrounded by mud, interrupted by a small island thick with saw grass and low, scrubby trees, and beyond the island was the Chocowin Sound. We stepped onto the porch, which felt like you might fall through.

"Why would you want to live way out here?" I asked Michael.

"Any reason I shouldn't?"

Which was the kind of thing Michael tended to say these days, like everybody was supposed to know how it was between him and Madeline and leave him alone. So I gave him that. He did not know yet what I knew, that Madeline passed by me almost every day on her way to see Jackson Price, how she would sit on the edge of his desk waiting for him to finish whatever it was he might be doing, because Jackson was always busy, a man of action that Jackson; you would never catch him sitting still. He shouted into the phone at people while scribbling notes on his legal pad, and Madeline's thighs would be inches away from his fingers. Michael did not need to know that.

He went around to the side of the house, dusted off the sill of a broken-out window, and stepped through. I heard the sound of penny loafers on floorboards before he opened the front door, and I stepped inside. The day was cold and gray and let only a stale light into the room. Inside, the air was clammy, and there was a smell of overwet wood. Directly in front of the door was a steep, narrow stairwell leading upstairs, and on either side, low-ceilinged rooms, both with fireplaces smudged with soot and stripped of their mantels. The kitchen, robbed of its stove and most of its cabinets, stretched across the back of the house. Upstairs were three tiny bedrooms and the only bathroom. On the drive down, Michael talked and talked about the *potential* of this house, and I mean, that was the word he used about a hundred times, but I had to admit, I didn't see any. So he pointed out the floors and explained how little it would take to get them back in shape, and he praised the condition of the plaster underneath the many layers of wallpaper, and he tapped on a door to show me how solid it was. He took a chisel from his back pocket and began working on the wallpaper, his plan being to tackle it a little at a time until, eventually, it would be gone.

"Need help?"

"No."

I went back outside to wait for him on the porch. I had to admit there was a lonesome sort of beauty to the place, but there was something about it that was too harsh even for me, like the difference between split rail and barbed wire, both fences, but the one making your skin crawl. Maybe it would have been different in the summer. Maybe under a blue sky and a summer sun this place could be somewhere you would want to be although, as Michael would point out later, then you'd have snakes. There was always something.

I took a folded envelope out of the pocket of my jeans. It was a letter from Margaret, the first one I had gotten from home, although I had written plenty. Well, a few. I had written two, maybe three, short notes, both of them saying as clear as could be that I was fine. I had been carrying Margaret's letter around with me for a couple of weeks, reading it over and over, as if there might be something I was missing.

Dear Ruth,

 If you don't come home, Mama and William are going to die. So you better!

Your Sister, Margaret

Well, somebody get out the violins. For starters, nobody was going to die, and what I wouldn't give to tell Margaret right to her face. I could feel my heart racing already. If anybody was

SOME DAYS THERE'S PIE   137

going to die, it was going to be me, of a heart attack from having to put up with my sister. I swear I could hardly breathe, but that's what she did to me, Margaret and Mama both. They made it so I could not breathe.

I heard footsteps on the stairs behind me and tucked the letter back into my pocket. Michael closed the door, locked it, then climbed back out the window. He was wearing shorts, as always, as if he had something against long pants, as if skinny legs were part of his uniform along with those scuffed-up loafers, no socks, and wrinkled dress shirts that he never tucked in. If it was cold out, he would put on an old, navy sweater with sleeves too long for his arms. He sat down beside me on the steps, took a plastic baggie out of his pants pocket, and began rolling a joint. It was hard not to stare at his fingers. Michael had beautiful hands, and more than once I had to stop myself from reaching out to touch them. They moved slowly, as if through water, purposefully, with their own rhythm, but there was a little sadness to it, and maybe that's how it is sometimes with beautiful things. There was a sense that Michael was shy about his hands, as if they would not have been hands of his choosing. It worried me how much dope he smoked. I could not say anything, not with the amount of beer I drank, and don't think Michael wouldn't point this out. *You're one to talk*, he would say, although I believed there was a difference. For one thing, I had certain rules where he didn't. He would just as soon light up at breakfast and keep it going all day, while I wouldn't think of taking a drink before supper. He said it did not affect him.

"So, Ruth. Do you think Jackson is good-looking?"

I looked at him. I picked up a couple of dirt clods and began tossing them at a tree that had fallen near the porch and said, "I don't believe I want to talk about this, Michael."

"Tell me the truth."

"The truth? Okay. I don't know how the man makes it past his mirror every morning. Mere mortals would stand stock-still and stare."

"Shit."

"You asked."

"Victor thinks I ought to forget her."

"I think Victor is a very smart man."

"You do?"

I rolled my eyes. Somebody better stop me if I ever fall in love and get this dense.

"But Madeline needs me. Nobody understands her, especially not this Jackson joker; I mean, what does he know? I'm the only one. You wouldn't believe how many people think she can do no wrong, for one thing. They *expect* her to be perfect." He shook his head. "It's a lot of pressure."

"I cannot imagine."

He smoked. I tossed more dirt clods, but after a few minutes of watching them explode against the tree trunk, I began to wonder if any tiny creatures had made their home in its rotten bark, crawling perhaps from the marsh to this new landscape, another world, another planet. My brother, William, would think so. He would stop me from pelting their home with my dirt-clod bombs. Sometimes my brother, William, was smarter than people who only think they are smart. I missed William, I really did. I felt awful for leaving him, but I didn't think what Margaret said was right. He was not going to die without me.

Michael leaned back against the steps. He closed his eyes and tilted his face up as if hoping for the sun to warm him even though the sky was a solid sheet of still, gray clouds. "So, Ruth," he said. "What about you?"

"What about me?"

"You don't ever say much about yourself."

He slipped his hand around my ankle. Maybe it wasn't anything, just a hand on a sock, but you never know. I looked at it for a minute then moved my foot away. "There's nothing to say."

Michael stubbed the joint out on the bottom of his shoe and stood up. He shook out his legs as if they were stiff from sitting, and he sighed. "Madeline tells me I need to loosen up."

"Rose tells me the same thing."

"Rose does?"

I nodded.

"I never have understood what you see in that old lady." He reached down his hand and pulled me up. "You ever eaten oysters at Sutter's Cove? If we leave now, we'll catch the sunset."

But once we were back in the car, all I could think about was how there was not going to be any sunset with all these clouds. Why couldn't he see that? All you'd have to do was look up and know it was true. I could have told Michael, but he would not listen, and the closer we got to Sutter's Cove, the more it gnawed at me. There's times you can pretend and other times you can't, and all it takes is one niggling detail to send you over the edge, and it was not just the clouds. Every time I looked at Michael I wanted to slap that hair out of his face. How can he drive with that hair, I thought, and the radio was too loud. Michael always listened to the radio as if he were deaf. I turned it down; he turned it back up, without thinking about it either, as if some random wind had come in the car and turned down his radio and not a real live person sitting next to him. I spoke up. "This isn't a good night for oysters, Michael."

"What's wrong with it?"

"Maybe another night. How about I just go to Rose's tonight."

"Rose's?"

"You could drop me off."

To get to Sutter's Cove, you had to turn south off Highway 53 about three miles before you reach Rose's house. Michael was driving fast, and I could not be certain what he would do. When we got close to the Sutter's Cove road, he slowed down as if he might turn, and I held my breath, but then he did not turn. When I got out at Rose's, he did not cut off the car. He did not even look at me.

"Bye," I said.

But he sped away.

11 | SWERVING ON A PLANE

It was getting on toward Christmas, which wasn't bringing out the best in anybody. "I'd just as soon skip it this year," Rose said, but Carol told me that's what Rose said every year. Carol was trying to stick a garland of pine branches over Rose's fireplace, but it kept sliding off like a snake, escaping. "How'd we get it to stay last year, Mother?" she called to Rose.

"I have no idea, but don't you go banging nails in my mantel," Rose shouted back. She was in the kitchen with a pot of coffee and the Sunday paper, having already declared that she was not going to help.

"Hand me that string," Carol said to me.

With Carol, you never thought to ask a thing like, *What string?* If there was string, and Carol asked you for it, by golly it was your job to find it. I pictured her at the hospital, the mere sound of her white shoes clearing the hall. String. I found it on the floor next to a large box marked X-MAS which Carol had set in the middle of the floor but, when I reached for it, the box suddenly burst into a jarring rendition of "Jingle Bells."

"Shut that thing off," Carol said.

"What is it?" I asked.

"It's my walking Santa, and Mother will shoot him if she hears it."

I looked in the box and found him under smaller boxes of colored glass ornaments, green plastic wreaths with red velvet bows, and a manger scene carved out of wood. He was kicking his feet back and forth, back and forth, a crazed walker going nowhere, one arm waving up and down, ringing a single bell. I picked him up and turned him off.

"You got a lot of Christmas decorations," I said.

"I try," she said. Then she hammered three nails sideways into the mantel to keep the garland from slipping.

I was with Rose; I could do without Christmas. What got me mad was how you're supposed to stop everything and feel different just because of one stupid day, and if you don't, something's wrong with you. It's everywhere, at school, in the stores, on TV, like a threat that you better be festive. You better be good. Mama did try. I would not have admitted it then, but I know that now. She would bake a turkey and a pumpkin pie, but when we sat down at the table, it would just be us all over again.

But for me the worst part of Christmas was the basket of food and toys the Baptist church used to send over every year. I always begged Mama to tell them we didn't need it, but she said that would be rude, so here it came, Christmas Eve every year, delivered by the mothers of classmates I knew. I imagined them waiting in their cars, hiding in the backseat, giggling. One year there was a doll for me. It was not a hand-me-down either. Somebody had gone to a store and bought it brand-new, a sort-of rag doll, soft all over except for her face, which was hard plastic. She wore a white dress with the daintiest blue flowers all over it, and I remember wishing I had a dress like that. She had painted-on yellow hair and a face with shy eyes and a smile that looked somehow too old for a doll, as if everything about her suggested a little girl except that smile. As it turned out, that was the Christmas I had begun to feel too old for dolls, and worse, I was embarrassed that nobody had noticed, so I gave the doll to William, who loved her. He played with her all morning, had her sit with us at dinner, then took her to bed with him, tucked under his arms tight as could be. As for me, I cried myself to sleep, wishing I had not given her away, which was another reason I dreaded Christmas. It was like a memory factory, and who needs that?

Michael was going home for Christmas even though he said he did not want to. His home was in Virginia, and he told me that when he got there, his dad would start pressuring him to go to law school like his two older brothers. *Why else would anyone major in history?* was the kind of thing Michael's dad liked to ask, which was the kind of thing Michael could not stand. But it was Christmas, so he would figure out a way, because that's another thing you did at Christmas. You stood things.

When Carol finished with the garland, she took me into the dining room to arrange a candlestick display out of large wooden spools. "Alma found these," Carol explained, handing me a spool. It was surprisingly heavy, solid, smooth with wear. "She's good for collecting things nobody else wants, but this time she got it right, giving them to me. I knew exactly what to do with them." The candles, three red and three green, looked as old as the spools, dented in places, and some of them bent, but never once lighted. Carol wanted to put them on felt stars like she had seen in the *Ladies' Home Journal.* She showed me the picture. She had already made the pattern out of the top of a shoe box just like the article said. She took the felt out of a paper sack and said, "I was thinking, put the green candles on red stars and the red candles on green; what do you think?"

"Hand me the green," I said, although we had to take turns

cutting because there was only one pattern. When it was my turn, Carol stuck her head through the kitchen door. "You could make us some hot chocolate," she said to Rose.

"Why?" Rose said.

"For the Christmas spirit," Carol said.

"I'm not in the Christmas spirit," Rose said.

Carol just stood there in the doorway. I was about to show her my green star but decided maybe this wasn't the best time. In a minute she looked at me. "She canceled another doctor's appointment."

"Oh." I honestly did not know, and I told Carol, "Next time, tell me. I'll get her there."

"Why do you think she would go with you, if she won't go with me?"

I shrugged. Carol did not know it, but I was on her side when it came to getting Rose to the doctor. It's not like you want to give in to every little worry, but you want to think you have a hand in things, like if a car's coming at you, you swerve out of the way. Maybe. Maybe not, but there's a chance, which is how come I never understood why anyone would get on an airplane. There's no swerving on a plane. Rose liked to bring up her friend Louise and the bath-oil beads as proof against life holding any guarantees, and maybe she was right; maybe she had no need for doctors, but I couldn't see why it would hurt to find out. Carol sat back down at the table. She unfolded a piece of red felt and held it in her hands, but that's as far as she got.

"She's probably fine, Carol."

"She's not fine."

We moved on to pinecone reindeer. Carol had a picture in a magazine of these too, plus a pattern, and she was showing me how to cut out antlers when Rose came in the room carrying two cups of hot chocolate.

"You want to help?" Carol asked her.

"No."

"You could wrap some presents," Carol said. "Look here at what I got Jacob." She pulled a bright green sweater out of one of several shopping bags piled in the corner and handed it to Rose. "I about broke my neck finding it, had to look all over town because Alma told me it had to be all cotton and it had to be green or he wouldn't wear it. Can you imagine? Nine years old and already picky. I'd tell any son of mine he could wear whatever his Aunt Carol gave him."

"It's too little," Rose said. She held the sweater out in front of her. It had a white snowman on the front.

"It is not," Carol said. "Alma told me what size."

"I don't care what size it is; it's not going to fit Jacob."

"I looked all over town for that sweater, and I'm not taking it back."

She pulled it out of Rose's hands and stuffed it back into the bag, then took her hot chocolate and sat down at the far end of the table. I showed Rose how to attach antlers to the pinecones, but the eyes were trickier. Neither one of us could figure out the eyes. "You think they stick up on top or on the side?" I whispered.

"Looks better on the side to me," Rose whispered back.

Which brought Carol back down to our side of the table, pointing at the magazine and saying, "Can't you read?" She snatched away my pinecone reindeer and put his eyes on herself. She also redid my antlers. "I'm not taking that sweater back, Mother," she said.

"That's fine," Rose said. "It's still too little."

On my way home that night I stopped by the new Revco. I found the Christmas cards in the center aisle. Most were in boxed sets, but I did not want a whole box; I just wanted one, and I was surprised at how picky I turned out to be. I passed over the cute ones; I did not want to be cute, and I did not want to be too serious either and nothing religious. So I was saying no to this one and no to that one, as if it were life and death here, as if it mattered, but finally I found the one I wanted. It showed a picture of a cardinal in the snow. There was a little sadness to it, but that was okay, too.

I took it with me to Jack's by the River, the bar across the street from my apartment, owned by a friend of Victor's named Jack Henry Sabatino. It was dark in there and quiet, with navy blue, sailboat-print curtains over the windows and matching chair cushions. On each table was a small brass ashtray shaped like an anchor and a candle in a red glass with netting. Jack Henry had draped pine garlands around the rim of the bar for Christmas. I sometimes ended up at Jack's by the River at night, with Victor or Michael or both, often late, after the other customers were gone. Jack Henry kept it open as long as we wanted since we were neighbors, but tonight I came alone, and Jack Henry nodded and brought me a beer but did not interrupt. I spread the card out on the table and wrote:

Dear Mama, William, and Margaret,
    Merry Christmas!
I miss you all, but I'm fine. I'm happy.
Please be happy, too.
Love, Ruth

At the office the next day, Deborah Hoffman came out of the advertising department with a life-size plastic Santa Claus. She wanted me to help her arrange it in the lobby then string a chain of cardboard bells around the walls, and I was glad to, because I felt sorry for Deborah. Most people went the other way when they saw her coming to keep from having to hear about her husband the Marine and her three boys. All you had to do was half smile at her and in she'd start: *You won't believe what Brad's done now.* There was no stopping her, either, and you were supposed to keep them all straight, which one was Brad and all the rest. I never had any problem with Deborah because it seemed obvious to me; *somebody* needed to hear about Brad, and when I got tired of listening, I simply walked away. It never fazed her. We strung cardboard bells along the walls of every department then hung a cluster of mistletoe over the door to Ed Stivers's office.

It was supposed to be a joke. Stivers did not notice because he was behind his desk yelling at a reporter, which we were used to. Deborah and I were back at our desks when he stomped out of his office and bumped his head against the mistletoe.

Who put this crap here?

Over in advertising, you'd have thought Purdy would be happy since ads pretty much sold themselves this season, but he wasn't. It happened every year, Rose said. Christmas was Purdy's dark season. People said it behind his back as if it were a kind of joke, *Purdy's dark season*, but it was true because, despite the belts, green with red reindeer, the rest of his clothes tended to be on the dark side like black turtlenecks and navy corduroys, and he moped around with a dark expression on his face. He was drinking more, anybody could tell that, and unlike other times of the year, he did not try to hide it.

"You just have to stay out of his way," Rose said, "and it will be over soon."

But when Friday came, my paycheck was short $21.62. I figured there was a mistake and went back to the business office, but there was no mistake. It was Purdy who did it, docked my pay for time off the job—putting up Christmas decorations. It wasn't an even $21 or $22 either; that's what galled me the most. It was $21.62 as if he had counted every minute. Purdy had docked Deborah's pay, too, it was all over her face, but she wouldn't talk about it.

"What do you think we oughta do, Deborah?"

She shrugged.

I looked, but Purdy was already gone for the day. "Maybe we could talk to him tomorrow."

But fear was what was all over her face, and it made me wonder if this might not sit well with the Marine husband.

"You okay?"

But she pushed past me and fled out the door.

Christmas Eve, I walked into Rose's house and smelled turkey in the oven, which I knew meant trouble because Alma and Dean were vegetarians. I turned to Carol, who sat at the kitchen table reading *Better Homes and Gardens*.

"They don't have to eat it," she said when I asked.

Cecil was there. Rose had found him living in the back of a crab house at the end of Chocowin County, and while the crab pickers were glad to step over him back and forth to work, not one of them would have asked him to Christmas dinner. He complained of a toothache, but Rose could not get him to a dentist until after Christmas. He was stretched out on the sofa in the living room with an ice bag on his face, watching Rose and Jacob as they sat on the floor under the tree shaking presents.

There was a little bit of Jacob that reminded me of William. Not that Jacob was slow, in fact, just the opposite because I got the feeling Jacob knew more than he let on, but that was part of it, the idea that Jacob lived in two worlds, one that he showed and the other he didn't, just like William. William never could learn things school could teach, like reading and arithmetic or even sitting still and listening to the teacher, but there was another part of William that knew things. Like when I was sad, William knew without me saying anything. He would just be there, patting my hand and looking at me as if he would tell me what to do if he could.

I used to be able to reach William in a way no one else could, and when we were little, we even had a language of our own. I don't remember all how it went now, but it was something like, everything began with an "s" like *spar* for car and *spog* was dog and *spree* was tree. I think it drove my mother crazy to hear us laughing at what she could not understand. I outgrew wanting to play with William, but by then I had become like a second mother for him. Mama would say things like, *You tell him, Ruth; he'll listen to you,* but it didn't seem right, and it made me mad. I was tempted to tell her, *But I'm not his mother.* I did worry about William missing me, more now that it was Christmastime, since he had never known a Christmas without me, but when I caught myself, it helped to think, he has a mother, and it's not me.

I sat down on the floor with Rose and Jacob and placed my package under the tree. I had bought Rose a notebook because I thought she should write some of her stories down. On the cover of the notebook was a picture of a rose, as if it had been made just for her. Alma and Carol finished setting the table, then Alma called outside to Dean.

Dean was sitting by himself on Rose's patio, hunched over from the cold, his coat up over his neck, his hands in his pockets.

"What's he doing out there anyway?" Carol said.

"Talking to himself," Alma said.

I noticed Carol and Rose give each other a quick look, and

Alma saw it, too, but nobody said anything. Jacob also stopped what he was doing and looked at his mother, but she did not meet his eye. "Run on and wash your hands," she told him. When he left the room, Carol said, "If you ever want to come back home . . ."

"I know." Alma interrupted her.

Jacob picked Rose's present to open first. It was a model of a World War II battleship, and you should have seen his eyes, like he had landed in heaven without having to die, but Dean, his eyes got tied up in a knot, dark knotty eyes, smoldering. You knew what he was thinking. *A battleship, an instrument of war, does not belong in our house, in our house of God, in our Godly house.* But Alma put her hand on his shoulder and smiled. "How very thoughtful, Mother."

Carol handed Jacob her present. He opened it quickly and, since he was a polite child, said, "I love it, Aunt Carol!" He lifted the sweater out of the box and held it up so everybody could see, but what everybody could see plain as day was that it was too little. Nobody said anything. I handed Rose my present, but before she could open it, Carol blurted out, "I hunted all over town for that sweater."

"It's perfect, Carol," Alma said. "Thank you so much."

"It's not perfect, Alma; are you blind? Come here, Jacob," and Jacob did. He walked over to Carol, sweater in his hand. She turned him around to hold it up to his back, as if a wiser soul could make it fit, somebody who knew what they were doing.

"I'll take it back, Carol," Alma said. "Don't you worry about it."

"You won't find another one," Carol said. "I can't tell you how many stores I had to go to just to find this one, but you were the one who said he had to have green."

"There are several children on the farm who could wear it, aren't there, Jacob? It's a beautiful sweater. Anyone would be thrilled to have such a nice sweater."

"I didn't buy it for the other children on the farm," Carol said. "I bought it for Jacob. I'll get you another one, Jacob. Can you handle red?"

"Yes, ma'am."

"See?" Carol said to Alma.

"I like red," Cecil said, and she glared at him, too.

Cecil gave Rose a wind chime he had made from sticks and old metal scraps. Stuck inside one of the tubes was a poem written on a small piece of folded paper. Rose pulled it out, read the poem, then handed it to me.

Christmas.
I have seen it in snow,
like the picture you get when you say the word,
the postcard sent to yourself.

Colored lights on cactus,
on palm trees,
will do if all you want is to shop.
They also work for the birthday of that boy.

But if Christmas means coming home,
then a Rose from Texas is all I need.

Alma gave everyone a jar of pickled peaches, except Rose also got pickled okra. Carol gave socks to everybody. Rose gave me the gold necklace with the dolphin on the end of it.

Dean did not get over the battleship. He stacked his small pile of presents next to his chair and would not open them, but my guess is, he took most of it out at dinner on the prayer, the longest I ever had to sit through, in which he went through the life of Jesus, starting with his birth and going to his death, including a description of each and every nail which I, for one, could have done without before a meal. Then he asked for forgiveness and told us, in a voice shaking with rage, that God had not sent his only son to die for our sins in order to boost the nation's economy. It took some work to follow him. I looked around the table to see Rose and Alma looking at each other, and Jacob tearing his paper napkin into tiny pieces. But Carol had a bead on him like a hornet with radar, and when he finally finished, she spoke up. "Dean, are you sure you don't want some of this turkey? Looks like everything else here's gotten cold."

Rose coughed. Alma cleared her throat. Jacob and I kept our eyes on our food and chewed quietly, the clinks and scrapes of stainless-steel forks on china being the only sounds in the room. Then Carol turned to me. "Did you not want to go home for Christmas, Ruth?"

"My parents are in France," I said. I swear it just popped out.

"France?"

I was in trouble. "They go there every year," I heard myself saying. "For Christmas. They go to France for the holidays. It's like a tradition."

Carol studied me. "What do they do over there for Christmas?"

"I have no idea. What I mean is, it's a new tradition. I never actually got to go myself." I looked to Rose for help, and quickly she turned to Jacob. "Did I ever tell you about the time I hid from Pancho Villa?"

"The bandit?" Jacob said, lighting up. Surely he had heard the story; everybody had heard that story, but Jacob was like me. He could always hear it again.

"The bandit," Rose said. "You betcha. We lived a ways outside of town, so we missed a lot of what went on there, but one day we looked up, and here came a man running down the road, shouting, *Pancho's coming, Pancho's coming.* We had been waiting for this, see, my mother especially, because Pancho Villa and his gang had been crossing the border, and we all knew that one day he might get to Agua Vista. My mother grabbed the four of us children, and we ran to Daddy's shop and hid under the printing press. All day long we stayed there, me and my brothers and sister. Daddy had to help guard the town, although I will tell you that my father, your great-grandfather, was not the kind of man who would shoot people. I was more afraid for him than for us, but it turned out not to be Pancho after all. Just a herd of goats somebody had spotted in the distance, churning up dust."

"What?" Carol said.

"Goats," Rose said.

"I heard what you said, Mother, but that's not what you always told us."

"Well, it's the same thing."

"It is not," Carol said. "It's not even close to the same thing."

"We weren't any less frightened, and that's what counts. It could have been Pancho."

Carol could barely speak. "You have told me all my life how you were almost killed by Pancho Villa, and now you're telling me it was goats?" she sputtered.

"She didn't mean anything by it, Carol," Alma said.

"She always told me it was goats," Cecil said.

"Shut up, Cecil," Carol said. "Mother, you tell me and Alma, your daughters, your flesh and blood, the same story the same way a hundred times but you wait until *she* comes along to tell the truth," and here she pointed to me.

"I think it's better this way, Carol," I offered. "It's better with goats, really. This way it's funny."

Carol stomped out of the room. We heard the back door slam, then a car backing full speed out of the driveway.

"You see now why I could never live with her," Rose whispered to me.

12 | SAY IT'S NOT A CHEVROLET

One cold January morning, Roger Bailey of Bailey's Chevrolet walked into the *Lawsonville Ledger* and caused a commotion without saying a word, but you would have to know Roger to understand how he did this. Roger came by every day. Sometimes he had business and sometimes he didn't, but it did not matter. We were part of his day, like lunch. He would bound in the front door and, first thing, tell me a joke.

Quick. What happens to ducks when they fly upside down?

I give up.

They quack up.

Quick. When's a bicycle not a bicycle?

I don't know.

When it turns into a driveway.

A new joke every day. Roger had a voice that carried, so there'd be people as far back as the business office chuckling or rolling their eyes, depending on what they thought of Roger. Me, I put up with him. When he finished with me he moved through the advertising department like so much wind. *How're ya doing?* People stopped work to talk to him. Women ducked to keep from getting kissed.

Usually he wound up at Stanley Becker's desk talking about golf. Stanley was a young man in the advertising department who graduated from N.C. State in marketing and believed he could sell anybody anything. He was not shy about standing in the middle of the advertising department handing out his secrets for success, and here was one: *Never disagree with a customer.* Here was another: *Your smile is your best weapon.* But his favorite was, *You can sell anyone anything if you find out what makes 'um tick.* Golf, Stanley believed, made Roger Bailey "tick," and the two of them played a regular Wednesday afternoon game, but on this morning, Roger walked past both me and Stanley, through advertising without a single hello. No jokes, no kisses, no *How're ya doing!* By the time he got to Purdy's office, everybody was staring. *What's wrong with Roger?* We could see them talking through the glass walls of Purdy's office. Roger would not sit down, and Purdy got a look on his face like somebody was in trouble. Then they called for Rose.

It was Stanley who figured it out. He fished through the Sunday sports pages then groaned. "I knew it."

Deborah Hoffman and the other salesman, Lloyd Baines, gathered around him. "It's the full-page Bailey," Stanley explained. "I should have known. I never should have given her that account, but I swear I thought she could handle it." So they looked, and there it was in forty-eight-point type, a brand new Chevrolet selling for $1,100. Instead of $11,000. "I gave that account to Rose to be nice," he said. "See if I'm ever nice again."

Lloyd admired the mistake, which was brave for Lloyd. He had been at the paper longer than Purdy and, like Purdy, was a drinker, but it seemed to go harder on Lloyd, a small man with pale eyes and skin as thin as a butterfly's wing. He rarely spoke his mind about anything, but all of a sudden he piped up, "I got a picture of all them people swarming Bailey Chevrolet trying to get their hands on that car."

I laughed from all the way across the room, but not Stanley. Stanley did not laugh. He said, "Rose is too damn old for this job. You can't be sloppy in this business anymore. These days you have to be sharp. Somebody ought to tell her that," and he looked straight at me.

"Maybe it was typesetting," Deborah offered, and it could have been. No one in the office had a high opinion of the type-setters, especially Purdy, who was often heard saying things like, *What's one more zero, or one less, to people like that?* But it wasn't typesetting. Stanley checked it out. "Nope," he said. "They got it straight from Rose's copy. Eighteen hundred dollars for a brand new Chevrolet. Loaded. Rose must have lost her mind."

We looked back to Purdy's office, and there was Rose. She had her head in her hands, and she was crying.

She would not quit crying. Purdy and Roger hovered around her, but it was as if she couldn't care less the way she sat there, weeping like an autumn rain, the kind that keeps falling without hardly making a sound. After a while Roger left just the way he came in, without a word, and nobody spoke to him either. Still Rose cried. Purdy stepped out of his office, panic on his face. He looked at me and held up his hands. *What do I do?* I left the phones ringing and went back there.

"You want me to take you home, Rose?"

She did not answer.

"The ad was wrong," Purdy said. "All we did was tell her, and now look."

People started to gather. *Something's happening to Rose;* like a wave rolling through the building, people in layout coming to see, people from down in the business office. People were whispering.

What's wrong?

Is she sick?

She's got cancer, don't you know.

Ed Stivers came out of the newsroom and stood in the hall. The phone on my desk was ringing, and he kept looking at it, then back to the crowd, back and forth like that, trying to figure it out. Then the phone quit ringing.

Rose would not stand up. "Let's go, Rose, please!"

The phone started ringing again. Stivers shouted, "Why isn't anybody answering the damn phone?"

"I'm taking you home," I whispered to Rose.

"Good idea," Purdy offered.

I looked straight at him. "How about you shut up and answer the phone."

He did. Rose walked. And we left. It made me a hero. I don't know how long after that day people came up to me and said, "Way to tell him, Ruth!"

Weeks.

Way to go!

People I didn't know gave me the thumbs-up sign when I walked down the hall, and I suppose it was because nobody ever talked to Purdy like that, but I don't know why not. Purdy wasn't going to do anything to me. For what he did to Rose, he ought to feel lower than a whipped dog; even I knew that.

Rose stopped crying when I got her home. I made her lie down on the sofa and brought her a pillow and blanket, which she took the way a child would, gratefully, without having to say thank you every little minute. I would have brought her a beer, but I couldn't find one, so I poured her some ice water.

"You want me to turn on the TV?" I asked her.

She shook her head no.

Now that the windows stayed closed for the winter, Rose's house always smelled musty like old ice or rusted plumbing and furniture never moved, and it was dark, like Mama's, although the reason Mama's house was dark was because she never opened the curtains. They were dark, brown-plaid curtains she had made herself, and I know that if anybody ever stretched them out, the dust from twenty-five years of hanging there would fly all over the place. The brightest light in that house came from the TV, which, between Mama and William, didn't have an OFF button that I could see. Rose's house was dark because it was turned the wrong way, and even on the brightest day, it seemed to hide in its own shadow. She said it was built like that on purpose for the coolness of it, and maybe so, but I found myself always wanting to turn on another light. I sat down and lit a cigarette.

"You want one?"

Again she shook her head.

"You ought not to listen to Purdy, Rose."

She nodded.

"He's an asshole."

She smiled.

"What did he say to you anyway?"

"Nothing." She waved her hand through the air as if to wipe it away. "I don't know what came over me."

"Probably a crying attack. I have them all the time."

She shrugged. "Well, I don't."

"You got any beer?"

"No, honey."

"That's okay."

"I've got lemonade, but you'll have to make it up."

"You want any?"

"Not now."

"Me neither."

She closed her eyes, and right then it seemed like something went out of her. I don't know what it was. She was Rose, then she was only a shell of Rose, and you could not grab hold of what was missing any better than you could put air back in a balloon. It shook me up. It was a feeling like you think you're on solid ground, then you look, and it's not ground at all; it's nothing but a little boat, and the harbor's gone.

"Are you sick, Rose?"

She didn't answer.

"Rose?"

She opened her eyes and looked at me. "Would you do something for me, Ruth?"

"Anything."

"I'm sorry to be so much trouble," she said.

"You're no trouble, Rose."

"There's a box in my closet."

"You want me to get it?"

"If you don't mind."

Rose's bedroom was next to the kitchen in a small room that Raymond had used as an office. Carol turned it into a bedroom after Rose got sick, so she could quit going up and down stairs, and it was big enough for a bed and a dresser but not much more. There was one closet, missing its door. When I walked in, it hit me, which box? There were at least ten, fifteen, maybe twenty stacked on top of each other in a row along the wall, filled with books and newspapers, old *Chocowin County Criers*, and other loose papers. The boxes looked old, their seams thinning, some splitting, and the papers spilling out were yellowed and covered with a fine layer of dust. It was like she had saved everything she had ever owned or done or been, filling up the space around her, starting in the corner and moving out. Photographs covered the walls in a random pattern or no pattern, just wherever the nails happened to be hammered, more pictures of Carol and Alma in all different stages from babyhood on up, but there was one picture of a large, square-headed man with features that made you think of Carol. This would be Raymond. There was also a picture of Larry, although it was not on the wall with the others. It was on the dresser in a silver frame. I knew who it was right off, and I had to give it to Rose. He was an unusually handsome man, with dark skin, silken hair a color like night, and clear blue eyes. I could not swear to it, but it was in the eyes. He looked an awful lot like Alma.

Leaning against the wall next to Larry's picture was a stack of old *Chocowin County Criers*, and I looked through them. There were the expected feature articles on children and on old people, on fishermen and farmers, but there were other articles, too, and as I flipped through them, I began to think that Rose's work as a reporter might have been more important than anyone was giving her credit for now. There was one on a conflict of interest involving the sale of a tractor and a county commissioner, and like Jackson, Rose had written about an illegal meeting held by the county commissioners. A number of articles featured the Chocowin County sheriff, who tended to pull people over on the highway for no good reason, but even more were about the county health department, including three written in 1967, which were separated from the rest as if, just recently, she had gotten them out to look at them. I unfolded the top one and read the headline. **Segregation at Health Department.** The other two had similar headlines: **County Officials Deny Segregation,** and **State Vows to End Health Department Segregation.** I carried them to Rose's bed and sat down.

I knew about these particular articles, some of the last she wrote before selling the newspaper, because she had told me the story behind them. At that time, there had been two waiting rooms at the health department, one for white people and another for black people. There were no signs. Nowhere was it written down; nowhere was it said out loud; it was just the way it had always been, something that had always bothered Raymond, although he had never done anything about it. Rose got the idea to write the articles from a young, black woman named Eliza Jones, who worked for her one summer. Eliza had grown up near Scoot, where men grew up to be fishermen and women grew up to work in the crab house, but not Eliza. Eliza went to the University of North Carolina at Chapel Hill and learned to be a lawyer. Rose had told me about Eliza, and the way she talked about her, she must have been very smart. I once had Rose tell me I was smart, too, but I did not take it to heart.

Rose decided the best thing to do was march Eliza over to the Health Department to sit in the white waiting room. Eliza did have a cough at the time, so it was not like they were lying. They figured Eliza would never make it out of the waiting room, and that's what they wanted, for Eliza to get kicked over to the other side. Instead, a nurse called her back, examined her, and Eliza walked out with a prescription for antibiotics.

Rose wrote the articles anyway, and all kinds of people ended up getting in trouble. Clear up to Raleigh people were coming down, and newspapers from all over the state picked up the story. The North Carolina Press Association ended up giving Rose an award for her work, although Rose was not the one who told me about that. Carol was. She said she was as surprised as anybody when she saw the certificate. "It came in the mail in a cardboard tube, but Mother could have gone up to Raleigh for it. She could have gotten some credit for once. She could have met the governor, but she wouldn't do it."

"Why not?"

"She did not like him."

"Ruth!" Rose was calling me.

"Just a minute." I found only one box in Rose's closet, but it was huge, and when I tried to pick it up, it would not budge. I shoved it across the floor, but it ran aground on the rug in the middle of the room.

"Are you all right, Ruth?" Rose called again.

"I'm fine," I yelled, but she came on in anyway.

"Not that box," she said. She lifted a small shoe box off the shelf, then pointed to the one at my feet. "That one's too heavy."

"No kidding."

She opened the big box and peeked inside. "Magazines, no wonder."

I followed her to the kitchen, where she took the lid off the shoe box. Inside were pill bottles of many shapes and sizes. Rose riffled through them until she found the one she was looking for.

"What is that?" I asked.

"I don't know exactly. Alma gave it to me. It's some kind of vitamin."

"I don't believe in vitamins," I said. "I don't believe in God, and I don't believe in vitamins."

"Alma told me this one was a picker-upper. In case you're ever low."

"Is that what this is, Rose? Are you just low?"

"It's green," she said, holding a pill between her fingers.

I helped Rose cut the pill in two so she could swallow it better, then I put the bottle on the windowsill along with the others. Already there were blood-pressure pills, heart pills, and pain pills, and although I had never thought about it until that day, it made me nervous to see them lined up in a row like that. On the windowsill next to the bottles were a glass full of sandy seashells, a sun-warped color snapshot of Jacob, a bottle of hand lotion, a jar of peanuts, and a piece of stained glass shaped like a lighthouse. Rose once told me that life is what you put on the windowsill above your sink, and when she said it, I had thought she meant really, but she did not mean really. She only meant that small things matter. Sometimes more than big things. "There's a lot you're going to miss if you don't know that," she had said. I strained to remember what might be on my windowsill: a bottle of aspirin, a melted-down candle, an opened package of Junior Mints, and a beer can filled with slimy water and one wilted flower left over from summer, but I could not figure out what in the world it might mean.

Just then we heard a car in the driveway, and Rose groaned. The back screen door slammed shut. "All right, Mother, what happened?"

Carol. She took Rose's temperature, felt her pulse, pushed on her stomach, peered into her eyes, and I don't even know what all else, but I will tell you this; I have never seen anyone move so fast. "You don't appear to be sick," Carol said. "Does somebody want to tell me what happened?"

I started to tell the story of the Chevrolet ad, but Carol cut me off.

"I know all about that. Screw him. Did Roger Bailey make you cry, Mother?"

"No."

"Did Purdy Hughes?"

"No."

"What then?"

"I think she had a crying attack," I said.

Carol looked at me like a day gone bad. "I have never heard of such a thing."

"I have them all the time," I said.

Carol turned back to Rose. "You want some lemonade Mother?"

"Not right now, thank you."

"Why don't you come help?" Carol said, pointing to me.

I followed her into the kitchen and watched as she pulled a can of concentrate out of the freezer and held it under a stream of hot water in the sink.

"She just told you she didn't want any lemonade," I said, but Carol had down pat the art of ignoring people, especially me. She had come from the hospital, her uniform, a stiff, white pantsuit, gave her the look of somebody important, and it made a difference. You put a woman like Carol in jeans, she'll just look dumpy. "Get me some ice," she said.

I did not exactly want to but did anyway. I jerked open the refrigerator door, and just as I did, the blue Chinese doll with the bobbing head fell on top of me. I yelped. It hit my shoulder, tumbled to the floor, then rolled. Carol peered at it lying on the floor as if it might come alive; we both did. I had been watching those bobbing-head dolls teetering on the top of that refrigerator for months, but they never did fall. Not until now. Carol grabbed it before me. I imagine it took every bit of willpower she had not to toss it in the garbage can.

"I hope it's not broken," I offered.

"Why?" she asked.

"You okay in there?" Rose called from the living room.

"We're fine," I called back, then I turned to Carol. "Do you remember those articles Rose wrote about the health department waiting rooms?"

"Ancient history," Carol said.

"They're lying on top of Rose's dresser. I was just wondering why she might have pulled them out."

"Because . . ." Carol said slowly, as if enduring the obvious.

"My mother was the best newspaper reporter this place has ever known. She was better than Ed Stivers, way better than that silly Jackson Price. She does not want to forget it, and I don't blame her, but that's part of the problem. It was a long time ago. Maybe it's not fair that everybody else seems to have forgotten, but you can't make people appreciate you. You have to go on. You have to say, that was one part of my life, now here's another, but Mother won't do that." She put the Chinese doll back on the counter next to the sink and opened the can of concentrate. "Mother cannot go on like this. I hope you can see it now, Ruth."

While she filled the can with water, I picked up the doll and snuck it back to the top of the refrigerator where Rose liked it.

"It's going to get worse. I see it every day at the hospital. I've told her she can move in with me, but she won't listen." She dropped ice cubes into three glasses. "So I want you to tell her."

"She seems okay to me, Carol."

"What do you call what happened this morning in Purdy's office?"

"I don't know."

"Did you know that just last week she woke me up in the middle of the night because she couldn't find her keys? Why she needed car keys at three o'clock in the morning, I have no idea, but I had to drive out here to help her look for them."

"I wonder why she didn't call me?"

"Are you her daughter?"

"No."

"That's why. Did you know that she threw away every single one of her brand new blood-pressure pills in a day?"

"How do you know?"

"The bottle's empty." She picked up the bottle on the windowsill and shook it. Nothing. "Either she threw them out or swallowed them all, which would have killed her. How about the time she locked herself out the house? Except instead of calling me like she should have, she hauled a ladder up against the house and climbed in the kitchen window."

I remembered seeing the ladder but thinking nothing of it, propped up there against the house, and I began to wonder what else looked normal that might not be.

"She could have killed herself," Carol was saying. "What's going to happen when she starts the house on fire?"

"She shouldn't smoke in bed," I said.

"Are you kidding? She shouldn't smoke, period."

"I'll tell her that."

"Like I haven't," she snapped.

She marched back into the living room, glasses of ice-cold lemonade in her hands. I followed, but Rose was not waiting for us. She had fallen asleep on the couch.

13 | AND ALL OF THEM WERE BLUE

Some people claimed that after Raymond died, a man showed up at Rose's house, a man nobody had ever seen before, a mystery man. Not everyone believed it, but those who did said he stayed right there with Rose and Carol, who was only six years old at the time. It was not long after the funeral either, because people were still bringing food, and Rose would not let them come inside. She simply took their lasagnas and their chicken soup, their cakes and broccoli casseroles, saying thank you and closing the door. But some said they saw him plain as day, sitting in the living room like a brother or a cousin or an uncle from far away. So why not introduce him? He could have been a new chair the way she forgot to mention him, and that was no way to treat your brother.

It was Larry; I knew that. Larry found out that Raymond had died, and how he had died, and did the first thing that came to him, never once thinking Rose would turn him away, and she didn't. She opened the front door, and there he stood. Maybe she thought about it for about two seconds. He stayed three weeks. "But this time," Rose said, "I didn't want to marry him." Nine months later, Alma was born.

This is where the story gets confusing, because if you count up the months, there is no reason to believe that Alma could not be Raymond's child, and lots of people counted up those months. So the story split, some saying Rose had been pregnant when Raymond was killed, others saying it was the mystery man who was Alma's father, the real story being that nobody knew. And Rose never told, which over the years helped her grow into a person who did not do things like other people did. There's an awful lot of freedom in that. The way I looked at it, this was not a woman who would make a mistake on the ad copy for a car dealership, then go home and die over it.

But that's what it seemed like. Rose was not the same Rose, and it wasn't just one thing that made me say that. There were the circles under her eyes that told me she wasn't sleeping good, and she quit even trying to brush her hair, and she'd show up for work with her shirt inside out, not every now and then, but two or three times a week. Around the office there was talk that she was getting senile, although the strongest theory was that the cancer had come back, and this time it was going to kill her. I told them they were wrong, but I didn't know. She would not take walks with me anymore. She would not go to Dickie's for lunch. All she ever wanted to do was go to work then come home, where I would find her sitting in the dark, drinking coffee, and putting together a jig-saw puzzle.

"How can you see what you're doing?" I would ask.

"I can see all right."

"Let me turn on a light."

"I don't need a light."

"What's wrong, Rose?"

"Nothing."

"Have you eaten anything?"

She only shrugged.

"You ought to eat, Rose."

"I don't have a taste for anything, Ruthie."

"Yea, well I think eating's a goddamn chore, but you have to do it anyway. How about we go over to the mall and get us a Chick-fil-A?"

But she wouldn't.

Carol hired a carpenter. His name was Clark. Clark's job was to build a second bathroom onto Carol's house, so when Rose moved there, she would have her own.

"That's fine," Rose said, "but I'm not moving."

I thought she at least ought to go see it, and I told her so, but Rose said, "I don't need to see it."

"You ought to anyway. I'll take you over there."

"Nah."

"What if she's only bluffing, Rose? Then you wouldn't have to worry about it."

"She's not bluffing. Carol doesn't bluff; she doesn't know how. Anyway, I'm not worried."

"I don't know, Rose. If somebody wanted to move me where I didn't want to go, they'd be hearing about it. I'd be over there every day having a fit."

"She can't move me if I don't let her," she said.

But I still didn't know. Carol scared me the way a bulldozer would if it were aimed my way, and Rose, she could slip into a thing the way you do when you're not careful. Rose was not careful. She liked to tell people not to worry, and that's fine, but you can still watch your back. Then one day I got her to go with me.

Carol lived in a neighborhood of small brick houses set close together with sidewalks and old trees and settled-in concrete porches. Patches of hard sand infiltrated the grass. This was not a place where people were likely to come and go; the streets did not look big enough for a moving van. Men and women on their porches waved as we passed by. Rose waved back. She said, "Those people were old when Carol moved in," but I kept my mouth shut. Rose was sitting in the front seat of my car looking like she invented old.

Carol's house was on a corner. It was the only yellow brick house on the street, the rest being one shade or another of red. It had black shutters and a small porch surrounded by a black, iron handrail entwined with flat metal roses. Carol was not home. We found Clark in the backyard eating a baloney sandwich.

"Hello, Clark," Rose said.

"You know him?" I asked, surprised. In all our talk of Carol and the new bathroom, Rose had never mentioned she knew the man doing the work, although I don't know why it seemed important. He was an old black man with grayish skin and long, vein-lined muscles. He wore dark green work pants and a shirt a lighter shade of green, buttoned at the wrists and all the way up to his neck. He tucked his sandwich inside a paper sack and stood up.

"Back still bothering you?" Rose asked him.

"It's this shoulder here giving me the fits these days, Miss Rose, and a flare-up in the fingers every now and again. How about you?"

"Healthy as a horse; you know me. How's Opal?" she asked about a woman I had to guess was Clark's wife, since neither of them bothered to tell me.

"Not too good," he said.

"I am sorry to hear that. You tell her I asked about her, hear? You tell her I'm coming down soon for a fried crab sandwich."

"I'll just do that, Miss Rose, I will."

"I didn't know you two knew each other so well," I muttered.

Rose offered Clark a cigarette, which he took. She took one, too, "to be sociable," then handed one to me. Rose had promised Carol she would stop smoking, but I was not going to tell. We stood, the three of us, smoking and looking at the ground. Clark had been digging a trench, although he had not gotten far. It was staked out roughly in the shape of a rectangle, marked with string.

"You're wasting your time, Mr. Clark," I said. "Rose is not moving in here."

He did not answer but offered me a full grin, the way you do to somebody speaking a foreign language, but you want to be nice anyway.

"So how much is she paying you?" I asked.

"I don't know as I ought to say, exactly."

"Tell Rose," I said. "I'll close my ears."

"I don't know exactly if I ought to," he said.

"It's okay, Clark," Rose said. Then she whispered to me, "We don't need to know that."

When we got back to my car, Rose told me, "Don't worry. That bathroom won't be ready for a long time, if I know Clark."

"You never told me you did."

But Rose leaned her head against the back of the car seat, closed her eyes, and was asleep by the time we got to the end of the street.

I called Alma. *Something's wrong with Rose.*

Alma never went anywhere without Dean, so I was surprised when she and Jacob pulled up in Rose's driveway in their creaky, wood-paneled station wagon one evening as the sun was going down behind the soybean field in streaks of purple and red. Rose was bent over a puzzle of a New York City street scene. Each piece looked like somebody had dropped five or six buckets of paint, and the colors had splattered every which way. Jacob burst through the back door and ran toward his grandmother. Rose hugged him, then turned to Alma. "Why'd you come?"

Alma sat down on the sofa and smiled. She wore no coat, only a cotton dress with tiny flowers of dark maroon and black that fell almost to her ankles. As she rubbed the thin fabric between her fingers, I noticed again how small were her hands, almost like a child's.

"Dean?" Rose asked.

"Dean doesn't know."

Rose took this in. You could see her taking it in, but she also seemed to know how much she could get out of Alma and not ask for more. As I watched the two of them together, I realized that Alma was like her mother in ways Carol never would be. Or me. I noticed, for instance, that when she came into the room, Alma had been careful not to turn on any lights. When I got up to flip on the switch, she shook her head.

"No?"

"No," she said. Which was the kind of thing Rose would have done. Just because it's dark doesn't mean you have to turn on the lights.

I sat back down. Alma made a pot of coffee and gave each of us a cup with lots of milk and sugar. Rose stared at it. "I didn't think you drank coffee."

"Every now and then. I brought some banana bread. Jacob, would you mind getting it out of the car for your grandmother?"

"I don't want any banana bread," Rose said.

"Honey, would you just please . . ." she whispered to Jacob, and he left the room.

Alma sighed. "So. How are you doing, Mother?"

"Fine."

I tried to get Alma's attention to let her know not to believe it, but Alma just nodded. She smoothed out her dress again as if she were brushing crumbs no one could see. "I have something to tell you, then."

"Shoot," Rose said.

"It's a secret," Alma said.

"Who am I going to tell?" They both looked at me.

Then Alma whispered, "There's something besides banana bread in the car."

Turned out it wasn't anything, just another one of Alma's quilts, so you tell me, where was the big secret? I looked to Rose to see if she could figure it out, but Rose studied Alma's face and gave nothing away. Alma told us she had been working on this quilt for six years with scraps of material she had saved and moved with her across the country and back.

Well. I sure had not called Alma to talk about sewing. I lit a cigarette and started fiddling with Rose's puzzle, only half-listening to Alma talk about her quilt. She wanted to enter it in a contest in Asheville, except Dean would not let her. "Dean will take one look at my quilt and claim God made it; now isn't that like something he would say, Mother? He's going to make me give it to the church just like everything else." She looked down at her hands. They were shaking.

"Do you want to leave it here with me?" Rose asked her.

She shook her head. "That's okay." Then she whispered. "God did not make that quilt. I did."

Good grief. At this rate we would never get around to talking about Rose.

We heard the back door slam, and Jacob came back. Rose

stood up. "Let me help you with that, sweetie," she said, and the two of them went to the kitchen to cut banana bread, leaving me and Alma alone in the dark.

"Alma," I whispered, but she did not answer. I gave up on the puzzle and sat down beside her. "Alma," I said it again. "Carol's trying to get Rose to move in with her. She thinks Rose can't take care of herself anymore."

"I know," Alma said.

"She's not fooling around, Alma. She's already hired a carpenter to build a new bathroom. I swear if Rose doesn't watch it, she's going to end up there."

"I know."

"Rose doesn't want to go, Alma."

Alma sighed. "Carol would take good care of her."

"But Rose doesn't need taking care of."

"Mother won't do what she doesn't want to do."

"You mean she won't move to Carol's?"

"Yes," she said, but I could tell there was more.

"You mean she won't get better unless she wants to."

"Yes."

I decided that if anyone could help Rose, it would be Cecil, and I tried to find him. I had heard Rose say he was known to wander up and down the coast as far north as Norfolk and as far south as Charleston, so there was no telling where he was, but one day Victor told me he had seen him in a neighborhood across from the post office downtown. "I'll take you there," he said.

To get there, we walked through a neighborhood of old houses not far from the architect's office where Mrs. Pickle's boardinghouse had been. Michael came with us. He said he wanted to check on the Parker House, but he and Victor often walked through the old parts of Lawsonville to see how people were fixing up the houses. There was usually something wrong, the wrong kind of window, the wrong trim, the wrong color. "What would drive a person to put an eighteenth-century porch railing on a nineteenth-century house?" Victor exclaimed, though not as if he expected an answer.

The houses along the streets north of the post office had never been restored, and Victor looked at them the way you would look at abused children; if you could wrestle them away from their parents, they'd have half a chance, but that was a difference between Victor and me. The deeper we got into the neighborhood, the more I realized I did not care about the houses; it was the people I saw, men with stringy muscles and dirty T-shirts pulled too tight over their chests as if that were an advantage. It was like seeing a dozen Homer Birdsongs, cocksure and tobacco-stained, and women grown fat from too many Big Macs, their voices like shotgun spray aimed at children who ignored them, filthy children who watched the world the way foxes would and learned quick. As I walked along the sidewalk and looked up at those people on their porches, I knew who they were.

A child on a Big Wheel blocked the sidewalk up ahead, and without thinking, I fished through my pockets for something to give him, candy, change; I don't know what I was looking for, but it did not matter. Then I heard Michael say, "There ought to be some kind of spray."

Victor started to laugh, but choked it off when he saw my face. "You don't mean that," I said.

Michael glanced at Victor, then shrugged.

"You better take it back," I said.

"Come on, Ruth, he didn't mean it," Victor said.

Michael reached over and tousled my hair.

I slapped his hand away. "Don't touch my hair."

"I like your hair."

"Stop it," I yelled.

"Okay, okay. I take it back. Jesus!"

Victor trotted ahead. "That's the one," he said, pointing to a newly painted blue house at the end of the street. "I saw Cecil working on a car in that driveway just last week."

But the woman inside said Cecil was not there. "He was here," she said, "but he's gone now." She was a large, heavy woman, nearly blond, with deep frown lines. She blocked the way in as if I might try to barge through anyway.

"It's important I find Cecil, okay? So if you see him, will you tell him it's about Rose?"

The woman did not say anything.

"Rose Lee."

"What's wrong with her?"

It was my turn not to know what to say. Victor and Michael were still on the sidewalk at the bottom of the steps. I could see them both silently measuring the house with their eyes, calculating what it would take to rescue it from this woman. "Nothing," I said. "Nothing's wrong. Will you tell him?"

"I don't know no Rose," the woman said and closed the door.

Victor took me to Dickie's and bought me a plate of french fries. They were the fat kind that burn your fingers if you try to pick them up too fast. They came with a little paper cup of ketchup and one of tartar sauce which, along with coleslaw, was a house specialty, but I was not hungry. Dickie said she had not seen Cecil either.

"What's wrong with letting Rose go to Carol's?" Michael said. He was spooning the last of a chocolate milk shake out of a tall glass, and Victor and I just stared at him. "I mean, I don't see what's so bad about it. My dad moved my grandmother to a nursing home, and she was fine. Dead now, but fine then."

Victor looked at me, and I looked back. He knew what was so bad, but he shook his head as if to say it was not worth trying to explain it to Michael. He pointed to my french fries. "Are you going to finish those?" I shoved the plate to his side of the table. "You watch," he said between bites. "Rose'll be fine. She's a lot tougher than you think, right Michael?"

"You're asking me?"

"Did anybody ever tell you how she got me my job?"

I knew the story. Rose had told me about how Victor snuck into the church one summer day and started playing the organ, and the music that came from the open windows and doors drew people off the street and into the church until there was no more room, so they stood on the sidewalk to hear. If you listened to Rose, Lawsonville nearly stopped the day Victor first played the organ. He was hired on the spot.

Victor shook his head. "Not exactly," he said. Michael was rolling his eyes. Victor finished the last french fry, licked his fingers, then leaned over the table. "I had come from what we might call, because I strive always to be polite, a messy entanglement." He glanced at Michael, who was nodding. Michael knew this story. "All I will say, Ruth, is this. It was horrid. Never put your heart in the hands of a rich man."

"Don't worry."

"We were on his yacht, docked here on our way from Fort Lauderdale to Norfolk when I jumped ship. Just walked off, no money, no idea of what I was going to do, and no hope of going back home to Mobile, no ma'am. Not after all I had been through. There is no telling what would have happened to me if not for Rose. She's the one who talked them into hiring me. I still don't know how she did it."

"It didn't hurt that you could play the fire out of that organ," Michael said.

"No, but these folks were not used to taking in stray queers."

"He's lucky they didn't tar and feather him," Michael said.

"Now they swear they don't know what they would do without me."

"You haven't seen anything until you see the old ladies down there make a fuss over Victor," Michael said. "They treat him as if he were their own son."

"They've taken me on to raise." Victor and Michael both smiled at this idea, one they had obviously considered before. Then Victor said, "People tended to listen to Rose more back then."

"Maybe they owed her something," Michael said.

Victor turned in his seat to face him. "You are always thinking the worst."

"Maybe I'm just getting old and cynical."

"Old? I think you could stand a little growing up."

"Rose rescued me, too," I said, and that got their attention. I could see them both on the edge of their seats. Well, not literally on the edge of their seats, but they had that look in their eyes, wanting to find out what Rose had rescued me from. I felt my face turn red, knowing my story was not nearly as interesting as they imagined. I shook my head and stammered, "That's why we have to help her now."

Victor studied me for a minute longer before he said, "You're right, but what I'm telling you, see; she's tougher than you think."

We left Dickie's and followed the sound of chain saws until we reached the old Parker House, then we stopped and stared. None of us could say anything. The giant oak tree that had stood in the front yard was down. It lay in huge logs like centipede sections snaking out from the stump in different directions. Sawdust covered the grass, and a bulldozer sat quietly to the side. Already you could see the stakes where the gas station would go, blocking the house completely from the street. I knew Victor and Michael and others had fought hard to keep that house from being demolished, too, but I could not see how it mattered now. The oak tree had been a hundred years old. We stood there watching, not speaking, for a long time, lone mourners at a funeral for a tree.

It was Victor who moved first. "Let's go," he said, although it took a few minutes for us to turn our faces and walk away. Victor said he knew a shortcut, and we followed him, behind a bank building, through the parking lot of a lawyer's office, past the Methodist church. The church was the smallest in town, a red-brick building almost as old as St. Paul's Episcopal, that sat back from the street, surrounded by willow trees. A small graveyard was on one side, enclosed by a short, black iron fence. Roots from the old trees that shaded it crawled under the fence and wound around the gravestones. Victor stopped at the gate and turned to me. "You remember me telling you about the sea captain's wife? The one who died of a broken heart? She's supposed to be buried here. I found the burial record in the courthouse, but I have never found the grave."

We stepped over the fence and began walking, each of us following a different path, stopping to read the names and dates of people we never knew. Toward the back of the graveyard, the dates were harder to read, some of them worn completely off the stones. Others you could make out by kneeling and feeling the stone, and for each one I did some quick math between the first and second dates to see how old the person was when he died. So many had died young. I stopped in front of one.

Abigail Rivenback
Born July 19, 1892
Died November 7, 1903

I cannot tell you what it was about this gravestone; any number of them could have affected me the same way, but I was suddenly struck with the thought that, in 1903, there had been a November 8. There had been a November 8, and 9, and 10, and however long you want to count, for everyone except Abigail Rivenback, and so it was: For everybody dead and gone, there is a next day for the rest of the world.

But so what? I say, just because you can ask the question doesn't mean there's an answer, but some people won't quit. Okay, fine. You can believe in God if you want. You can believe God wrote the Bible, that the world was created in seven days, and that Jesus died for you. You can believe in Heaven, you can believe in Hell; you can believe in Santa Claus and the Easter Bunny, too. You can believe your dog used to be a person. You can believe the pope is somebody. You can believe God wants your team to win, that he hates your enemies, that he listens to your prayers, and on the third day He rose again, because it's all the same to me. Some people would say I don't have any faith. I say there are worse things.

But if pressed, I would tell you there might be something worth waiting for, which was why I was worried. I was beginning to think Rose might not be waiting for anything anymore.

That night I found her huddled under a blanket, working another puzzle, this one a picture of an ocean, and everything in it was blue. The water was blue, the sky. There were hundreds of tiny pieces scattered faceup on the table, and all of them were blue.

"Let's you and me go to the mall and get a Chick-fil-A," I said.

"You've tried that already."

I sat down next to her. "What is this, Rose?"

"Nothing."

"Are you sick?"

"I don't think so."

"You want a drink?"

"I don't drink."

"You could start."

She filled in a hole in the sky with a piece of blue and rubbed it flat. She drank the last of a cold cup of coffee. She smiled at me. Then she picked up another piece of blue.

"This isn't even half fair, Rose."

"I know, hon."

14 | CAKE, HAM BISCUITS, AND RED, RED RUSSIANS

Purdy could not live with himself. It was on his face, a kind of wishing look, as if he wanted somebody to tell him it was okay what he did to Rose, but nobody would. Because picking over somebody's time card is one thing; it's something else to make an old lady cry. Even Purdy understood this. He had crossed a line. You get mean enough, and people don't care anymore.

But there's just so long a person like Purdy can hang-dog it, and one day he called me into his office. I figured I was in trouble. That morning Roger Bailey had called while Purdy was out, and I had taken a message. I knew who it was; only a deaf person would not recognize that voice, but I pretended I didn't. *Bailey. Now how do you spell that?*

You know damn well how to spell it.

Then he hung up.

I decided that was my only defense: *But he hung up on me, Mr. Hughes!*

Purdy's office made me nervous anyway. Stivers's office had a couple of plain, black office chairs and a desk. On the wall, somebody had tacked up a picture of sand dunes, torn from an old calendar, and that was it. But Purdy's office looked like a rich person's living room, with dark, heavy furniture, red leather chairs, an oriental rug, live plants in blue-flowered planters, and pictures of golf course holes on the wall. On the bottom of each frame was a small, gold plaque: *13th Augusta National; 18th Pebble Beach.* Every time I went in there I was scared I was going to break something.

But I was not in trouble. Purdy stood in the doorway and urged me to come on in. He held the chair so I could sit down. Then he sat down on the other side of his desk, looking almost giddy when finally he said, "Let's give her a party."

"Who?"

"Rose, of course."

"What for?"

"We'll call it Rose Appreciation Day," he said. "I should have thought of this years ago."

Now there was in Purdy's eyes an alertness that made me think he had not been drinking. If he had been drinking, I could count on him forgetting this conversation, and I would not have to worry with it. I could say, *Boy, Mr. Hughes, that sounds like a great idea,* and it would not matter. But I was going to have to be careful, with Purdy not drinking and all, so I said, "I don't know, Mr. Hughes. I don't know if a party would exactly do much for Rose," but even as I said the words, I could see Purdy purely beaming from the genius of his own idea. In his mind there was only one problem standing in the way of making it work. "What do we put on the cake?"

"Put a rose on it," I said, figuring there was no use fighting it.

Even Carol, when she found out, thought a party was a great idea. "What's the matter with you, Carol? You don't even like Purdy."

But she cut me off quick. "Mother deserves this," and she went out and bought herself a new dress in green silk. For Rose, she picked out one in maroon.

Rose did not look good in maroon silk. It washed her out worse than the flu, but it hardly mattered, because it was dark in the ballroom on the sixth floor of the Ramada Inn, where Purdy insisted the party be held. There had been some argument over when Rose ought to arrive. Rose thought she would simply get there when the party started and sit down, but Carol wanted her to make an entrance so the crowd could part and let her through. It was a picture she had in her mind, the crowd parting then applauding. Purdy sided with Carol, but he worried over the timing. "Don't come in too late or it won't work," he warned, but she did not listen. By the time Carol got Rose to the Rose Appreciation Day Party, people were already eating ham biscuits. They were dipping carrot strips into ranch dressing and spreading cheese on crackers. They were already drinking whiskey sours and vodka tonics. Carol beamed as the elevator doors opened and she walked Rose slowly across the ballroom to a chair at the front of the room, but I think more people would have noticed if she had sat her by the bar.

Purdy stood beside Rose's chair. He had been drinking since that morning, and by now his face was splotched red and white, and he was sweating. His eyes did not focus, but every now and then they slipped into a wild panic as if he did not remember why everybody was there. He tapped his glass, but the sound of it startled him, and as people pressed into a semicircle, he looked as if he wished he had not done that. He started to say something then motioned to Stivers, who bounded up to the front of the room.

"Once," Stivers boomed, "Rose stood on a dead man."

The crowd burst into laughter because everyone knew this story. Not only did they know the dead man story but a dozen other stories that had turned Rose into somebody they thought they knew. Stivers didn't even get it right. He said Deputy Bud Snow had to drag Rose off the corpse, which was not even close to true. Rose had gotten off just fine by herself.

As he spoke, Stivers motioned to Rose as if he wanted her to stand up, but she wouldn't. She sat quietly looking down at her fingernails, which somebody had painted frosted pink. Her hair had been molded by the beauty parlor into something Dickie called the Seashell, and somebody had put too much rouge on her face. I couldn't watch. I found Michael and Victor at a table near the back of the room. "He doesn't believe half what he's saying," I said.

"It's not that bad, Ruth," Michael said.

"You know what the guys in the pressroom are saying? Purdy will fight to the penny over every minute of overtime you claim, but all of a sudden he has enough money to throw a party and invite the whole town. And you know what? They're right. Even Rose thinks they're right."

"You're taking it too seriously," Michael told me.

"Have a ham biscuit," Victor said. "They're lovely."

"I ought to leave," I said.

"Rose might need you, Ruth," Victor said.

"Looks like to me Rose has all the friends she needs," I said, which was not true, and I knew it, but there were so many people. I could not even see Rose through all the people, but not a single one, I bet, cared about Rose the way I did.

"I'll get you a beer," Michael said.

Stivers must have finished his speech because there was a final roar of laughter followed by loud applause, and the crowd began to filter back through the room. The bar was in the center, and as I watched Michael make his way there, I noticed Madeline directly in front of him. She was wearing a thin, black dress that came to her thighs, so the first thing you noticed were her extremely long legs. You noticed her dress and her legs and the fact that she was standing next to Jackson Price, holding his hand. I grabbed Victor's arm to show him, but he acted as if he had known all along. "It's unspeakable," he said, "but I'm glad. Michael needs to see this. He deserves better than a woman like that."

Michael must have seen them, too, because just then he stopped. You could see him trying to decide what to do but, in the end, he walked right on. Just as he passed Madeline, she reached her hand out as if to touch him on the arm, but he jerked away, turning his head so if she spoke, she would be speaking to the back of his hair. He brought back my beer and a gin and tonic for himself and slumped down in his chair.

"I ought to get up and walk right out, is what I ought to do," he said, but he didn't. He sat with his hair in his face and drank his gin.

Suddenly there was a commotion over by the bar and when I looked, there was Cecil yelling at the bartender. Behind him was a second bartender, a younger man with a look on his face like he was ready to run if a fight broke out. I moved in close enough to make out that what Cecil wanted was a free drink, not understanding the concept of a cash bar, but before I could get to him, a policeman showed up. I recognized him. He was the same bristle-haired, shiny-shoed officer who had brought Cecil out the night Rose and I had gotten him out of jail. He took hold of Cecil's arm. I got there right before Cecil hit him.

"He's with me," I told the policeman.

"I got a call," the policeman said.

"Well it was a mistake," I said, then turned to Cecil. "What do you want, Cecil? You want a beer?"

The policeman looked at the bartender, then back at me. Cecil went limp and hung his head down, but there was no doubt he would strike like a snake if he had to. I knew it. The policeman did, too. The policemen looked like he was ready.

I put down a ten-dollar bill on the bar. "This man wants a beer," I said. I searched the crowd for a friendly face, but I got the feeling everybody around us was pretending we were not there. I saw Roger Bailey talking to a group of young women, but he looked away when he saw me staring. "Make that two," I added. Still the bartender did not move until the policeman signaled his okay. I pushed the money across the bar and said, "Keep it," then led Cecil out of the ballroom through a set of arched doorways into a hall. On one end were the elevators; on the other, two benches covered in red velvet. Between the benches stood a tree in a brass bucket. We sat on a bench under a pear-shaped light where we could not see the party anymore, although we could hear it. Cecil pulled his hat down over his ears. He smelled awful.

"Don't you want to take off that coat?" I asked him, but he shook his head, no.

"Rose said I could come," he said.

"Where'd she find you?"

He shrugged. He was jittery, even for Cecil, jiggling his legs, biting at his lower lip, and every few minutes he would peer down the hall as if he heard somebody coming, but there never was anybody there.

"I've been looking all over for you, Cecil. Didn't anybody tell you?"

I told him about Roger Bailey and the Chevrolet ad and about how strange Rose had been acting ever since, and he shook his head. "Rose ought to quit."

"And do what?"

"That would show 'em, all right. That would show those bastards."

"But what about Rose?"

"Rose? She'll be fine."

I sighed. "Want something to eat?"

He shook his head no, but I went back into the ballroom anyway and brought him out a half a dozen ham biscuits and a brownie. He chewed slowly, and we did not talk. I smoked a cigarette, knocking the ashes into the brass bucket. I handed Cecil a napkin, but when he finished, he wiped his fingers on his shirt then whispered, "I don't belong here."

"You better than anybody, Cecil. Let's go tell Rose you're here."

"Why would I want to get kicked out of there again?"

"Rose won't let them kick you out."

"Rose can't do everything. I gotta go now."

He would not let me stop him. I watched him get on the elevator, but instead of pressing the button and facing outward, Cecil pressed the button, then turned his back to the doors as they closed behind him. I felt sick. Not the kind of sick where something hurts, but soul-sick, which feels like somebody's knocked the wind out of you. Like something's gone that shouldn't be gone. And it wasn't just Cecil, and it wasn't just the party that raged on behind me, although that was part of it. It was because of all the people everywhere and in every time who seem to know the inside way of things. And all the people on the outside who don't.

———

A couple of years before Marianne Johnson was killed by a lumber truck, she gave a party and invited the whole class. Had I not listened to Margaret, I would not have gone, but Margaret told me this was my chance. I wished I had asked her, *chance for what,* but I was young then, thirteen or fourteen, and still willing to believe that Margaret might know more than me. Marianne lived on the road near Umbrella Rock in a big house with a huge stone porch that overlooked the valley. At one end of the porch was a glass wall with French doors that led inside. At the other was a door that led downstairs to a basement recreation room, but I did not understand this right away. From time to time I would see people go through the basement door, but I did not pick up on the fact that they did not come back. I did not think about it, because I was too embarrassed that nobody was talking to me. There are some bad things in this world, but near the top of the list has to be standing in a crowd and not having one soul to talk to. I tried to look busy eating Fritos, but there's just so long you can keep that up.

Finally Marianne herself came over to me, but I was so relieved, I did not understand what she was saying at first. Something about her parents and something about the basement. Then she placed something in my hand. It was a small whistle, although you would not know it was a whistle, not from the look of it, a sort of ceramic disk painted red and black, but she showed me how it worked, and the sound was tiny like a faraway bird.

"Blow this if my parents come out," she said, nodding toward the French doors. Then she gave me a look that said, *Understand?* That's when I noticed that all of a sudden no one else was on the porch, just Marianne and me, then she, too, slipped through the door that led to the basement recreation room, where who knows what was going on, and yes, I did understand. I was alone. Not part of the party at all. I had never been a part of the party. I was the guard.

I spent a little time wondering what I ought to do if any parents did come out, thinking how easy it would be to forget to blow that whistle, but after a while, I simply laid the whistle on the table with the Fritos and the dip and the cookies and the brownies and walked to the end of the driveway, where I waited for two hours for Margaret to pick me up.

She was furious. Not because of what Marianne did; I did not tell her that. If Margaret had found out what Marianne had done, she would have known what a lost cause I really was. I listened to her tirade all the way home and through the front door and into the kitchen, where I sank into a chair. She said I was hopeless. She said if I wanted to shoot myself in the foot, that was fine with her. Mama was waiting for us at the door. She watched us cross the room. She watched me sink into the chair and Margaret head straight to our bedroom and slam the door behind her.

"I never wanted to go to that stupid party anyway," I yelled to the closed door.

Mama, I will remember this until the day I die, just sat back down in front of the television.

I was still sitting on the bench outside the ballroom, staring at the elevator, when I was startled by nearby voices. I turned to see Ed Stivers and the man they called Fingers talking to each other in whispered voices at the other end of the hall. I could hear they were talking about the hospital but could not pick up enough to make sense out of what they were saying. Fingers was holding a cigar in his mangled hand, and he was smoking it, and the smell was thick like I was standing with my face in a filthy smokestack and breathing in. Stivers, I noticed, held two drinks, one in each hand. When Fingers returned to the ballroom, Stivers walked down the hall and handed one to me.

"What's in it?" I asked.

He regarded me before saying, "Alcohol." I took it as a dare and drained it. "Black Russian," he told me then. We watched the elevator doors open, spilling out a group of latecomers, then close. "Wait here," he said.

I watched as he disappeared into the dark ballroom, watched as he passed right by his wife, Joan. I saw it through a mirror on the other side of the hall. She was standing just around the corner from me, so close that, had I said her name, she would have turned to look. I knew it was Joan because of her hair, which was unusually short and made her head look too big. She was pinched in at the middle by a huge golden belt around a black pantsuit, and I could hear her. "You can walk down the street in San Francisco and find . . . and in New York . . . and the last time I was in Boston . . ." which was the kind of thing she always said as if she were bent on making sure everyone knew she was *not* from Lawsonville and that she would put up with it for *just so long*. In a minute Stivers was back with another drink for me.

"White Russian," he said.

"Don't they make them red?" I drained that one, too.

"I like a girl with a sense of humor."

"Good for you." I looked in the mirror to see if Joan was watching, but she was not. "I should go home now."

"Don't go." He sat down beside me on the bench. "I saw what you did back there with that policeman. You're a brave girl, aren't you, Ruth?"

"Not so brave."

"Wasn't that Rose's boyfriend?"

"Some people say so."

He nodded and smiled at me. "I understand you are from somewhere in Tennessee."

"It's a small town. You never heard of it."

"Try me."

"Summerville."

"Never been there."

"Of course you haven't. I told you, it's a really small town."

"I could tell you were from Tennessee, though, the first time you opened your mouth." He raised his glass as in a toast. "I'd marry you through a hole in the wall if you'd keep talking."

My glass was empty. He handed me his drink, something light brown. Scotch? I gulped it down.

"I used to live in Memphis," he said, drawing it out, this *M e m p h i s*, as if caught in a memory he had been wanting to bring up all this time. "I worked downtown within walking distance of the river, but everybody warned me not to go there. Don't go down *there*, was what they said, but I didn't pay any attention. It was the Mississippi River, for Christ's sake; you know what I mean? How are you supposed to stay away from something that big? I never had anything on me anybody would want to take except my life, and you can lose that anywhere. Are you a gambler, Ruth?"

"I don't know."

"You look like a gambler to me."

"It must be my hair."

"Is that what it is?" He smiled, and I'm telling you what. It got hot in that hall all of a sudden. I was dizzy and feeling the current of sweet drinks moving through my blood like honey. I looked in the mirror, and there was Joan looking back at me. You could have counted the seconds, one, two, three, four, five . . . all the way to ten, before she turned her back and walked away, deeper into the ballroom, where I could not see her anymore. Then, I don't know what happened. I bolted. I stood up and ran back into the dark, crowded ballroom until I found Victor at a table by himself and sat down. He handed me a napkin; I wiped the sweat off my face. "I have to get out of here, Victor."

"Yeah, Michael left, too."

Victor looked tired. His eyes were red, and there was a spot of sausage-ball grease on the front of his shirt. I put my head in my hands. "You shouldn't drink so much," he said.

"I know. Tell me something, Victor, what do you know about Ed Stivers."

"Ah," he said, studying me. "He is a handsome man."

"You think so?"

"I do."

"I'm surprised anybody else would think it."

"There's all kinds of handsome."

I nodded.

"Don't get tangled up with him, though, Ruth." He pointed to a man standing across the room, his friend, Jack Henry Sabatino, who owned Jack's by the River and was now talking to a woman in a silver dress. "You see Jack Henry there? He loves me more than anything in the world, but guess what? I love Michael. Michael, of course, loves Madeline, and Madeline, it appears, loves Jackson. So you tell me, could anything be more screwed up?"

"I don't know, Victor." I shook my head.

He sighed.

I reached out and put my hand on his. Then from out in the hall came an explosion of laughter, and the room emptied to see what it was. Carol was there and Purdy and Stanley Becker and Ed Stivers and Roger Bailey and Jackson Price and Madeline and Jack Henry Sabatino and as many other people as could squeeze into the hall. Stanley Becker was the loudest. He stood in front of a gaping set of elevator doors. They had opened before the elevator had reached floor level, so what you saw were the heads of a group of boys from the pressroom who had been riding the elevators, pressing buttons. They were going to have to climb out, but as they reached for hands to help them up, someone poured a drink over their heads. Then somebody poured a drink over Stanley's head. Victor stood on tiptoe to see better. I went looking for Rose.

She was all alone. Her hair had come undone, and a trail of black mascara ran down her face. Her shoes lay on their sides under her chair. I wondered how long in that crowded room she had been sitting alone, but now the room was practically empty. I pulled up a chair next to hers, and she grabbed my arm.

"They did this because they think I'm going to die, didn't they?"

It was like the whole room vanished with one question.

"Didn't they?"

"Yes."

It seemed enough, and she let go. It's a wonder what a simple answer will do, but I figured, if somebody's asking for the truth, you've got to tell them. Most people aren't asking.

"I have to go now, Rose."

She nodded.

I ran down six flights of stairs to the parking lot of the Ramada Inn and threw up in the bushes.

15 | GONE FISHING

The answer to Rose's problems came in the form of a giant of a man named Fred Fish.

Rose hated Fred Fish. I would not have thought Rose hated anybody, but she hated Fred Fish. *That man,* she called him; she could hardly say his name. She sort of spit it out, like her jaw all of a sudden didn't work right.

Fish was the director of the Chocowin County Health Department, a position he had held for more than twenty years, which put him in charge of the segregated waiting rooms at the time Rose had written those articles for the *Chocowin County Crier.* I did not figure this out right away. It was something I realized slowly as I began to piece together the stories she had told me. Rose said you could spot Fish a mile away because of his size, and it was true. The first time he came into the office with a press release, I knew who he was, and how sad is that, to think that the way you look is so alarming, people you've never met know who you are? He was well over six feet and massive in a way that scared me. His hands were bigger than my head. His chest was so wide it looked like you could not fit your arms around it, like the pictures of those redwood trees in California where people try to wrap their arms around but can't.

The articles about the health department turned out to be harder to write than you would think because, after Eliza Jones sat in the white waiting room and nothing happened, she was ready to say there was not a story. But that's the way Eliza was, smart but careful. Carol had told me you could count on Eliza not to do anything rash, and that was something, coming from Carol, whose idea of rash could include changing your hairstyle, but everybody seemed to think a lot of Eliza. So Eliza came back from the Chocowin County Health Department with her prescription for antibiotics saying they could not write the story because they did not have any proof.

"Let's do it anyway," Rose said.

Still it was hard. They first tried talking to people as they came out of the health department, which should have been easy but wasn't. As Rose explained, "The black people, they wouldn't hardly talk at all, either that or they would say, *It's where we sit, Miss Rose*, so you begin to ask yourself the question, if they don't consider it a problem, why should I? And white people, you ask them; they'd say, *What black side?* I'm not lying either, unless you got somebody who plain didn't care; then you'd hear, *Because I ain't sitting next to no nigger, that's why*. At least those people told the truth. But the real truth was, nobody was about to go against Fred Fish. People were afraid of him, and fear, Ruthie, that's all the truth you need."

Fish thought it was funny. Rose would sit him down to ask him questions, and he would laugh at her. He would not answer her questions, but he wanted to let her know there were no hard feelings. So Rose used pictures. She took pictures of the outside of the health department, the two separate doors. Then she and

Eliza dashed inside, took pictures of the people sitting in their waiting room chairs, then dashed back outside before they got caught. Those pictures showed people with surprised expressions on their faces, but there was no getting around the fact that they were either all white or all black, not both. Rose published the pictures along with interviews of the few people who would talk, and ended up with four articles in all. A man was sent down from Raleigh, and within a couple of weeks, there was just one waiting room, and it was open to everybody.

This was Wild West stuff. I told Rose I sure wished I could have been there, and she grinned because she knew it was so. After all, when does anybody get to go against the bad guy and win? When I got this story out of her, it made sense to me why Rose never came down on Carol's side when it came to Ed Stivers and Jackson Price and their crusade against the hospital. Even if they were wrong, she could put herself exactly where they were, because there had been a time when she saw things that weren't right, and she did something about it.

I got a picture of Rose in pin-striped pants speeding off in cars, marching down hallways, barging into offices, squaring off with the likes of Fred Fish. Rose said it wasn't like that exactly.

Fish was patient. It was the scariest thing about him, Rose said, because if he had struck back right away, you could almost understand it. Instead he backed down. He called press conferences with newspapers clear up to Raleigh to say he never meant for there to be two waiting rooms. "It's just something that came on naturally," is how he was quoted in the papers; then the next day he said, "Never again will there be discrimination under my watch." Summer ended, Eliza went back to school, autumn came, and winter, then one day the next spring, Rose got her first parking ticket.

The *Chocowin County Crier* was located in a small, brick building two blocks west of the county courthouse. The building was
still there, although it had long ago been boarded up and left to
rot. There was no parking lot, so Rose parked in the street. She
had been parking in the street for twenty years. The ticket was
issued by the sheriff, Lester Grant, and that, Rose said, was all
you needed to know.

"I told Lester, 'I've been parking here for twenty years,' but
he only smiled, and, Ruthie, his was a smile you don't ever want
to see. Think about Hitler smiling and see if you don't know what
I mean. Only it made me mad, don't you see. Made me so mad,
you could not have paid me to park anywhere else, so I kept
getting tickets, more and more tickets, a new one every day. I
don't even remember how long it went on, but I ended up owing
nearly six hundred dollars, and Lester, he was talking about sending me to jail when I finally gave up. They made me park behind
the drugstore, three blocks east."

And maybe if it had ended there, if it had stayed a matter of
parking and nothing more, Rose could have looked back and
laughed, one more story in a life full of them, but Fish did not
stop with parking. He condemned the building.

The *Crier* building was old, but welcome to Chocowin County.
There was hardly a new building in the whole place except for
the new bank branch and a Hardee's. "I never did understand
how he pulled it off," Rose said, but she ended up with no one
on her side. Not the county executive, not the county commissioners, not the planning commission, which consisted of only
four people anyway, three of them related to Fish.

By this time, Cecil was living on and off with Rose, and he
tried to help her fix what was supposed to be broken, the plumbing, the wiring, the roofing, but Fish always came up with something else wrong, and you cannot go on like that for too long

without the money to back you up. Cecil insisted she fight Fish in court except she had to go clear up to Lawsonville to find a lawyer who would go against Fish, and by then Rose was nearly broke.

"That's when Carol said I should give up," Rose said. "I was nearly seventy years old anyway, and she did not want to see me down to my last dime, you know? And I could understand her position, but I turned it right back on her. I decided that, at seventy, I could get down to my last dime if I wanted."

Although it did not matter, because it was around that time, Cecil got himself put in jail for writing a poem on the side of the health department building. She told me what it said:

Fishes in the ocean,
Fishes in the sea.
A Fish out of water
Is as evil as can be.

"Boy, Rose, he didn't mince words, did he?"

"Those were my thoughts exactly, Ruthie. I told him he could have been a little more subtle."

Rose bailed him out, and in the end, she was forced to sell the Chocowin County Crier, which was what Fish was going for all along.

She sold it to a man who promised to keep it going exactly the way it had always been. "But he didn't," Rose said. "He turned it into a shopper. You can still get ahold of one; they've got them for free outside the Piggly Wiggly, but that's all it is anymore, a shopper."

Rose came up to Lawsonville then, looking for a job at the Ledger. She had two decades' worth of newspaper articles to show plus an award for investigative reporting, but the editor (who was not Ed Stivers then, but someone else) said she was too old to be a reporter. I can't hardly tell this part of the story without getting mad all over again, but that's how she ended up with a job in advertising.

"Why did you take it, Rose?"

"I needed a job."

Like I said, don't get me started.

The way Fred Fish brought press releases to the *Ledger* was, he would come into the office, shove a piece of paper across my desk, then turn and walk out the door. He did not speak to anyone. He certainly did not take the trouble to carry it into the newsroom the way most people did. One day, he handed me a press release and when he was gone, I read it, but instead of taking it to the newsroom the way I was supposed to, I slipped it under the phone book on my desk. I took it with me that afternoon when Rose and I walked down to Dickie's Dinner to try a secret-recipe pound cake.

Dickie had called Rose that morning about this cake, and when we got there, she brought it out and sat down next to Rose. "I want you girls to try this now. See what you think's different about it."

Rose stared at the cake in front of her. "Chocolate," she said. "It's got chocolate in it."

"Well, I know that," Dickie said.

"I mean you can see it plain as day," Rose said, poking at the cake with her fork. "What's the big secret?"

Dickie was wearing pink, which put a glow on her face. She had pulled her hair back in the tiniest bun you'd ever want to see, the size of a thumb, a thumb bun. She said, "It's just that everybody's used to the lemon. Customers come in, order pound cake, they're wanting lemon, you know. This one's called a marbled pound cake, and you can see how the chocolate's kind of marbled there all through it. I thought I might try something new for a change."

"It's dry," Rose said, taking a bite.

"Don't tell me that," Dickie said.

"Not bad dry," Rose said. "But it's not going to beat the lemon if that's what you're after; it's just not."

I took a bite and thought it tasted fine and told Dickie so, but there wasn't any going back on what Rose had said. *Dry.* The killer word when it came to pound cake, and Dickie flew off toward the kitchen, her hair flinging loose from its bun.

Rose shoved her cake aside and fumbled for a napkin. I took out the press release. "I want you to look at this, Rose. It's about mosquito control in Chocowin County."

She read it then nodded.

"So the ditches you told me about, the mosquito control ditches that are really boat canals, Fred Fish is digging them. The same guy who ran you out of the *Crier*. I mean, I just put it together. It's illegal, isn't it, Rose, what he's doing? Those boat canals are against the law."

Again she nodded, but this time slowly, and she raised her eyes to look at mine. Then she smiled. It was spine-strengthening was what it was. It was what I had been waiting for. I said, "It'd be something if the newspaper got hold of that story, wouldn't it, Rose?"

"I've always thought so," she said.

"You ought to write it."

But Rose said no.

"Why not?"

"Because," she said, "I am not a reporter."

"Tough."

"Anyway, I'm too old."

I have heard it said that hyenas will latch on to an elephant's leg if that's what it takes to bring it down. They won't let go, not for nothing, which is how I got with Rose, because I had finally figured it out. Going to the mall for a Chick-fil-A won't cut it. You got to have something to do in this world. That's what was ailing Rose and what, I decided, would cure her.

And one day she surprised me.

His name was Ned. Ned worked for the State of North Carolina, Division of Environmental Services in Raleigh, which was the agency in charge of mosquito control all over the state. It's where the money came from. Rose also told me that Ned was a nice young man.

"How do you know he's young?" I asked.

"He sounded young."

She said she was lucky to have gotten Ned on the telephone, which is what Ned had told her. Lucky, lucky, lucky; we did not even know how lucky, because you would not believe how many people up in Raleigh were on Fish's side, and not just Fish, but health department directors up and down the coast. Because they all did it. They all dug boat canals in the name of mosquito control and made money doing it.

"They send a cut up to Raleigh; that's how they get away with it," Rose said. "Ned says his boss gets paid for every canal Fish digs."

"But Ned doesn't?" I asked.

"He says he doesn't," Rose said.

"Maybe he's just jealous," I said.

"Maybe. But he told me he has been waiting for a call from a reporter like me for years."

"A reporter like you, Rose? Does that mean you're going to do the story?"

We were driving down Highway 53 toward Scoot. Rose had her face pressed up against the window, which was driving me crazy, because she was mumbling into the glass, and I kept having to lean sideways to hear her. She did not exactly answer me, either. All she said was, "Ned claims it's too dangerous to talk over the phone."

"Dangerous? What does he mean, dangerous?"

"He said he would meet me at the Econo Lodge in Lawsonville at six o'clock tomorrow night; the only problem is, that's the night I promised Carol I would eat with her. We can't let Carol get wind of any of this; she'd shut us down faster than a hurricane."

"I'll go," I said.

"I should be able to join you there by seven."

"I still don't see what's dangerous."

She dismissed the notion with a wave of her hand.

We were going to Scoot for fried crab sandwiches at Clark and Opal's house. Rose said she used to go there with Raymond, who always said Opal's sandwiches were his favorite. Opal mashed in a lot of pepper and a little egg with the crab before it was fried, but Rose added that, no matter how hard she tried, she could not do it like Opal. "Nobody can."

I knew Rose was fond of Clark, but I couldn't help it; every time she said his name, I got nervous, thinking about Carol's new bathroom. Rose had been right, Clark was coming along slowly on it, but he was coming along. You would see Carol these days, and under her arm she'd have tile samples which she would pull out and show you—*What do you think, the blue or the pink?* She carried around copies of *Southern Living* and *Better Homes and*

Gardens, dog-eared to pictures of new bathrooms. It seemed to make Carol happy to show you the pictures, to talk about bathroom fixtures, and if it made Rose nervous, you would not have known. It looked to me like we were in a runaway car heading for a crash the minute that bathroom was finished, but Rose didn't see it.

Once in Scoot we turned down a dirt road I thought would never end. A gully ran down the middle, so deep in places it felt like balancing your tires on the rim of a railroad track. Clark and Opal Johnson lived at the end of the road in a small, block house that backed up to a large marsh that had a mosquito control ditch running through it. You could see it in the distance. "That," Rose pointed out when we stopped, "is the real thing. A mosquito control ditch built for the purpose of controlling mosquitoes."

"Looks like a boat canal," I said.

Rose had brought a camera, and when she got out of her car, she began taking pictures of the marsh. I looked around. There were two other houses like Clark's across the road and three trailers, but Clark's looked kept up the best. There were daffodils in the yard and a small gravel walk to the front door. Six or seven dogs came to meet us.

"Now you'll find people who'll say you don't fry a crab," Rose said, as we walked toward the house. "Dickie's one. I tried to get her to make me a fried crab sandwich one time, and she flat out told me, no. You fry fish, shrimp, and oysters, she said, but never crab unless it's one of those soft-shell kinds, but that's a different story. I say food's food, and you ought to be able to fry any old thing you want."

Clark met us at the door. He looked as if he might have dressed up for our visit in clean black pants and a brown paisley-patterned shirt buttoned to the neck. The house was clean but crowded, as if Clark and Opal had pushed all the furniture they owned into one room. There was a thick smell of grease but also something sour and mediciny. Opal was sitting in a wheelchair in the middle of the room. She was an ash-colored woman with ash-colored hair that hung down to her shoulders in irregular lengths. Even sitting I could tell she was a tiny woman, smaller than Rose, like a twig doll with clothes pinned on. She had on a red-and-white-checked dress and a dingy white sweater. She rocked back and forth, fingering the sweater, and did not look up when we came in. Rose looked at Clark but did not say a word.

"She's been going down, Miss Rose," he said.

Rose pulled up a chair and sat next to Opal and held her hand, but Opal did not look up, keeping instead the rhythm of her rocking and the pick, pick, pick of her fingers on the sweater. "You didn't tell me it was this bad. How long has she been like this?"

"It's hard to say for sure. A year, maybe."

Clark made the sandwiches, and I went to help. He spooned patties of crab mixture into the frying pan, and we watched as they sputtered and sprayed a mist of grease into the air. I backed away. We watched them smoke up and burn. He got them out fast with a spatula and dried them on paper towels. Grease dripped off the stove top onto the floor.

"How're you coming with Carol's bathroom?" I asked Clark then.

"Pretty good, pretty good," he said. He wiped his hands on his pants, then thought better of it and wiped them on a paper towel.

"Well, slow down then," I said.

"Carol can have as many bathrooms as she wants," Rose said. She wheeled Opal into the kitchen and parked her in a corner next to the table. "It's no concern of ours."

Clark slipped the patties into hamburger buns and served them with ketchup at the small, cramped table. They tasted sweet and salty at the same time, and I ate every bite. While we ate, Clark told Rose about the neighbor who stayed with Opal when he was gone and of the nurse who came by once a week to check on her. The nurse was sent by Carol, as it turned out, which seemed to surprise Rose. "She never told me."

"She don't like to worry you," Clark said.

"She should anyway," Rose grumbled.

Then she told Clark about Fred Fish and the mosquito control ditches, which surprised me, since we were supposed to be keeping it a secret, although it seemed to me Clark knew the story already. As he nodded, I got the feeling there were pockets of people all over Chocowin County who knew all kinds of things, who had always known, like a club of knowing, and not just about Fred Fish. There were all manner of stories I did not know.

Clark chuckled. "It'll be like old times, won't it, Rose?" He looked at me. "Rose here's the one who got them to build the bridge on 53 just before you get to Scoot. Before then, anytime it rained the highway flooded because, I don't know; whoever built it in the first place didn't pay attention to that marsh next to the road, right, Rose? That *big* marsh. Right next to the road. Maybe they were blind."

Rose was grinning. "Maybe."

"Maybe they had a hole in they head."

Rose and Clark were both chuckling now.

"Come a good rain, we'd be stuck out here for days, sometimes weeks," said Clark. "You had to have a boat to get to town, but after Rose wrote them stories . . ." He snapped his fingers. "You should have seen how fast they moved."

"Their sight was restored," Rose said.

Clark looked at me. "You should have known this lady once upon a time."

From the corner, Opal made a choking noise. Clark looked embarrassed and, excusing himself, hurried to her. He held a cup under her chin and helped her drink through a straw, ice cubes knocking hollow against the side of the cup. When she pushed the cup away, he wiped the dribbles off her chin. Rose leaned over the table and held her head in her hands.

"It's all right, Miss Rose," Clark said. He patted her shoulder.

"What can I do, Clark?"

He shook his head.

He walked us to the car, but before we got in, he stopped. "I hope you get him this time, Miss Rose. You know we're all with you down here. I hope you teach old Fred Fish a lesson he won't forget." But when he helped her into the car, I heard him whisper to her, "You be careful, hear?"

Rose was quiet most of the way back, but when I pulled into her driveway she sighed. "They weren't the same, Ruth. Nobody can make a fried crab sandwich like Opal. It's just something, you know . . ."

"I know."

". . . that's gone."

16 | UNDERWEAR SPY

Rose was right. Ned was young. I met him at the Econo Lodge, Room 207, in his underwear. "Rose?" he asked, when he opened the door.

"No, I'm Ruth. Rose will be here in a minute."

I did not know whether to go in or not, a man in his underwear and all, but he left the door open, so I walked on in, except here was the problem. I didn't know where to sit. Right away, the bed's not going to be your first choice when there's a man wandering around in his underwear. It was white boxers. I couldn't decide whether he was trying to tell me something or just making himself comfortable. I made a point not to look and found a chair by the TV. Ned was a stocky man with reddish hair and freckles, a whole lot of freckles in places I wasn't sure I ought to be seeing. Every few minutes he would walk over to the window and peer out through the small crack in the curtain like they do in the movies. I wondered if he considered himself a spy. Ned the Spy in underwear.

"Are you a reporter, too?" he asked me.

"No."

"Rose is lucky she got me on the phone."

"So I hear."

He was still in his underwear when Rose knocked on the door. She had been at Dickie's with Carol and smelled like fried catfish. She wore a bright pink blouse with a matching scarf I had never seen before, lipstick the same color, and sunglasses, although the sun was almost gone. I had no idea what the sunglasses were for. I wondered if Rose thought she might be a spy, too, but when she got in the room, she took off the glasses and gave Ned and his underwear a look like you're not going to want to see if you're anywhere past ten years old. I was glad I wasn't Ned.

He edged over toward the bathroom and began to pull on a pair of jeans. I fished out a cigarette from a half-empty package and was in the process of lighting it when he turned around. "You're not going to smoke, are you?" he said.

I looked at him, then down at my unlit cigarette, then at him, back and forth like that a few times before looking to Rose, but she was not paying attention to me. Ned was pointing his finger at her. "First off," he said, "you never saw me. You don't know my name. You can't quote me, and you can't tell anybody where you got your information."

And Rose said, "Okay."

"I mean it," he said.

"I know," she said.

"So, okay then." He sat Indian-style on the bed and began to tell us how it worked. Although local health departments dug and maintained the actual mosquito control ditches, the money and equipment came from the state, and the rules were clear. If the state bought you a dragline for mosquito control, you used it for mosquito control. Nothing else. "This is taxpayer money I'm talking about here," Ned said. "And last I heard, the taxpayers of the state of North Carolina are not lining up to buy every little ditch-digger his own dragline. It's got to be state business or no business."

It was also the state, he explained, who decided where to dig the ditches. Inspectors came down every couple of years to decide this, and after they decided, they drew maps, and it was these maps the health departments were supposed to follow. Ned had filled a plastic motel cup with ice and water which he swirled in a circle as he talked, almost, but not quite, tipping it onto the bedspread. I found myself waiting for it, wanting it to spill.

"Well, a man like Fish, he's going to look out in the parking lot and see that dragline and get an idea," Ned explained. "He's going to think, maybe he could do a little business on the side. Dig somebody a boat canal, and if anybody asks, say it's for mosquito control. So tell me, what's the difference between a boat canal and a mosquito control ditch?"

"I been here before," I said. "Is this a riddle?"

"A map," Rose said. "One's on the map, one's not."

"You got it," Ned said, pointing to Rose. "Now let's see if you can guess how Mr. Fish gets paid."

"Cash only," Rose said.

"You're a smart girl," Ned said.

"Ignore him, Rose," I whispered.

She didn't answer either one of us.

"A percentage goes to Raleigh, although most of the inspectors don't know that. I'm not supposed to know it either, but it's been going on so long, half of them have forgotten it's illegal," Ned said.

"You're sure it is?" I asked.

I was still holding my unlit cigarette, which I had probably ruined by stroking it between my fingers in a sort of nervous twitching so that lumps of tobacco now showed through the thin paper. I was wondering what Ned would do if I lit it anyway. I was wondering if he had ever *seen* Fred Fish. With all his big talk, I wondered what he would do if he ever came face-to-face with somebody that big. He glared at me. He said, "Tell me again what it is you do?"

There was something about Ned. Like the way he introduced himself as an entomologist like he assumed I would not know what that meant. *Entomologist,* he had said with some brand of a Yankee accent as if to imply I didn't talk right. I could go a long way without knowing something like that. I excused myself and went outside to smoke.

I didn't know why we needed Ned. What was wrong with me and Rose, was what I wanted to know.

Everything was happening so fast. I held on to the balcony railing and looked up, but the Econo Lodge sign flooded the sky, and there were no stars. I sat down on the cold concrete and leaned back against the bricks of the motel wall and remembered those nights Chuck and I had sat on the bed, watching TV, eating Chinese food, and drinking beer, and I had thought: *This is my life now, the way it will always be, nailed down,* but I had been wrong. And before Chuck, it had been me working at Durwood's without any idea of how to do something different. I did not know what I wanted. I never planned anything. I did not even know I was going to run away with Chuck until the exact minute I got in his car.

Of course, there's people who won't believe that.

I know, because people had been telling me I was bound to leave Summerville someday. I had teachers who said things like, *You ought to make something out of yourself, Ruth.* Even Durwood, who would just as soon I never leave, once told me, *Wait until you get your traveling shoes.* Even Mama. She never said any particular words I could point to, but sometimes when she looked at me I got the feeling she was steeling herself for when I was gone, but I did not understand it. People seemed to think they knew more about me than I knew myself, which can get on your nerves. So maybe running off with Chuck did not surprise anybody, but it surprised me.

Not that Chuck and I had not been kidding around. When they buried his brother, Chuck did not sit with his family but stood next to me at the edge of the cemetery. We told each other jokes, and sometime during the middle of it all he said, "You're just what the doctor ordered." I told him, stop being so corny; try something else, but it did not faze him. He just smiled and said, "How about you come away with me?"

"Well," I said. "I just might."

After the funeral we drove down the mountain, and he bought me a beer, and we leaned against his car in the parking lot of the 7-Eleven and talked. He told me about Wuffer Works. I told him about Mabel Jones's fried pies. I promised to write him, and he wrote down his address for me on the back of an envelope. That seemed to be a pretty fair picture of where we were except, when he dropped me off at home that night, he said, "I meant that about you coming away with me."

"Yeah, well. Maybe." But I swear I didn't mean it.

The next day I was back at work at Durwood's when Chuck came in for a fried pie, except there weren't any. And for the first time ever, I got mad about it. Chuck didn't care. "I didn't really come for pie," he said.

But I wanted him to have a pie, and I turned to that mean Mabel Jones and said, "If you're going to sell pie, you ought to sell pie. Every day, not just when you feel like it."

"I am not," she said, "nor have I ever been, in the business of satisfying your boyfriends."

My boyfriends! If she was talking about Homer Birdsong, she was way out of line, but before I could answer, I heard her mutter something completely surprising. "Just like her daddy."

There it was again. "What? What do you know about my daddy?"

She pretended to price jelly. And maybe I should have quit there, but I didn't. I kept at it, and Chuck slid somewhere behind the gingham aprons and cast-iron muffin tins mumbling something about how I ought to just drop it, and Mabel Jones closed her mouth up so tight it'd take a crowbar to pry it open, but I did not quit. I put my hand on her hand so she could not price any more jelly. Then she told me. She told me that, right after I was born, my father left my mother and moved in with a school-teacher named Virginia Crow. Ginny Crow. Miss Ginny. People all over knew who she was. She taught fourth grade, and every-body said she was a good teacher. I was lucky not to have had her, although I remembered wishing I had.

Or maybe it was not luck. Maybe it was the work of people like Durwood and others who knew better. Who knew a lot more than me and would not for anything have let me get put in a classroom with Miss Ginny as my teacher. My father was living with her when he died, although it was Mama who put him in the ground. I tried to make myself imagine what kind of shame you would have to bear to take in ironing for people who knew that. What kind of pride. Mama never told me. Margaret never told me. I could forgive William.

"Don't worry," I told Mabel Jones right to her face. "I don't believe you one little bit." Then I stomped out the door. Chuck followed me. He drove me over to an empty school playground, where I threw rocks against a chain-link fence until it got dark. When I finished, he said, "You really can come with me, if you want."

Now I was hundreds of miles away from there, smoking a cigarette on the cold floor of a motel balcony on the other side of a wall where Rose and a stranger named Ned were planning who knows what, and maybe that was good, and maybe not; I couldn't hardly trust myself to say. The way my life was going was like a ball rolling off a steep slope, watching it speed down, not knowing what it's going to bump into, not knowing when it will stop or where or even if it will. But that wasn't what was bothering me.

Right after I was born.

That's what Mabel Jones had said. The more I tried to forget it, the more it stuck, like something in your throat you can't get out. You can say what you want, but Mama wasn't the only one Daddy left. All those people who said I was like him; I'm sorry. They were wrong.

I stubbed out my cigarette and went back inside. Rose and Ned were bent over the bed, arguing over a map. "I am telling you it's too far to walk," Rose was saying.

"It's not that much farther, and at least we know where the road starts," he said. "How do you know there's even a road over here?"

"I know," Rose said.

"It looks like the middle of nowhere to me," he said.

"It *is* the middle of nowhere, but I know a path."

"You're sure?"

I sat back down in the chair by the TV. "Rose is always sure," I said.

Ned walked around the room with his hands in the air, saying, "Fine, that's just fine," over and over. Rose started folding the map back, but it would not fold straight, so she sort of smashed it smaller and stuffed it in her purse. As I walked her to her car, Rose asked me, "Why didn't you make him put his pants on?"

"I didn't want to hurt his feelings."

"His feelings are the last thing I'd worry about."

When we got back to Rose's, we found Cecil sitting on the back steps with a dog. A bruise covered one side of his face, but he was more upset over a lost hat. He kept touching his head as if maybe he was mistaken; maybe it was still there after all.

"What hat?" Rose said. "And where did you get in a fight?"

"Savannah."

"Georgia?"

He shrugged. "They'll never find me here." He put his arms around the dog. It was a yellow dog, skinny, with legs that looked too long for his body. He nudged at Cecil with his head.

"That's not *their* dog, is it?" Rose said.

"Not anymore." Cecil started to apologize for showing up like this, but Rose would not let him.

"You come get something to eat," she told him and led him into the house.

"I've got Jiffy Pop," I said, showing them the package to prove it. I had bought the Jiffy Pop remembering how Margaret and I used to buy it for William, who was never disappointed, who squealed with excitement the hundredth time as much as the first. I liked it that something you saw on television worked just as well when you got it home, which was not the way I figured most things worked. I half expected the foil wrapper to stay flat or cave in on itself or break, but Jiffy Pop always surprised me. As I watched Rose help Cecil into the house, it suddenly seemed pitiful to me that a package of popcorn could represent all there was of trust in this world.

Cecil went straight to Rose's bathroom and threw up, so he ended up not needing any Jiffy Pop. Rose laid him on the couch with a cold washrag on his forehead. She sent me for blankets because Cecil was cold, and I must have pulled out every one in the house. A mountain of blankets. Cecil could not seem to get enough blankets. We had left the dog outside, but he would not quit barking. "Maybe you ought to let him in," Rose said, and the dog purely hurled himself inside, skidding across the kitchen floor and out to where Cecil lay on the sofa as if he already knew his way around.

"Smart dog," I said.

"His name's Peanut," Cecil said, turning his head so the dog could lick his face.

"He doesn't look like a Peanut." I sat down on the floor, and Peanut came over to me and licked me on the face.

"I didn't mean for you to have to bring no dog in the house, Rose. I'm sorry," Cecil said.

"It's all right, Cecil. Should I be worried about the law coming after you this time?"

"Not this time," he said and closed his eyes.

Rose opened a map and spread it across the half-finished puzzle of the ocean and began to explain the plan she and Ned had worked out. "We're going to have to catch Fred Fish actually digging the boat canal or else we won't have proof. Clark's found out for us where Fish is going to be digging, so all we have to do is show up."

Cecil opened his eyes. "I am through tangling with Fred Fish," he said.

"You aren't tangling with Fred Fish," Rose told him.

"You ought not to either," he said.

Rose stood up, wadded the map in a ball, and tossed it on a chair. "I'm going to buy you a new hat, Cecil," she said.

"It won't be the same."

Peanut started barking while I was popping popcorn, and I looked up to see a car pull into Rose's driveway. Rose came and looked. It was Alma's station wagon, we could tell that from the window, but the only one in it was Dean. He came on into the kitchen slowly, as if he knew he was not welcome. *Where's Alma, where's Jacob,* you knew it was all Rose could do not to ask, but with Dean there was a kind of dance you had to do or else he would not talk. Peanut stood in the doorway between Cecil and the kitchen and growled. Dean stood with his back against the sink.

"You want to sit down?" Rose asked, but he shook his head no.

"Where's Alma?" he asked.

Rose took it in. You could see it on her face; she understood that Alma was missing, that neither one knew where she was. "Jacob?" she asked.

"He's gone, too."

"How long?" Rose asked.

"I don't know," he said although it pained him to say it. "Since this morning, I guess." He peered into the living room at Cecil, and Peanut backed up and growled.

"You're welcome to search," Rose said, stepping out of his way.

Find me a man who would not be offended by such a thing, and I'll show you Dean. Dean did not know to be offended. He barged through Rose's house, slamming doors and scooting furniture out of the way. My bet is, he would have searched Rose's house even if she had not offered.

"She hasn't called?" he asked when he was through.

Rose shook her head, and though she was telling the truth, he did not believe her. She had poured herself a cup of coffee and was sitting at the kitchen table. I sat next to her eating popcorn. "I'll let you know if she does call," Rose said.

Now this really wasn't true, and I knew it. Dean knew it, too, but there was nothing he could do, although he did not seem to know how to leave. He took the glass of lemonade Rose offered but then put it down, untouched, on the kitchen counter. You could almost feel sorry for him.

It was Cecil who finally got him to leave. Cecil wrapped a red and gold blanket around his shoulders and came on into the kitchen. It was one of Alma's blankets, given to Rose years ago, and you could see it in Dean's eyes how you could have shot him and not hurt him as bad as seeing this man's body touching Alma's blanket. Cecil looked like some wild man in robes, hair splayed out, skin a sickly pale, and the faint smell of vomit encircling him. He looked at Dean. He looked at Rose, then back to Dean. Then, staring at Dean, he said to Rose, "You reckon I'm still contagious?"

Dean ducked his head, mumbled something not one of us could hear, then left.

There was no word from Alma at Carol's either. Rose called to be sure, but all that did was make Carol want to come over, too. "I told her to stay put, but she's coming anyway," she said. She was rubbing Peanut's ears, and then she stopped. "Carol's not going to like this dog," she said. Then she pushed herself up to make a fresh pot of coffee.

Carol did not like the dog. She came through the back door then braked. "You're going to get fleas. How're you going to sell this house with fleas?"

"Who says she's going to sell it, Carol," I said, holding up the bowl in front of me. "Have some popcorn."

"It's all right, Carol," Rose said. "You remember when Alma told us about that craft fair in Asheville?"

"No," Carol said.

"You remember, the craft fair. She wanted to enter a quilt, but she was afraid Dean would not let her; don't you remember?"

"She wasn't there," I reminded Rose.

"Where?" Carol said.

"Here," Rose said. "The last time Alma was here, she told us about a quilt, although I'll admit I wasn't listening carefully. You remember what she said, Ruth?"

"When was this?" Carol asked.

"I don't know. Ruth, when was it?"

"Why wasn't I here?" Carol asked.

"Are you going to keep on like this or listen?" Rose said. "I am trying to tell you that Alma is most likely at a craft show in Asheville, which means she's fine. Jacob's with her, and they're both fine."

Cecil, who had returned to the sofa, called out, "When has Alma ever not been fine?"

"You keep out of this," Carol called back then turned to Rose. "What is he doing here?"

"He's sick," I whispered.

"Tell me something I don't know," Carol said.

Rose poured Carol a cup of coffee and filled it halfway with milk. Carol stirred three spoonfuls of sugar into it, sat down, and fingered a handful of popcorn. "Why didn't you tell me about Alma?"

"I didn't know she would really do it," Rose said.

"She went without Dean?"

"Looks like it."

"I didn't think she had it in her."

"I know you didn't."

The two of them, side by side at the kitchen table, held their coffee cups between their hands like squirrels.

It was late when I got home, and me with work the next day, although I knew Purdy would not mind. I had seen it before. If you had circles under your eyes, they only matched his, and anybody who came on to work anyway was okay by him. Maybe it was like a badge in Purdy's eyes to stay up all night, to drink all night, to do whatever it was you had to do in this world to keep sane and still do your job.

I parked my car on the street in front of Victor's house but did not get out right away. I was so tired. I could see myself climbing the steps to my apartment, see myself unlocking the door, walking inside, then heading straight to the refrigerator for a beer, and I dreaded it. I saw myself picking up the can of beer, dreading it, and opening it anyway as if I did not have a choice in the thing. How it was just an automatic me. I got out of the car and felt the breeze off the river, cool still, but with a hint of warm air stirring. Spring back home meant Mayapples pushing up in the woods like great armies gaining ground, a regiment here, another one over there, until they took over. I wondered if Mayapples even grew here.

I did not notice Michael until I reached the porch. He was sitting in one of Victor's big wicker chairs, and he did not say anything until I reached the top of the steps. Then, "Hi, Ruth," or I would have passed right by.

"You startled me."

"Sorry. Want a beer?" He handed me a bottle, Michelob, not altogether cold. Michael had one of his own, empty except for one sip that he took when I sat down, which maybe I would not have done had I not been so tired. And maybe I should not have anyway because Michael had a way of looking so pitiful you found yourself doing things you didn't want to do just to make him quit. I watched the reflection of the lights on the river and drank the beer.

Michael pointed down the street to the bar across the street. "Madeline's in there with Ed Stivers. Victor told me. He just came from there, and he saw her."

I thought maybe Michael had spoken wrong, and I asked, "Don't you mean Jackson Price?"

"That's what I said, but Victor said clearly it was Ed Stivers, and anyway, he described him, a smallish man, balding, and that isn't Jackson. As Victor so nicely put it, she's dumped the reporter for the editor."

"Maybe she graduated," I said.

"You know what she tells me?" Michael said. "She tells me she can't be in a relationship until she finds herself. Her words. Makes you wonder exactly what part of herself she's trying to find. Do you know how much older he is than Madeline?"

"He's married, too."

"He's an old man."

"Maybe they're just talking," I said.

"What is it about these newspapermen, Ruth?"

"Nothing that I can see, Michael."

We watched as a single car drove across the bridge, a flash of red taillight, but the sound of it stayed in the air as if the silence, interrupted, was slow to forgive. When the echoes of it were gone, Michael stood up slowly. He moved over to me, and with so little effort as you would be amazed, curled himself up in my lap. Michael was skinny, but I was skinnier, and if it had not happened so fast I would have told him, *Wait, this won't work,* but before I could say anything, it was working. He rested his head against my shoulder. I put my arms around his back. And maybe we would have looked odd to anyone passing by, and maybe it is odd to think of it even now, but while it was happening, there was the sense that there was nothing else to do.

17 | RAIN DANCE

Dean was standing in front of Carol's house in the rain when Rose and I drove up. Soaking wet, clothes sticking to his skin, hair like clumps of black seaweed dripping to his shoulders, Dean paced ankle deep through the water at the edge of the street, head bowed, mumbling.

"How did he know she was here?" Rose asked Carol when we got inside.

"God told him," Carol said.

Alma had come in on a bus from Asheville that afternoon. "She's back here," Carol said, leading us to the spare bedroom. This was the room Carol had been getting ready for Rose, yet here was Alma unpacking a suitcase. She sat cross-legged on the floor, taking folded clothes out of the suitcase, unfolding them, folding them again, then putting them in the dresser with a little pat. Jacob's clothes in two drawers, hers in the other two. "We could put another dresser in here, you know," Carol said. But Alma just kept folding clothes, pressing them flat, laying them in the drawers. A sheet of plastic hung over the hole where the door to the new bathroom would go when it was finished.

"Dean's out there in the rain," Rose said. "You want me to let him in?"

"No," Alma said.

Carol said, "We can take care of him, Alma, don't you worry," but Alma just said, "I'm not worried," which worried us. *You ought to be*, is the thing we all were thinking.

"I'm going to talk to him," Carol said.

She was still dressed in her nurse's white, down to the stockings on her legs, and against the gray fog of the day, she looked like an angel. Not the feathery, fragile kind, and not in the least angelic, but motherly, an angel that will take care of you as long as you don't talk back. She carried a black umbrella. I watched them out the window, Carol under the umbrella, Dean under the rain. The street was like a shallow river washing over their feet. When they finished talking, Dean went back to praying. Carol shook out the umbrella on the porch before she came back inside.

"He says you can enter your quilts in any art shows you want if you just come back home," she told Alma.

Alma stopped folding and put her hands on her knees as if she might be thinking about it. Then she looked up at Carol. "Nah."

"You want me to tell him?" Carol asked.

"I told him once already. He's not deaf," Alma said.

Carol said, "He also wants Jacob."

Rose had taken Jacob into the living room to watch television, and I joined them. Jacob had never been allowed to watch television before, which had always been a sore point with Carol, who liked her shows, but you could not turn on the TV with Dean around, sighing deep, noisy sighs in the background. Rose and Jacob were sitting on pillows eating egg salad sandwiches. Alma sat down beside Jacob, and for a minute it looked like she might stay and watch TV with us; then I heard her whisper. "Do you want to go back with your daddy?"

"No," Jacob whispered back.

Alma looked up at Carol and shrugged. "See?"

"I'll tell him," Carol said.

But Alma stood up and said, "It's okay, hon." She patted Carol on the arm. "I'll talk to him."

She went out, no umbrella. I don't know what it was about these people and the rain, but by the time she got to Dean, she was as drenched as he was and did not seem to notice. She wore a thin, yellow dress, which clung to her, and when she placed her hands on her hips, you could not help but notice the perfect curve beneath them. With Alma you could not tell; maybe she knew exactly what she was doing.

Dean stomped in the river that was a street. He kicked arches of water into the air with his boots. You could see it; here was a man used to getting his way. He had Jesus on his side.

The problem was, so did Alma.

Alma came back inside, changed into dry clothes, and the next time I looked, Dean was gone. Nobody saw him leave either; he was just gone. We all looked at Alma, who only shrugged. "Dean can't have Jacob unless he goes to court, which he won't do, and the reason is, he can't. He and his friends on the farm have never paid a dime of income tax for as long as I can remember."

Jacob was staring at his mother. I noticed he watched her all that evening, secretly, eyes darting her way then back, the way you would watch a stranger you did not trust.

Dickie arrived with a chicken potpie in a casserole dish under foil, and I joined her in the kitchen. Carol was scrubbing the kitchen counter with a washrag. She picked at it with her thumb-nail, then scrubbed, then picked again. "Why is it Mother can't make a sandwich without getting food all over everything?"

"She's just old, sweetie," Dickie said.

"It's not because she's old; she's been this way all her life. I never knew until I grew up that kitchen counters weren't supposed to be sticky. I thought they came sticky, like a test, so you'll turn out stronger for it. You face a sticky countertop every day, you can face anything."

"Hand me the lettuce; I'll do the salad," Dickie said.

She sent me into the dining room to set the table, but then came behind me straightening each and every piece of silverware I put down.

"We could eat on trays," Carol said, standing in the doorway, watching.

"Don't be silly, Carol," Dickie said, but all the while the two of them were sending eye signals to each other, an entire conversation on the fringes of the room. I did not try to keep up.

I went back to the living room, where Rose and Jacob had turned off the television and were now sitting on the couch with a road atlas turned to a map of Texas. I sat down with them and looked at where she pointed. She was disappointed that Agua Vista was too small to be on this map, but she knew where it was located just outside of Brownsville, and she showed us where. I had not remembered that Texas plunged so far south, and looking at the map, it was like looking at an entirely different country dangling off the United States, this huge swatch of land with Mexico on one side and the Gulf of Mexico on the other. She showed Jacob all the places where Pancho Villa had crossed the border, telling him the story all over again, getting him to see this time what it was like not to have a television or a radio or anything to warn you, and his eyes were bright, imagining the danger, but I was picturing instead a very young Rose playing on a beach with her big brother, Frank. She had told me about a game they played with each other. Frances was a baby and too little to play, and their brother, Tommy, was too impatient for it. Tommy preferred to be swimming, the one who loved the water more than anyone, but she and Frank could play for hours. They piled towers of sand at the same spot, twenty-five paces from the end of a boardwalk, then watched the water eat them away, counting the seconds out loud until they crumbled. Frank kept the numbers in his head, a running tally that ended when he died. Rose said she still remembers the fastest time, four seconds, although Frank was sure they could get it down to three. Maybe it was the idea that they had time—but then they didn't—that made Rose remember a childhood game she otherwise might have forgotten. A silly game, she called it, almost apologizing, but we both agreed that there are things you know as a child you cannot know when you grow up, things you see, you can't see anymore. I know, because I spent summers playing elves and fairies under a tree in my backyard, until the summer I went out there and could not understand how anyone could think an acorn was an elf.

Rose moved her finger up the map and pointed to Port Arthur, where she and Larry had lived briefly, and she showed us Bland, where she and the rest of her family moved after Frank and her mother died. Jacob put his finger where Rose's was, and they traced the half-moon along the coast between Bland and Agua Vista, and I wondered if he was thinking something like what I was thinking, seeing himself standing in the sun next to that boundless blue ocean.

At dinner that night, Alma did not say a word about the chicken potpie. When Jacob asked her, "Should I pick the chicken out?" she simply said, "No. It's protein. It'll be good for you." And I noticed that there was an easy swing to the way Carol and Alma talked to each other, like some remembered rhythm that Dean had merely interrupted twenty years before. They worked it out, how exactly Alma and Jacob could move in with Carol, as if here it was, tucked away for all these years, the plan for when Alma left Dean. As I listened, I thought about how funny things turn out, because all this time I had been worrying about how I was going to stop Carol from moving Rose, and now it was not going to happen. Just like that. Alma, not Rose, was going to move in with Carol. Alma, not Rose, was going to use the new bathroom. Things are hardly ever what they seem. Rose seemed comfortable with this, but I never got used to it.

Parson's Lane was a dead-end dirt road about halfway to Scoot on the southeast side of Chocowin County. It would have been hard to find even if the road sign had not been run over and flattened but Rose knew the way. The nearest town was Scarboro, which was six houses plus a Handy-Andy Store and gas station in the middle of acres and acres of soybeans and potatoes. At the end of Parson's Lane was an old dock, although you had to park your car and walk down a wooded path to find it. There's people who went there to fish regular, Rose said, except now you found empty beer cans along the creek bank thrown by teenagers who came there to drink. This was Thompson's Creek, which ran into the same marsh as Sinking Creek, only from the other side. It was near midnight when Rose and I got there.

"Ned's never going to find this place," I said.

"That's okay."

"Then you tell me why it is we need him, Rose."

"Because, we're going to find Fred Fish digging a ditch with the state dragline, and Ned will be able to look at that ditch and say if it is for mosquito control or not. It won't be; we already know that, and I am going to quote him."

"I thought we couldn't quote him."

"Anonymously."

I pulled off the road, cut the engine, and here came a pack of dogs out of the dark. Three of them were big, two like shepherds, and the third, a Doberman who walked crooked. The fourth was a small mutt with knots of straggly hair who yapped worse than any of them. I would not get out of the car.

"They're not going to hurt you," Rose said.

"So you get out."

"A barking dog won't bite, you know," she said.

"Whoever told you that garbage?"

"It's what I know." She opened the door, but then I noticed she took a MoonPie out of her purse and gave the dogs each a bite.

"That's cheating," I said.

"What's cheating?"

"You're feeding them. Of course they're not going to bite you if you feed them."

"Who told you that garbage?"

"Okay, Rose. Feed them for me."

I slid out of the door on my side. The dogs stopped barking, all except the little one, who would stop for a minute, then start all over again as if he momentarily forgot what his job was, then remembered, but even he eventually wandered off. Until Ned pulled up. Then they all started up again, and Ned would not get out of his car. Rose had to make him.

"I hope you know what you're doing," he said.

"Rose always knows what she's doing," I said.

We sprayed for mosquitoes, and I sprayed twice, once with Rose's can, once with Ned's, to make sure, because the mosquitoes were like flying piranhas here. Then we started toward the woods. Rose did not take the path to the dock, which was well formed and marked by a rubber hanging from the branch of a skinny tree. Instead she broke through the woods to a smaller path you could not see from the road. We carried flashlights, even though the moon was bright enough to light our way without them. It was what Homer Birdsong would have called a gibbous moon, which was almost full but not quite, a moon still rounding out, and I was all of a sudden struck by the notion that Homer had considered himself smarter than me just because he knew the names of things, and what a dummy I had been to believe him. I was glad for the moonlight whatever the moon was called, and I told Rose, but she shook her head. "It's going to make shadows," she said.

"So, what happens if we get caught?" I asked.

"We can't get caught," she said.

"But what if we do?"

"We won't."

The path soon ran into an old logging road. Not everybody would have known where it was. Ned had spotted it on the map, but he had wanted us to start where the road began, two miles before you got to Scarboro, which to Rose was two extra miles we did not need to walk. Rose was the one who knew about the path, but these were the things Rose knew, and I wondered if maybe it was this knowing the back of things, the shortcuts, the forgotten stories, that gives you the right to call a place home. Rose always said she was from Texas, but surely this counted for something, this Chocowin County with its places and its people and its stories, this Chocowin County that Rose had made, as much as anywhere else, her home.

We spread out. Moonlight flooded the road, making it easy to see where we were going. Ned walked fast and had gotten about ten feet ahead of us when Rose suddenly sped up and passed him. In a minute he slipped ahead again, but again Rose passed him. The third time she stopped. I stopped beside her, but Ned kept going. Rose crossed her arms and watched until he was out of sight.

"He'll come back," she said. "He is bound and determined to be the leader, but he has no idea where he's going."

We listened to the droning of spring peepers. The wind was up, rustling trees. There was the occasional crack of a falling limb. Rose was still as ice. Then Ned came back, just like Rose said. Footsteps first, angry, prideful, then Ned himself in the moonlight. He stood braced before us. "Why aren't you coming?"

Rose did not answer him. She simply started up again, and this time Ned did not try to get ahead, which was a good thing because it was not long before Rose stopped again. She lifted a limb of a small pine tree and scooted around it. Ned and I followed, and, lo and behold, there was another path. Nobody could have seen that path, the way it started behind one tree that looked exactly like every other tree. I started to ask her. "How in the world . . ."

"Shhhhhhh," she said.

We walked single file, crouching. Sometimes the path seemed to disappear, and Rose would step aside and let Ned hack us through, but always Rose would pick it back up again, as if she could sniff it out. She made us turn off our flashlights and stopped often to listen. I whispered, "You okay, Rose?"

"Shhhhhhhh."

We heard it before we saw it, the low rumbling of an engine running, a noise you are not likely to hear in the woods in the middle of the night, then lights off to the right. We had to go off the path to see what it was. The lights came from spotlights hung on poles along a straight line from the creek to the backyard of

Ted Hardaway, the dentist. Someone was working a dragline—
Fred Fish, no doubt. There was not one other person I knew of
who was that big.

Ned dropped to the ground and began crawling on his belly
soldier style in the direction of the lights. I looked at Rose. She
looked back at me, and we both rolled our eyes, watching Ned.
He was acting like a boy in his backyard playing army, but what
got to me was, in a backyard game, somebody's going to say,
Bang, you're dead, only you're not. What I was picturing was three
hundred pounds of Fred Fish crashing toward us through the
forest on giant feet, slinging trees. Rose and I crept over to a large
fallen log and knelt down. The log was wet, sodden, as was the
ground. I could not see where I was putting my knees or my
hands and had to force myself not to consider the possibility of
spiders crawling over the back of my legs or the top of my fingers.

"Snakes out yet?" I whispered.

"Shhhhhhh."

I was sorry it was Ted Hardaway getting the boat canal, because he seemed like a nice man. I remembered him from when
he brought me a sack full of toothbrushes to hand out during
Dental Health Week. He talked like a preacher would, cavities
being the devil, and you could see how dental health was more
to him than a job.

Ned crawled back and crouched with us behind the log. "You
think we can get decent pictures from here?"

"I'm not getting any closer," Rose said.

"I'll do it," he said.

"This is close enough," Rose said.

Now I knew they had talked about this, because I had heard
them. I had heard Rose say plain as day, "We only need one of
us to take pictures, and I'm the one." I don't remember what Ned

said back. Could be he said nothing, which is one sure way to disagree. All I know is, at some undetermined moment, both of them drew out cameras. Rose knew enough to have loaded high-speed film in hers, but Ned used a flash, and he kept at it, flash, flash, flash, flash, like fireworks shooting straight out of the woods, like shouts in the dark, *Here we are, here we are, look over here!* I was fixing to grab him by his shirttail and pull him back down when Fish turned off the motor. That got him and Rose both down.

A second figure stepped out from the shadow of the house, Dr. Hardaway it looked like, and he and Fish scanned the woods in our direction. We could hear their voices, but no particular words came through. Then Fish picked up one of the lights and turned it toward us, the beam skimming the air just over our backs like a blade. I held my breath. I could see Rose next to me on the ground, but I could not see Ned. I mashed my face into the wet leaves. I could hear Rose's rattling breath and knew she was strug-gling not to cough. I heard the buzz of a mosquito circling my head. Eventually Fish put the light back on its pole, and he and Dr. Hardaway stood over the ditch smoking cigarettes. They talked some more, tossed their butts into the creek, then Fish got back on the dragline and started the engine again.

"Let's get out of here," I heard Ned say, and he took off. He ran fast, breaking limbs, trampling underbrush, headed for the logging road, path or no path. I helped Rose up. This time she followed me, holding on to my sleeve as I picked our way back, sticking to the path because I knew that in the long run it would be faster that way. Then I can't account for what happened. Maybe it's like animals on a stampede who forget to think, or can't think, or won't, but when I reached the wide, moonlit ex-panse of the logging road, I took off. Faster I ran and faster, propelled by the fear that, if I looked over my shoulder, I would see Fred Fish roaring up behind us. "Hurry, Rose, hurry," I called, but I did not wait for her. I would have run all the way back to the car if I had not heard her fall.

"Ned!" I screamed for help, although I could not see him in the empty road ahead, then ran back to Rose. She was crumpled on the ground on her side, coughing deep, hacking coughs, and she did not want to talk.

"What is it, Rose? Where does it hurt?"

"It's her arm," Ned said, running up behind me.

"Wrist," she sputtered, as if, even in pain, she would not give him the last word. "Help me up."

Ned took one side, and I took the other, and we held her under her armpits and lifted her up. "Let's go, Rose," I said, but she shook us away. She took a few steps by herself then stopped and sucked air like somebody just remembering to breathe. It had to hurt. She was sweating. Ned and I looked at each other.

"I could try to carry her," Ned said, but Rose shook her head and pushed off again. This time she walked with her good hand on my shoulder, the hurt one pressed against her belly. We walked slowly while Ned went ahead, clearing the path. I continued looking behind us for Fish, but there was never anything but the shadows of trees. It took a long time to reach the car, and by then, Rose was drenched with sweat. She let me settle her into the front seat, where she leaned her head back and closed her eyes.

"Goddammit," Ned said when I closed the door.

"Go on home," I told him. "I can handle it from here."

"I can't be seen at the hospital with a reporter," he said. "There's going to be too many questions. I could lose my job, you know."

"I just told you I can handle it." The dogs came back, and Ned lunged at one of them. "Don't do that," I said.

"Why not?"

"Because it's a fool thing to do. Talk to them." I held out my hand and said, "Good doggie." I reached to scratch the crippled Doberman behind his ear, but he ducked and slunk away. "They won't hurt you."

"You're as crazy as she is," he said, pointing to Rose. Then he leaned up against his car and covered his face with his hands. "This is going to get back to Raleigh, I just know it."

"Not if you don't say anything. When the story comes out, you act as surprised as anybody."

"There's not going to be any story now. How can there be a story with her around?" He nodded toward Rose. "You guys are a circus, you know that? A goddamn freak show. I should have known."

Rose stuck her head out the window. "So, Ned," she called. "In your professional opinion, was that a state-sanctioned mosquito control ditch you just saw? Off the record, of course."

"No, ma'am."

"What was it then?"

"A private boat canal for certain."

We watched as she braced a small notebook against the dashboard with her knee and wrote something down. Ned rolled his eyes.

"Please go home," I said.

He got in his car. "It's probably broken, that wrist," he called to me. Then he turned the car around and drove away.

I slid in beside Rose. It was hot in the car, and I cracked the windows, and the two of us sat listening to the chorus of frogs. She was breathing deeply and did not seem to be in a hurry to go anywhere. Occasionally she coughed, but when I started to put the keys in the ignition, she put her hand on my arm. "Wait just a minute."

"What is it, Rose?"

"There's days, Ruthie, all I do is look back and regret." She closed her eyes.

"I can't believe you would have anything to regret, Rose."

"Maybe I wouldn't change much, but I sure wish I'd gone home to see my daddy before he died. It seemed like something always came up," she shook her head. "Frances would call and tell me how his health was failing, then she'd hand the phone to my father, who would swear he was fine. *Don't come, Rose, if you've got work to do,* he would say, and I let myself believe him. He was proud of me, see. There was Frances, the one who took care of him, who had made his business flourish despite him, and yet I was the one who had gone out in the world and made something of myself. I never told you, but he sent me money the whole time I was married to Larry, which was the reason I was never in any money trouble. It was just-in-case money, so I'd never be trapped. My whole life, I always had choices." Rose was breathing deeply, and I waited until she was ready to talk again. "I'd tell myself I could always go to Texas in the spring. Or next summer. Or sometime, but it was just an excuse. Then it was too late. I went to the funeral. He is buried next to Mother down in Agua Vista. We're all there, Mother and Daddy and Frank Jr. and Tommy. Frances too. She died on the very day of my own surgery, can you believe it? I could not have gone to her funeral if I'd wanted. And I would have wanted. I swear she did it for spite." Rose started coughing again. I put my hand on her back to steady her. She braced her hurt arm on her belly, but every time she coughed, she winced.

"Does it hurt, Rose?"

"Not too much, Ruthie."

"I guess we ought to get you to a doctor."

"I hate to be so much trouble."

"Don't be ridiculous."

She nodded. Then she said, "What are we going to tell Carol?"

"Beats me."

"How about we tell her I fell down the stairs."

I shook my head. "That won't work, Rose. You would just be proving what she's been saying all this time, that you can't live by yourself. No, ma'am, you can't be falling down any stairs. You don't think we could tell her the truth?"

"Ha!" was all Rose said to that.

Rose's wrist did end up being broken. We told the doctor and all the nurses in the emergency room of the Lawson County Hospital how she fell walking down *my* stairs, and we promised that she would never do anything like that again. And they believed us.

19 | WHEE, WHIM, AIN'T YOU SORRY FOR HIM?

But Carol was a bully for truth. She could pin you down like a bug specimen on a corkboard until you found yourself saying things you did not mean to say. You might fool her on some little thing, but tromp through the woods in the middle of the night to see a three-hundred-pound man on a dragline, and Carol's going to find out, and when she did, she blamed me. "How could you let her do it?" she yelled.

I lived by the rule that you don't have to answer obvious questions.

Rose spent three days in bed on pain pills with her wrist in a cast propped up on a pillow. I fed her soup and Jell-O and ginger ale, driving back and forth from work, taking turns with Carol and Alma. But on the fourth day, Rose did not take a pain pill. I took the· day off, and five minutes after Carol left for work, I picked Rose up, and we drove down Highway 53 to see Fred Fish. It was early spring, the kind of day when spring feels like a surprise, when you look around and say out loud, *What in the world, when did it get so green?* My exact words. Rose decided, instead, to sing.

"*The man in the moon has a rheumatic knee, Whee, whim, ain't you sorry for him* . . . You sing with me, Ruthie."

"I can't sing, Rose."

"Sure you can. *The man in the moon has a rheumatic knee, Whee, whim, ain't you sorry for him. The elephant danced and got stung by a bee, Whee whim ain't you sorry for him* . . ."

"I don't know the words," I said.

"Neither do I. I'm making them up!"

The Chocowin County Courthouse was a two-story redbrick building in the middle of Rhone, the county seat. It was the only two-story building in the county and took up a whole block on the corner of Highway 53 and First Street. There was talk of putting a traffic light at the intersection, but it would be the first and only traffic light in Chocowin County, and most people were of the opinion that it would spoil everything. Plenty of towns all over America could boast that they were one-light towns, but how many could claim to be no-light? Much less a whole county. Three flags flew in front of the courthouse, the American flag, the North Carolina flag, and a flag made especially for the twenty-fifth Annual Shrimp Festival. It had replaced the Confederate flag, which had flown over the courthouse for ninety-six years until the governor of North Carolina himself suggested it was time to bring it down. The Shrimp Festival flag was blue with a white shrimp boat on it and, as somebody pointed out, better than a bare pole.

Inside, the courthouse smelled like an old school, too much wax and old dust. Our footsteps echoed on the wide, wooden floor. There were doors along the halls with large brass nameplates and windows at eye level made of green, bumpy glass you could not see through. We opened the one that said RECORDS.

Miss Phyllis worked in records. Miss Phyllis Smith, although hardly anyone knew her last name; she had been Miss Phyllis for so long. But Rose was old enough to remember when Miss Phyllis was Miss Smith, a sharp, young woman who came to Chocowin County from Spartanburg, South Carolina. Miss Phyllis had never had much use for Rose. In her eyes, there were no such things as newspaper reporters, only snoops, poking their noses into places they did not belong.

"Good morning, Phyllis," Rose said, when we walked in the room. A heavy wooden counter separated the customers from the files, but Rose walked right through the thick, swinging doors. Miss Phyllis barely looked up. The floorboards creaked under a thin, beige carpet, worn through in places, and showing years of coffee stains and the vacuumed-over tracks of muddy boots. Huge, wooden filing cabinets lined three walls. Rose took me straight to one on the right. The drawer was heavy and crammed so tight you could barely get your finger between the file folders. I got Rose a stool to sit on. She could have worked faster if she had asked Miss Phyllis for help, but Rose had already told me she would not ask Miss Phyllis for anything, and in time, she found the map. We laid it out on a nearby table.

"Now look at this, Ruthie. These green lines show mosquito control ditches already finished." She traced the green lines with her finger. "See, there's the one that runs by Clark's house. You can see how most of them are on the east end of the county closest to the sound, and I suppose there's a reason for it. It might be important; remind me to ask Ned what it is. The red lines here show where ditches have been approved but not dug yet. And this"—she pointed—"is Ted Hardaway's land."

There were no lines, green or red, even close, and I said, "Rose, you're a pure genius."

"It's better than that," she said and pointed to the date.

November 1978. "This is a brand new map, only five months old, so Fish cannot claim the map is out-of-date, because that's what he is going to do, don't you see. It will be the only defense available to him. He will say the ditch is fine; only the map is wrong, but we can make sure he does not get away with it." She dug through her purse for her camera and took a picture of the map.

"Can I help you, Rose?" It was Miss Phyllis, standing over us. She looked like a walking sausage, short and wide, her bosom and belly pressed to bursting against her light brown dress. "You can't take the maps out of this room," Miss Phyllis said. "It's the rule."

"I know that Miss Phyllis, and thank you for reminding me," Rose said. She pulled a crumpled copy of the front page of the day's newspaper out of her purse and pressed it flat against the table. Then she placed it so the date of the newspaper showed next to the date on the map and snapped three more pictures. She scooted the stool over to the table, and before Miss Phyllis or I could stop her, she stood on it.

"Wait, Rose," I said, grabbing her leg.

Rose leaned over the map with the camera for what you might call an aerial shot, while I held on to her leg, and Miss Phyllis yelled, "You get down from there! Do you hear me? You're going to break your neck. Rose Lee, I'm going to call the sheriff if you don't get off of there right this minute."

Rose got down. She smiled at Miss Phyllis and said, "All done." She stuffed her camera back into her purse and put the map back in its folder and closed the drawer.

"Good-bye, Phyllis," Rose said as we left. "You can call Mr. Fish now."

I was right behind her. "What'd you say that for, Rose?"

"Because she's going to do it anyway."

The health department was not in the main courthouse building, which to Rose meant something. It was behind the courthouse, as if to suggest that Fish could do anything he wanted, and nobody would know. The building was a squat, brown building and looked like the kind of place that, once built, was never bothered with again. Where a gutter was broken, it stayed broken. Rust stains were left to spread. The sign out front had been used for target practice, and all that was left between the holes was:

Cou y of Ch co n

eal h Dep rtm n

There was no front door, just like Rose had said, only two side doors. "How did you know which was which?" I asked Rose. She pointed first to the right, then the left, "That one was for the whites, and the other was for the blacks. If we had time, we could peek in there and find it that way still; how much you want to bet? Let me just say, I would not be surprised."

Fish's office was farther away still, in a trailer in back of the health department next to a large, gravel parking lot, where you could see a dump truck, a backhoe, two bulldozers, and a dragline. From a distance, the dragline looked like a giant, yellow insect that had crawled up from some dinosaur time, sleeping now. Rose pointed and said, "That's the one he used at Dr. Hardaway's." Then she took a picture of it.

He was waiting for us. From the trailer doorway he loomed bigger even than I had remembered, like a wall or a force of nature you don't want to mess with, but at least he was smiling. "How're ya doin', Rose?" he said. Then he offered us a Coca-Cola.

"I'm fine, Fred; we don't need a Coke," Rose said.

He did not move. He pointed to the cast on her arm and said, "Still living dangerously, I see."

"I fell," she said. "You want to talk out here or go inside?"

It was dark inside the trailer, with a musty smell like worn-out boots and bug spray. The walls of Fish's office were covered with mounted, stuffed ducks and the head of one deer, plus a number of dusty photographs of Fish shaking the hands of people who looked important. We sat down on a dirty, orange couch that sat so low to the ground, you'd swear the legs had been sawed off. The room was small and crowded, and our knees touched Fish's desk. He stood on the other side and smiled down at us.

"Sure you don't want a Coca-Cola?"

"We're sure, Fred," Rose said. "How about telling me what you were doing at Ted Hardaway's place last Thursday night."

"Thursday?" he said, tapping his fingers together. "You're taxing the old memory there. I'm not as young as I used to be, you know, then neither are you, are you, Rose? Did you say Thursday?"

"Yes, Fred, I did. Last Thursday night."

"I don't believe I was at Hardaway's on Thursday, Rose. Wednesday maybe. I don't know. Tuesday? But Thursday? Nope, nowhere near Hardaway's. I was asleep in my own bed last Thursday night; you can call my wife."

"We've got pictures, Fred."

Fish nodded and set his jaw. Sweat was building on his forehead and neck. I glanced over at Rose. It was like sitting in a V position on that couch, and I knew it had to hurt her back, but you would not have known it. She looked like she could sit on that couch all day if that's what it took.

"What are you doing here, Rose?" Fish asked.

"I'm working on an article for the newspaper about mosquito control ditches, which I am sure, Fred, you will agree is a matter of concern to everyone around here. How about you tell me how you decide where to dig those ditches."

"You're not a reporter anymore."

"Then you don't have anything to worry about, do you?"

"You're too old for this, Rose."

"Does that mean no comment?" She took a notebook and a pen out of her purse and wrote something down.

"I'm too damn old for this," he muttered. He braced himself against the desk, which shifted under his weight. He leaned forward, pinned his eyes on Rose, and said, "You're right, Rose. But that is a mosquito control ditch we're digging at Hardaway's, paid for and sanctified by our boys in Raleigh, and maybe I was there Thursday. Maybe not; it's hard to say. Who knows, I might be there tonight."

Rose wrote this down in the notebook. She wrote slowly so he had to wait for her to finish, then she asked, "Any reason you're working at night?"

"It's cooler."

"At midnight? I've checked the map already, Fred. There are no plans for a ditch near the Hardaway property."

"It must have been an old map."

"And I suppose you've got a newer one?"

"I can get it. Easy. I can have it shipped down from Raleigh in a week. Now if you'll excuse me, I have work to do, but you come on back next week, and I'll have you that map, and you can quote me on that."

"I will, Fred," Rose said. "I sure will."

On the way home Rose sang her song again, and this time I tried to sing with her. *"Whee, whim, ain't you sorry for him!"* We made up seven new verses and sang them at the top of our lungs all the way home, and if there was anybody still thinking something was wrong with Rose, I was not one of them. I sure wish Carol could have seen it.

20 | OF MOSQUITOES AND OTHER BLOODSUCKING CREATURES

"You got pictures?"

Ed Stivers had Rose's mosquito control story in his hands, but he was not reading it. He was only pretending to read it, and when Rose handed him the roll of film, you could tell he did not want to take it. It was going to be harder to get rid of her if she had pictures.

We had waited until the end of the day to talk to Stivers because you never wanted to come up on him busy. His desk was covered with papers, stacks on top of stacks, which is where Rose's story would have landed, to be looked at the next day or the next week or never. Rose didn't have that much time. But at the end of every day, Stivers was alone. Usually he was the last person to leave the building, Purdy being the first, and talk was that Stivers stayed as long as he did because he did not want to go home, a hint that there was something wrong with his marriage, fuel for gossip, but I always thought there was more to it. It was in the evening when Stivers wrote his editorial for the next day's paper, two-finger typing on an old, black manual typewriter, the office quiet and dark except for one small desk light shining on his work. I could see not wanting to give that up.

Stivers placed Rose's story on his desk in front of him and rubbed his head above his ears. It was a nervous habit and could mean almost anything. "Why did you do this, Rose?"

I was surprised. Rose and I had anticipated trouble from Fred Fish. We had talked about it, and we had come up with ways to get around it. We also had figured on trouble from Miss Phyllis and possibly Ted Hardaway; and there was always Carol to think about. You never knew what she would do, but Ed Stivers we had counted on. Ed Stivers was sure to be on our side. In one very real way, Ed Stivers was our best weapon, because Rose could write all the articles she wanted, but until they showed up in newsprint, they weren't worth anything. Rose looked surprised but covered it quick. She asked for a cigarette.

"I've got one, Rose," I offered, but Stivers beat me to it. He sat down, but Rose would not sit down. Stivers said, "Okay, Rose, you did good. Real good. I'll put Jackson on it first thing in the morning."

"What do you need Jackson for?" Rose asked him.

"He'll need to check out these sources. You'll need to tell him who this anonymous is, for instance, and by the way, who is it?"

"None of your business," Rose said, blowing smoke out of the side of her mouth like she had practiced it. I had never seen her do that before.

"I see," Stivers said. "But Jackson will have to write this story. I'm sorry, but that's the way it has to be." Then he picked up a sheet of paper from a pile in front of him, a man moving on.

"I've already written the story. See there?" Rose pointed to the paper as if she needed a visual aid. Both she and Stivers had begun to speak slowly, like teachers talking to students who do not catch on quick. It was like watching some dream play out, not real people talking.

"And you did a fine job, too. But you're not a reporter, Rose. It's company policy, you know that. There's no mixing between the advertising department and news. I can't do anything about it."

"Bullshit," she said.

Which may have been a new form of expression for Rose. I could hear Carol like background music in my mind: *Mother never cursed until that girl came around,* but I swear, I never put Rose up to cussing, never. Stivers did not even seem to notice. He selected what looked like a news release from the Lawson County Agricultural Extension Service and pretended to read it, but Rose stopped him. She leaned over his desk and picked up her story. Then she said, "May I have my film, please."

He did not want to give it to her. "Why don't you let Jackson take a look at these."

"I am sure Jackson is an excellent reporter," she said. "He won't need my help." She held out her hand. He looked up at her, and she looked down at him, and somewhere in that moment was Stivers's last chance to change his mind. And it was my impression that he was, at least, thinking about it, because it took him some time to move, but in the end he put the film in Rose's outstretched hand and turned away. When we left he was banging at his typewriter, so I'll never know if he watched us as we walked out of the newsroom, but I will tell you this. Rose never looked back.

I took her as far the parking lot and got her in her car. "Are you okay?"

"Fine," she said.

"What are you going to do, Rose?"

She would not look at me. She gripped both hands on the steering wheel, her face set dead ahead.

"We'll think of something, Rose."

She nodded.

"You go on home," I told her then. "I've got something I got to do." I let her drive away, then I marched back to the newsroom.

Ed Stivers looked like he had not moved from the exact spot where we had left him, still typing. I could hear the sound of it all the way in the back of the building, and let me tell you; it grated on my nerves. The closer I got, the more it grated, like a sound you will break down walls to stop. I marched right back into his office. "You asshole."

He quit typing and smiled. "Sit down," he said.

"No."

"Then let's go get a drink."

"Do you have any idea how much that story means to Rose?"

"Yes."

"It's better than anything Jackson ever wrote in his entire life."

"You are absolutely right. Now can we please go talk about it over a drink?"

"Does that mean you'll run Rose's story?"

He took off his glasses and rubbed his head above his ears. "Sit down," he said, but I still wouldn't. He flipped through some of the papers on his desk, a sort of absentminded flipping, thinking about what to say. I watched his fingers. Finally he stopped and looked directly at me. "Fish won't go down easy, Ruth. Do you understand what I'm saying?"

"Yes."

"No, I don't think you do. And do not misunderstand me. I am not afraid of Fred Fish, not for myself and not for Jackson. I am afraid of Fred Fish for Rose."

"Rose is not afraid."

"You think I'm kidding. I'm not kidding."

"Fish can't hurt her if he's in jail."

He nodded and appeared to consider my words but then said, "Fish will never see the inside of any jail. I want you to listen to me, Ruth, because I know what I'm talking about. Fred Fish won't even lose his job. He may have to quit digging ditches for a while, but that's all, because that's the way things work down here. Nobody cares what he does with his draglines."

"But it's illegal."

"As are many things. You're going to have to trust me on this. If I let Rose go ahead with this, it could kill her."

"It's going to kill her if you don't," I said. "You might as well tell her to go ahead and die."

He swiveled his chair around so that he was no longer looking at me but into the newsroom. On the other side of the glass was the city desk and the AP machine, humming and blinking on and off, the only other light in the room. On the far aisle were sports and society and the desks of two more reporters. Jackson's desk was directly in front of Stivers's door, which made it so the two of them could talk without getting out of their chairs. It was a well-known fact that the other reporters did not like this arrangement, but Stivers never cared what they thought. In the darkness, the newsroom looked nothing like the hectic place it was in the daytime, with people running, people yelling, phones ringing. It looked, rather, like the ruins of an abandoned place. I don't know how long I waited for Stivers to answer me. I wanted to say more, but I knew he was thinking, so I kept my mouth shut. Rose claimed it's often the best thing. Finally he spoke again. "I'm not sure Rose can do it."

"She's not sure Jackson can."

"Okay." He sighed. "How about if I let her co-write it? Rose and Jackson together, a double byline."

"She won't like working with Jackson."

"It's better than nothing."

"I guess so."

We shook hands, a deal made, but he kept hold of my hand. "Won't you have that drink with me now?"

We walked to Jack's by the River. The bar was dark, mostly empty. Jack Henry looked up when we walked in, and I remembered it had not been so long ago that Stivers had been seen in this very place with Madeline, but I could not decide if I cared. Jack Henry was drying glasses and talking to Victor, who sat on the last barstool. Stivers and I sat down at a table on the other side of the room. "I'll just have a beer," I whispered.

Jack Henry came right over with a basket of pretzels. "You ought to keep better company, Ruth," he said. "How're ya doin', Ed?" They shook hands.

"Two Dewar's, Jack. On the rocks," Stivers said, and Jack Henry brought two scotches in short, heavy glasses. He returned to the bar, but I could tell that he and Victor were watching us while they talked to each other as if they were making sure I was okay. I turned my back so I could not see them.

Stivers drank down his scotch then slowly, carefully, as if this were brain surgery, he set the glass precisely in the middle of his napkin. He tossed a pretzel in his mouth, then another. I told him again how much he had surprised me and Rose by refusing to print her article outright. "I mean, what's the difference between Rose's story and all those ones you've run about the hospital, except maybe Rose's is better."

"It's not better."

"I think it is."

"It's not better." He tried to take a sip from his empty glass. "No, the way I see it, the hospital is controlled by a small group of rich people who are getting even richer on the backs of sick, mostly poor, people. Others might disagree, but that's my opinion." He signaled to Jack Henry to bring him another scotch. "Only I can't prove it."

"Fred Fish is getting rich."

"Pocket change. It's not nearly on the same scale."

"So, it's a matter of scale, who's more crooked?"

He smiled, nodding, popping pretzels in his mouth. "You are a very smart girl, Ruth."

"I'm just trying to figure it out."

Jack Henry set two more scotches in front of us. Stivers had rolled his sleeves up, and I was beginning to notice how he was getting a very nice, freckled sort of tan. I watched him drink his scotch, tossing it back with his wrist rather than sipping it. I tried it but about knocked my teeth out. "Maybe you're right," he was saying. "Maybe it's time to bring Fred Fish down." He stopped and stared across the room as if still thinking about it. Then he looked back at me. "At least we've got something on him. Do you know, Ruth, that in all this time I have not found one thing on the hospital board that will stick."

"I kind of wondered. Those stories on the kids who died . . ."

"Big mistake. Big, stupid, mistake." He shook his head. "It's like a mirage. I can see it, smell it, taste it, but the minute I try to grab on to it, it's gone. You know what I do sometimes, Ruth? I drive through the neighborhoods where these rich people live. I pass through the gates of their subdivisions. Forest Glenn. Harbor Pointe. There's no trace of humor in names like that, you know? If somebody would just say, Westhampton Estates, then give me a little chuckle, I think I might be able to take it, but no. They carve those names on stone. I drive past lawns so smooth and green it looks like somebody's out there with tweezers picking out the weeds. You got time to worry about weeds, Ruth?"

Jack Henry came back with clean napkins and a third round

of scotch. "Nope," I said. "Never have. I might, however, rather have a beer?" But by then Jack Henry had walked away.

"A person has to have time, and he has to have money to worry about weeds. I drive by houses so big it's embarrassing. Wouldn't you be the tiniest bit embarrassed to live in a house that big?"

I stirred a scotch with my finger then drank it down, shuddered, wiped my mouth with the napkin. "I've never actually thought about it," I said, which was not true. I had thought about it plenty. Back in Summerville I used to have the same exact feeling walking along the road to Umbrella Rock, especially in winter when the leaves had fallen, and you could look up through the yards and get a true feel for the size of some of those houses. Some were the houses of people I knew, like Marianne Johnson and others, classmates at school who did not seem so much different from me that they could live in such a different way, but I can't say my feelings about them were always clear. Sometimes I thought, what could anyone need with such a house? Other times I just wished it was me who lived there.

"I drive through those neighborhoods to remind myself what I'm doing here," Stivers was staying. "Do you understand what I'm talking about, Ruth? Because you can forget. It's easy. You can forget where the real power lies in this country, tucked away behind those gates. You can even forget why it should not be that way, but not me. I don't ever want to forget."

Stivers raised his glass, and I noticed his hand was shaking. He saw me looking and put it down quickly. In the candlelight, he seemed tired; wrinkles I had never noticed before crossed his face beside his eyes, next to his mouth, and looking at him that way, I decided it was his mouth, the slightly crooked way he held it, that made him, an otherwise unattractive man, attractive.

"Rose would agree with you," I said.

"What about you, Ruth?" His fingertips managed to brush the top of my hand.

"You want to go?" I said.

I refused to look at Victor as we left the bar because I knew he would try to change my mind. I caught him in the mirror trying to signal to me, but I pretended not to see. Stivers walked me across the street and up the stairs. I was thinking; I did not own any scotch, but there was beer in the refrigerator, and I was trying to decide whether to make us cheese toast or one of those tomato sandwiches, the kind like Rose made, and I was wondering what radio station he listened to, but I never got the chance to ask because, as soon as we stepped inside my apartment, he grabbed me. He got me by both arms and kissed me, right there in the hall, lights shining like spotlights, the door not even closed. He kissed hard; I could feel his teeth against my lips, and he pushed me against the wall and quickly moved his hands to my breasts. Then, just as suddenly, he backed away.

"Take your shirt off," he said.

And I did. I still don't know why. I pulled my shirt over my head and let it drop to the floor. He stood in front of me and told me to turn around in a circle, and I did that too. Then again. "Slower," he said, and again even slower. I felt myself starting to cry. "No," I whispered.

I picked my shirt up off the floor and ran past him into the front room where it was dark. This time it was *my* hands shaking. I turned on the radio and lit a cigarette. Stivers came into the room, walked to a window, and stood looking out at the changing traffic light on the bridge below, red then green then yellow then red again. I sat down in a chair and watched him, his back arched toward the window, one hand on the wall for support, the colors from the traffic light reflecting off his white shirt. He stood there for a long time, long enough for me to finish one cigarette and light another. I noticed the smoke was following the music. "Watch this," I said, but he would not look. "Do you like jazz?" But he had already started for the door.

"Don't worry about this," he said.

"Don't worry, I won't."

But even then I knew it was not true.

Rose would not work with Jackson.

"Why not?" I asked her.

"I have written that story once. Why would I want to do it twice?"

I didn't care that she was right. There was more to it than just being right. *Why do you have to be right all the time,* was what I wanted to know.

Rose was bent over a Dairy Queen ad on her desk. I was hiding from Ed Stivers. I had woken up that morning with my head feeling like somebody had lodged the sharp end of an ax above my eyes, my stomach fixing to slough off and fall out, both of which I could take better than the memory of what had happened, or worse, what might have happened, the night before with Stivers, who was over there in the next room shouting at his reporters as if they were deaf. I was slumped down in a chair next to Rose's desk in the advertising department, which meant I had to lean through the window into my office to answer the phone, but I didn't care. Now Rose was telling me she would not work with Jackson, and I was going to have to start all over again. I sighed. "I guess I could talk to him one more time."

"It's over," Rose said.

"It's not over. How can it be over?"

"Honey, there are things in this world just not worth it."

"This is not one of them."

She held up her layout so I could see. "What do you think's more appealing, the soft-serve or the hot dog and fries?"

I went back to my desk and cracked open the window into the newsroom so I could hear better. Jackson was yelling at Stivers even though they could not have been more than a foot apart, but Jackson often worked on the theory that the louder you say a thing, the more you get your way. This time he was saying, "I'm not doing any story with that old lady."

I peeked through the window in time to see Stivers's face turning pure red right before he chose just that moment to look over Jackson's shoulder. Straight at me. You could have hung clothes on the line between us.

So maybe I shouldn't have smiled.

He took Jackson into his office and closed the door.

During lunch that day, the newsroom was empty except for Jackson, which was why he must have assumed he was alone or else he would not have picked up the phone. He was not alone. I was right there next to him at my desk on the other side of the glass, but that was another thing about Jackson. He figured I didn't count.

"Hey, Fingers. It's me, Jackson."

I heard it plain as day.

"What do you know about mosquito control in Chocowin County?"

I poked my head through the window on Rose's side. "Why does Jackson always call Fingers?" I asked her.

"Because he's lazy. But you can hardly blame him, and he's not the only one. These guys, if they've got somebody who will hand over information, why should they work for it? And Fingers, he's one good source of information, let me tell you. He knows a lot, more than he should."

"But he's a *Lawson* County Commissioner. He doesn't even live in Chocowin County."

"So?" She peered at me. "Why? Jackson isn't calling Fingers now, is he?"

I nodded.

"About the mosquito control story?"

"He just hung up the phone," I said.

Rose sunk down in her chair. It was like she could not help it. She closed her eyes and shook her head.

Jackson the racehorse, Jackson the slick, Jackson the stupid. This is what Jackson did not know. Fingers owned a fishing cabin on Adam's Creek east of Sutter's Cove in Chocowin County, where he entertained certain businessmen. Also some senators and even the governor of the state of North Carolina. It was as fine a place to hunt and fish as you will find, especially to fish, since all you had to do was step out the back door and there was the dock. Because running clear from Fingers' dock to the Chocowin Sound was a boat canal built by Fred Fish.

Rose knew, but she wasn't ever going to tell Jackson.

I wish I'd been there the next day when Jackson went down to Chocowin County. I wish I'd seen Jackson's face when he drove into the health department parking lot, and there was Fred Fish, waiting for him. Jackson hated that. He liked to walk in on people, start right in asking questions before they had a chance to think of answers. It had made him an award-winning newsman, this. In all her years, Rose had won one press award, but Jackson, not even thirty years old yet, had already won three. But this time Fish was waiting for him with a Coca-Cola.

I heard about it from Sid, the photographer. Sid had gone down to Chocowin County with Jackson because Jackson refused to take his own pictures. As Sid explained it, "Jackson likes it when he can attack and have me circling with the camera. It's like a war with this guy. What a buffoon."

Sid was always calling Jackson names like "buffoon" and "moron" and my favorite, "Jackson the Slick," although not to his face, and not to anyone in particular. Sid was the kind of guy you often saw chuckling to himself when no one else knew what was funny. He was a tall, lanky man with a long, brown ponytail, who wore boots, a black cowboy hat, black T-shirt, and a brown leather jacket with fringe. He chewed on gum and mint-flavored toothpicks ever since he quit smoking. He lived on a sailboat with a girlfriend named Rachael and did not seek the company of many people, although he claimed to like me. "Ruth," he would say out of the side of his mouth. "You're all right." Sometimes he offered me a toothpick.

Jackson took Sid with him to Chocowin County, and they both got Cokes, then Fish herded them into his Carolina blue Lincoln Continental. "And if I had known what was coming up next," Sid said, "I never would have gotten in that car."

We were in his darkroom where he showed me a picture emerging under a watery solution. "We must have visited every mosquito control ditch in Chocowin County," he said, "or let me put it this way. If there's one we missed, I don't want to know about it, and there wasn't a damn thing we could do, either. I mean, we couldn't just get out of the car and walk, although I swear, Ruth, I was close, especially when Fish began the lecture on the life and times of the salt-marsh mosquito. It was more than anybody ought to know about an insect."

I watched as Sid pinned the photograph onto a clothesline to dry next to the others, mostly pictures of mosquito control ditches that all looked the same to me. Two were of Dr. Hardaway's house. The only way you could tell it was Dr. Hardaway's canal was by the house in the background; otherwise, it was just another big, muddy hole.

"We went here last," Sid said, pointing to the picture. "Jackson, he leapt out of the car, walked over to the ditch, and said, 'This is a boat canal, Mr. Fish.' You have to understand that, by this time, Jackson had lost any patience he ever had, although with Jackson that's not saying much, but Fish, he was as calm as can be. He said, 'No, son. It's a mosquito control ditch,' and that's when he pulled out the map."

It was rolled up in the trunk of the Lincoln Continental. Fish spread it out on the hood, and there it was, a red line running right beside Ted Hardaway's backyard.

"Of course Jackson didn't know what it meant, red line, green line, so Fish got out the manual, which he also just happened to have in his car. It was fatter than a phone book and explained all about mosquito control in North Carolina. He turned to the section on maps. It was beautiful, man. A truly wonderful moment in journalism. I thought Jackson was going to hit the guy, and Fish could have won an Academy Award for acting like he didn't know what everybody was so excited about. You should have been there, Ruth, I'm telling you."

What Ed Stivers could not understand was how Fish got that map so fast. He pondered this at the top of his lungs for about an hour after Jackson came back, pacing back and forth between his office and Jackson's desk, where Jackson stood, too mad to sit down.

"There's no way," Stivers yelled. "He could not have gotten a new map that fast if he had drawn it himself."

"It doesn't matter," Jackson said. "He's got it. There's no story,"

"There's no way," Stivers screamed again.

In the end, Stivers and Jackson reasoned that it was Rose who had been mistaken. The map showing plans for a mosquito control ditch on the Hardaway property had been there all along. She had simply missed it, or else she had read the wrong map. There could be no other explanation, and when he came to it, Stivers calmed down. There was no story, but there never had been; that's what Stivers figured, and that was going to be what he believed.

Which might have been okay reasoning since Stivers did not know that on an undeveloped roll of film on the windowsill above Rose's sink there was a picture of a different map.

There was something else Stivers did not know, and that was that he had been right. There was no way Fish could have gotten a new map that fast.

But Fingers could have.

There's got to be a way to tell when hope's not enough anymore, some kind of sign, some kind of moment and you know. If there is, I wish somebody would have told me, because when it came to Rose, I never knew when to quit.

When I left Sid's darkroom late that afternoon, I drove to her house and found her already in her pajamas. Cecil was gone again. He had left with Peanut sometime earlier, a note scribbled

on a piece of yellow paper was still on the kitchen table. I picked
it up and read it:

> If there was a forever
> I would spend it with you,
> but there's not, so
> see you later.
> —Cecil

"What is this crap, Rose?"

She shrugged and started back toward her bedroom.

"I'm just saying there's more than poetry in this world," I
called, following her. She climbed in the bed. "Listen to me, Rose,
it's not too late."

"Yes it is," she said. In her thin, cotton pajamas, I noticed how
Rose's bones stuck out like a bird. Rose the bird. And maybe
birds can fly, but it also looks like they break easy. She patted the
covers around her. I propped a pillow under her wrist.

"It's too early to go to bed, Rose; it's not even suppertime.
How about I heat you up some soup. Does your wrist hurt still?
Where are your pain pills? You want me to get you one?"

"I gave them to Cecil."

"What did you go and do that for?"

"He wanted them," she said, then pointed to the window.
"Would you close those curtains, honey?"

"No."

She closed her eyes.

"Listen, Rose, all we have to do is develop the pictures of the
map. Sid would do it tonight if I asked him, and by tomorrow,
won't Jackson look like a fool."

"I don't have anything against Jackson."

"You don't have to have anything against Jackson, for heaven's sake, you just have to show Stivers you are right. Because you are. We are. I cannot believe he wouldn't run your story once he saw those pictures. It is not too late, Rose, I swear it."

She shook her head. "Yes it is."

"Stop saying that!"

She pulled the covers up to her neck, gripping them as if somebody might try to yank them away.

"I'm sorry, Rose."

She nodded. I closed the curtains for her and sat down on the bed. In a while she whispered, "It doesn't really matter, Ruth. It never did."

"That's where you're wrong, Rose. You could have beat Fred Fish, I know it, and that's not nothing. It's more than I've ever done. You don't know what would have happened, Rose, you just don't."

"Still, it would not have changed anything."

The drawn curtains had made an artificial darkness in the room, as if we were all by ourselves, me and Rose, like in a space capsule far away from anything familiar. Even my voice sounded as if it had come from another place. "Maybe," I said, "it would have changed me."

She reached her good hand up out of the covers, and I took it in mine.

"Are you dying, Rose?"

"Yes."

"Now?"

"No, hon, I don't think so."

I was trying not to notice, but Rose looked even smaller, a body shrinking in front of my eyes. She was wearing earrings shaped like watermelons, and they looked huge, green and bright pink, lying on the pillow next to her tiny ears. I remembered Rose telling me that her father had shrunk before he died, a small detail she knew only from the letters Frances wrote, the letters asking her to come home. Rose told me she would hold those letters in her hand long after she had read them the second, third, fourth time, trying to picture her father shrinking, but she couldn't. I said, "What happens when you die, do you think?"

"I don't know."

"Do you believe in Heaven, Rose?"

"No."

"Me neither."

The wind was up, and when we fell silent, we could hear it in the trees outside. When the wind changed like that, I perked up in an uneasy sort of way, as if something inside me knew to get ready for whatever was blowing in, even though I knew it did not make sense.

"You know what I think I hate most about dying, Rose? It's like you get cut off in mid-sentence, you know what I mean? Maybe I won't mind to die when it comes, but I don't want to be cut off in mid-sentence."

"I can see that."

"I want to finish the sentence."

Rose did not come to work the next day which, by itself, was not alarming, but she did not answer when I called either, and when I drove out there at lunchtime, I found she really was not there. Her car was in the driveway, but the doors to her house were locked. Rose hardly ever locked her doors.

I had to find it out from Purdy she was at Carol's. "Tell me again exactly what Carol said, Mr. Hughes."

"Exactly?" Purdy was leaning against my desk with his feet propped up on a trash can in front of him, balanced between the desk and the trash can like a bridge. He was eating an apple, a big, red one, and every time he took a bite, he slurped up the juice so it would not dribble on his chin. " 'This has gone far enough.' That's what she said."

"What is that supposed to mean?"

"She also warned me not to expect Rose back at work. I suppose that means she's finally quit?"

"I don't believe this."

"Why don't you call her?"

So I did.

"Mother is sleeping," Carol said, then she hung up.

Hung up?

"She hung up on me, Mr. Hughes."

Just then the trash can tipped over, and Purdy fell. He lay sprawled on the floor in the middle of wads of paper, chewing-gum wrappers, and Styrofoam cups. "Shit."

"Are you okay?" I held out my hand to help him up.

He groaned. I helped him put the trash back in the can, and when we finished, he pointed to the phone. "Call her back."

"Mother is still sleeping," Carol said and hung up again.

I held the phone out in front of me and stared at it.

"She hung up on you again?" Purdy asked.

"Looks like it."

He finished his apple, tossed the core into the trash can, and wiped his hands on his pants. He said, "If you've got something you need to do this afternoon, I could watch the phones."

Carol's azaleas were in bloom, a wall of fiery pink and white along the house. When I got there, I realized I had never been to Carol's house without Rose. I rang the doorbell and started counting. On the eleventh ring, she opened the door and stepped onto the porch. "I told you," she said. "Mother is sleeping."

"She can't sleep all day."

"I don't know why not."

"What's going on, Carol?"

"Nothing."

Carol looked as if she had slept in her clothes. She peered out at the yard as if surprised to see the sun, then a look of alarm came over her face, and she marched down the steps and began hacking at a weed that was climbing up the side of one of the azaleas. I followed her. "I'm taking care of her, now," she said.

"All this running around; I can't have it." She twisted and yanked until, finally, the weed came loose from the ground. She marched back up the steps. "She is not twenty years old anymore even if she thinks she is."

"Just let me see her."

"I told you, she's sleeping."

"I'll wait."

"Suit yourself." She threw the guilty weed far out into the yard then slipped back inside, leaving me to stare at a closed door. I sat down on the porch steps. It was a steamy day, thick and windless. All over everywhere you heard people complaining about how we had skipped spring and moved right into summer, and that's exactly what it felt like.

Dickie pulled into the driveway. She waved to me but did not stop to talk, which was odd, because no bit of small talk was too small for her. She carried a casserole dish and hurried around to the back of the house without even saying hello.

In a few minutes, Alma came out. She sat on the steps beside me, carefully spreading the hem of her dress over her bare, browned feet, then tucking her long hair behind her ears, first the left then the right. I waited. She whistled, "Whew, it's too hot to cook."

"It's too hot to eat."

"You too? Jacob won't hardly eat a thing these days. I think it's got something to do with this school business. He doesn't like it. He's never been to school, you know, not real school, but I think he'll be okay once he makes friends, don't you?"

"Sure."

"He seems to be having trouble making friends."

"I could talk to him, if you want."

She patted my hand. "It's good to see you, Ruth. It's always good to see you."

"Tell that to Carol."

Alma nodded. "Carol thinks Mother is sick."

"Is she?"

Alma did not say right away. She looked out across the yard, then stretched her arms out and examined her hands. She had put a ring on every finger, which was new. I tried to remember, but I don't believe I'd even seen her in a wedding ring before. "Something's wrong," she said. She explained that sometime during the middle of the night, Rose had called Carol, who knew immediately that something was wrong. Rose was short of breath. "I don't know exactly what that means," Alma said, "but you know Carol; she doesn't take chances. And maybe that's a good thing, you know. Not to take chances."

"What do you mean, short of breath?"

"I told you, I don't know."

"So is she breathing or not?"

"She's still alive, isn't she?"

"How the hell would I know, Alma?"

Alma put her hand on my shoulder. "I suppose I could say she is weaker than usual. She does not seem to want to get out of bed, and that's not like Mother, you know. Carol thinks maybe we ought to keep her here for a few days anyway, just to watch her. I think that sounds okay."

"So why can't I see her?"

"You can," she said. "Just not now." She stood up and started to go back inside then stopped. "I am only asking you to be patient, Ruth. Just wait, okay? Not long. When Carol sees everything is going to be okay, she will calm down."

I did not have an answer for that.

"Okay?" she asked again.

I looked away. "Doesn't Rose want to see me?"

Alma came back to sit beside me again. She brushed the hair

out of my face the way you would comfort a child, but I pushed her hand away. "It's only for a few days," she said.

I nodded. I could feel her watching me walk across the yard. I got in my car and held on to the steering wheel. It probably looked to Alma like I was thinking something big, something important, but I didn't have one single thing to think about. I didn't know what I was supposed to do.

Eventually I went home to find a red Pinto with a rear bumper sticker that said *Ciao!* parked in the street in front of the house where I usually parked. Madeline. I tiptoed upstairs so she and Michael would not hear me. I pulled a beer out of the refrigerator. I even went so far as to open it, but then it sat, untouched, all night long beside my chair releasing tiny, golden bubbles.

Purdy tried to cheer me up. He caught me staring at Rose's empty desk and came over and sat down in her chair. He waved. "You okay?"

I nodded.

"She'll be all right, Ruth. This is Rose, you know. Everybody thought she was going to die two years ago, but she didn't."

He started bringing me candy bars. Snickers. Milky Way. Three Musketeers. PayDay. It wasn't like I had an appetite, but I could usually choke down a Milky Way. Once, as he sat in her chair, straightening some of the papers she'd left on her desk, he said, "She might be happier this way. I never thought she particularly liked advertising."

"She didn't."

"See there?"

Both of us sighed. Then Purdy said, "I didn't want to hire her. She was just this old lady with no ad experience."

"That's not true."

"You can't count the *Crier*, Ruth. Those ads walked in the door down there; I mean, where was the competition? Besides, she had run that one into the ground."

"You don't know what you're talking about."

"At least that's what we thought back then. What did we know? I figured I'd give her a couple of months then let her go, but you know what she did?"

"Tell me again."

"Outsold everybody. Outsold everybody who had ever worked here; she brought in more ads the first month than most people sold in three. It beat all." He shook his head and was quiet for a while, remembering. When he spoke again, he was not looking at me, but out the window at the street in front of the building. He said, "I'll tell you something I wish I had not done. First thing Rose wanted when she started working was a couple of weeks off, and I would not give it to her. It was policy, see? You had to work at least six months before you could ask for a vacation. I don't know why I was so stupid."

I didn't say anything, just let him talk.

He said, "There was something about going to Texas. I can't remember the details exactly, but it had to do with her father. Two measly weeks. I know later she went to his funeral, but after that she never took one single vacation in the whole time she worked for me that I can recall." He sighed. "Sometimes, Ruth, I think somebody ought to shoot me."

"I can see that. When did she start talking?"

"What do you mean?"

"You said when she first started working here, she wouldn't talk to anybody. So when did she start?"

He shrugged. "I don't know. Not long. Rose is one of those people who can't stay mad forever, you know."

On my way home from work, I liked to stop by the river and sit on the benches where me and Rose used to sit. I could not believe how much I missed her. It was almost worse than if she had died, knowing she was somewhere, and I could not see her, and the more I thought about it, the more it occurred to me; what if Mama was thinking the same about me?

For my twentieth birthday, Victor took me to Jack's by the River. He got himself a frozen strawberry daiquiri, and me, I ordered ginger ale. I found I could not stomach anything stronger anymore, and we sat at the bar telling Rose stories. I told him about sneaking through the woods to catch Fred Fish on the dragline, about the article Rose wrote, and finally, about Ed Stivers and Jackson and Fingers and how Fish had managed to get away.

"That's too bad," Victor said. "But you watch, somebody's going to get that guy someday."

"It won't be Rose," I said.

"No," he said. "It won't be Rose."

A few days later, Cecil walked into the office and stopped at my desk. "Carol's a Nazi," he said. I got him a cup of coffee and let him sit in the reception area with me. I noticed he had gotten himself a bath somewhere and clean clothes. Gone were the maroon pants and navy pea jacket, and in their place, cut-off army fatigues and a T-shirt that said, *Miami Dophins*. In the cutoffs, I noticed, he had skinny, hairless legs. He still carried his big tapestry bag and, reaching into it, he told me he had made something for Rose. He took out a long, wooden instrument, a flute, he explained, painted bright colors the way Rose would like, red and green and blue and yellow. He put it to his lips and blew a trill-like sound. Then he played a few softer notes like the beginning of a slow, sad song. People stopped working to listen. Purdy

peeked around the corner, and I heard someone behind him gig-
gle. "It's beautiful," I said, but Cecil was embarrassed and shoved
the flute back into the bag.

I phoned Carol's house six times, and six times she hung up,
but then she let me talk to Alma. "If you can tell me for a fact
that Rose does not want to see me, I'll leave you alone. Otherwise,
Cecil's here, and we're prepared to camp out in the front yard."

When Cecil and I got there, we found Rose in Carol's bed.
Beside it was a folding cot where Carol slept, a neatly folded
blanket at one end. Rose was buried in a comforter of pale green
stripes. Along the far wall was a kidney-shaped dressing table with
a matching pale green skirt and a gold-framed mirror. Cecil stood
in the doorway, unsure of whether to go in, until Rose said,
"Don't be a ninny." He handed her the flute and a small piece
of paper. A poem, of course. She fumbled with the flute but could
not make it play, although her eyes teared up when she read the
poem. I wished I had a poem. I wished I had something I could
give Rose.

Cecil sat down on the cot with the flute and started working
out the notes to "You Are My Sunshine." When I walked over
to the bed, Rose reached out her hand, and maybe there was
something wrong with her breathing, but there was nothing
wrong with her grip. She held on, and I held on, and Carol stood
at the foot of the bed folding towels. "Old people get like this. I
see it all the time," she said, as if Rose weren't right there in the
same room with us.

"Like what?" I said. But Carol did not answer that. She turned
and walked on out the door with the towels.

"Drop it," Rose said. "She's just one who loves her mother."

"Well, love's a funny thing," I said.

From the bedroom we could hear the sounds of Alma making

dinner and of Jacob watching TV. I sat down on the bed beside Rose. She told me she was feeling better and, mostly, that she was sorry to have worried me. That was the worst thing about being sick, she claimed, knowing who's out there worrying.

"Listen. When you're ready to move back home, just say the word, you hear?"

She nodded.

"I'll handle Carol."

Then here came Carol again, this time carrying a bowl of soup on a tray.

"You don't need to bring that in here," Rose said, "I'm getting up."

"Are you sure you should?" Carol said.

"Of course I should." Rose tossed back the comforter and sat up on the edge of the bed.

"Dizzy?" Carol asked.

"No," Rose said.

Carol looked back and forth between me and Rose as if there were foxes she could trust more. Then she said, "Where's Cecil?"

Sure enough, he was gone. The flute was lying on the cot where he had been sitting, but I could not have told you when he stopped playing it, or when he had stood up, or when he had gone out the door. I looked out the window and caught sight of him walking down the street. "I never even saw him leave," I said.

Rose had joined me by the window. "He'll be okay," she whispered, but she stood watching until long after he had disappeared around the corner.

Rose and I waited for dinner outside on the back deck. Used to be, you could sit on Carol's deck and see to the right and to the left, but the new bathroom addition blocked the view to the left, and that was okay. Now there was a feeling of privacy out there, which Carol had not intended, but it worked out. From the sky, the light was fading even though it would be some time before the sun went down. Rose handed me a present wrapped in a paper sack, folded and closed with Scotch tape. Inside was one of the ashtrays she kept on her coffee table, dog-shaped, with the red-plaid beanbag body and the little metal bowl on its back. I couldn't hardly say anything.

"I missed your birthday," she said.

"I can't take your ashtray, Rose."

"You're not taking it; I'm giving it to you. Now you'll probably go and quit smoking."

"I ought to."

"Yes, you should."

"You ought to, too."

Rose and I watched a neighbor's cat creep into the yard. He was a big cat with mottled gray fur, and he moved slowly, with his eyes straight ahead, ears stiff, muscles twitching. At first we could not see what he saw, then, suddenly, he pounced. It was a small bird. He ran with it to the back of the yard then put it down in the grass in front of a large, white azalea bush. The bird did not move. The cat batted at it as if it were a rubber toy, then looked away as if it did not mean a thing to him. In trees all over Carol's yard, dozens of birds screamed.

"Bad cat," Rose hissed.

"I'm going to get that bird," I said, and marched into the yard. Only when I was almost next to the cat did I wonder what I would do if it charged me back, but I lunged, shouting, "Go away," and the cat ran off. I picked up the bird and took it to Rose and put it in her hands.

"It's a song sparrow," she said.

"Is it dead?"

She brought her hands to eye level. "I don't think so."

She stroked the bird the way you would stroke a pet, a dog or a cat, and she held out her hands for me to try it. I did once, but it gave me the creeps thinking how easily I could crush its tiny bones, so I let Rose do it. She was humming; I could not tell what song, then she stopped and said, "I almost died once, did you know?"

"No, Rose, I don't think I do."

She nodded. "Before my brother Frank died. Diphtheria. Frank had the influenza, but I had diphtheria, and everybody thought I was the one who would not make it. My mother would not let me go to Frank's funeral because of it. I will never forget; she said she could not bear to lose, you know, two of us."

Rose's voice weakened for a second. I waited.

"She got a neighbor woman to take care of me, Mrs. Loretta Almeida, I can see her now. She had a mole on her face that used to scare the dickens out of me." Rose stopped again and peered into the bird's face. "Would you look at this, Ruth, he's got his little eye open."

I looked, and she was right. "Maybe he can hear you, Rose."

She shook her head. "Frank was such a good artist, so talented. I always thought he was going to be the one, you know, to make it big. Everybody did. We all admired Frank. There's no telling how far he could have gone."

She took up stroking the bird again. "I remember as clearly as if it were happening right here, Ruthie, the day my mother and daddy got home from the funeral. It was dark in my room, but my door was open, and I could see them in the parlor. They thought they were alone. Daddy was sitting in a chair, holding his head in his hands, but when my mother walked by, he looked up, and they stared at each other for a long time. I was holding my breath; it seemed like forever. Then my mother, it was as if she suddenly folded down onto him, and he held her there against his chest. I don't remember a single sound, only the sight of them stays with me, but it was the saddest thing I think I ever saw. Then, of course, it wasn't long before my mother . . . she was gone, too."

The bird opened its other eye, and for a split second, I swear it looked right at Rose. Then, faster than a gasp, it flew away. One minute, near-dead, the next, flying high, and me and Rose looked at each other like we could not believe what we knew we had seen. We scanned the yard, but we never saw that bird again.

"You know what you ought to do, Rose? You ought to write a book. You don't even have to write it, just tell it to me, and I'll do the writing. That's what you ought to do."

She didn't say anything.

"It'd be a good book, Rose."

She nodded. Alma called for supper, and I stood to go, but Rose stayed where she was for a minute longer. Then she looked up at me. "No, Ruthie," she whispered. "I believe what I want to do is go on back to Texas."

23 | LEAVING TOWN, PACKING LIGHT

The problem with sneaking off to Texas with somebody's mother is, if she dies, you've got to tell them.

Carol. Rose and I are here in Mount Claire, North Carolina, and she's dead.

No. Better to start with Alma.

Alma. Rose and I decided to take a little trip. But she died.

Perhaps I should begin slowly.

Did you ever know, Alma, that Rose wanted to see Texas one more time?

We did not leave right away. A week went by, and I asked her, "When, Rose?"

"Soon."

Two weeks, then three, and I asked again, "When is soon?"

The truth was, by then I did not want to go anymore. The closer we got to leaving, the more I realized that if I took Rose to Texas, I would lose my job, and I did not want to do that. It was a feeling that snuck up on me, but as soon as the thought crossed my mind, I knew it was true: I liked my new life. I liked my job,

and what was even more amazing, Purdy liked the job I was doing. He told me so one day, although not right out. He said, "If
that Roger Bailey gives you any trouble, you let me know," which
was not how he had treated receptionists before me, no way. The
day a receptionist went against a client like Roger Bailey would
have been her last day on the job, but that's what he said to me,
plus there was the part about him giving me a raise. I liked living
by myself. I liked doing what I wanted, when I wanted, without
having to explain it to anybody, and I did not want to start over.

How could I start over, and where? In Texas? I could not
picture myself in Texas, but I sure could see how, if Texas did
not work out, I might end up back in Tennessee. This was the
problem with taking Rose to Texas; I did not know what would
happen.

Although all around me things were changing, even in Lawsonville. Jackson Price was the first to go. He left suddenly
to work for a big newspaper in Charlotte; no two-week notice,
no farewell party. On Friday he told us, and on Monday he was
gone. Then Ed Stivers announced he would be leaving at the
end of the summer to take a job with a newspaper somewhere
in Pennsylvania. His wife was happier than anyone had ever
seen her, already talking about restaurants in Philadelphia, although Purdy pointed out, "Where they're going is nowhere near
Philadelphia, but let's just let her find that out when she gets
there, eh?"

Then Deborah Hoffman quit her job in advertising to move
to Raleigh and work in her sister's Hallmark Card Shop after her
husband, the Marine, left her for a young woman he met in Long
Beach, California. Deborah's departure was the saddest for me
personally because, unlike Jackson Price and Ed Stivers, I could
not say for certain she would be okay. Sad also because I did not

think anyone would miss her. On her last day, I took her to lunch and asked all manner of questions about those sons of hers, and I listened to every word.

I told Purdy, "It's not even the same newspaper," but he said don't worry. "People come; people go, but nothing really changes around here. Stick around for as long as I have, and you'll see."

"I hope to," I said.

Madeline moved in with Michael. They invited me down for drinks several times, but I always came up with a reason not to go. Michael stopped me on the stairs one day just to tell me how happy he was. "I am so happy," he said, looking deeply into my eyes as if to prove he wasn't kidding.

"Great," I said.

"I give it two months, max," was what Victor said.

Alma joined St. Paul's Episcopal Church which, she said, fit her better than Dean's religion, whatever it was. Rose helped her get a job at the Humphries House. Alma got to wear a costume that made her look like somebody who lived two hundred years ago, and she spent her days talking to tourists and working on a real spinning wheel. I went to see her. It could almost fool you. One night she let me try on the costume, and Carol stood back and could not get over how me and Alma were the same size even though there was more than a twenty-year age difference between us. We giggled, and I could not quit looking in the mirror. Alma told me I looked beautiful, but she was probably just saying that.

Dean never tried to get Jacob back. After a few weeks, he no longer even asked to see him, which suited Alma and Carol and Rose, but I didn't know. I worried about Jacob. He hardly ever said anything, and I had begun to notice that he never, ever looked you in the eye. It was like he was somebody walking on a newly frozen pond, never sure when he was going to fall through, but as far as I could tell, no one else saw it. Sometimes I would go over there with a package of Jiffy Pop, and we'd eat popcorn and play a game of Parcheesi or else watch TV. That was the summer me and him got hooked on baseball. We didn't care who was playing; we'd watch. I bought him a glove, and one day he showed me how you throw a curveball, but I think I was the only one he showed.

Fred Fish must have finished the boat canal, because it was said around town that Ted Hardaway bought himself a new boat.

The day Rose was ready to go to Texas turned out to be the second of July, Larry's birthday. Larry was dead by then. He had died young, which Rose said could not have been a surprise to anyone, although there was no glamour to it. That was the surprise. He simply dropped dead from a heart attack in his own front yard. It was Eleanor who sent the news, Eleanor, who as Rose pointed out, *was probably a very nice person when you got to know her.* Eleanor had sent Rose the small, framed sketch Larry had drawn of a beach, which had hung all these years on her living-room wall. I remember the first time she showed it to me, she said, "It looks a lot like the coast off Bland, Texas. I never knew he could draw."

"So, Rose," I said, "you're sure you want to do this?"

"If you're sure it's not any trouble . . ."

Once again we were sitting on Carol's deck, Rose in a gauzy, orange shirt with bell-shaped sleeves that was way too big for her. She had shriveled these past weeks so that her body now seemed to end in points, her cheekbones, her shoulder blades, her elbows and hands, her tiny legs. She had taken to brushing her hair straight up like a porcupine, and there were places her skull showed through, but her eyes were still bright and clear. She was not forcing me. I could do what I wanted.

"It's no trouble, Rose, I promise."

"Because I could go by myself."

"If you want to go back to Texas, I want to be the one to take you."

"You're sure?"

"I'm sure."

The day before we left, I stayed at work late cleaning my desk. I threw away old papers, stuck pencils in the pencil holder, stacked note pads in the drawer. I straightened phone books, dusted the desktop. I peered around the corner and saw Purdy still sitting at his desk, which was odd. Purdy hardly ever stayed late. Next to the phone was a sticky spot that would not come up with a rag, so I scraped it off with an X-Acto blade then looked around the corner again. Purdy was still there. I walked over to his office. "Can I come in?"

He was putting a new watchband on his watch, the old one, broken, in front of him. I sat down. "Need help?"

"I've almost got it," he said.

"I'm going to take Rose to Texas."

He nodded, but kept working.

"Tomorrow," I said.

He looked up.

"And, Mr. Hughes, it's a secret, okay? So you can't tell Carol or anybody, but especially Carol, at least not until we get a decent head start. It's what Rose wants. So I have to do it, don't you see? Rose would not ask me if it were not important." I watched Purdy as he let it sink in. "I was thinking, though. Maybe I could still have my job when I get back?"

"You won't be back," he said.

"Yes I will, Mr. Hughes. I promise."

I could tell he did not believe me. I looked down at my hands, took a deep breath, and whispered. "I don't have anywhere else to go."

He nodded, then went back to working on the watch.

"Does that mean yes?"

"We'll see," he said. "If you come back."

"I'll be back, Mr. Hughes, you wait and see. And remember, don't tell Carol."

He let me stand up and turn around, but before I got out the door, I heard him say, "Be careful, Ruth."

I peeked into the newsroom to find Stivers, but he was not in his office. Earlier that day I had bought him a good-bye present, a wooden puzzle shaped like a dragon. I had seen it in the window of a small store downtown in the tourist section near the Humphries House. It stood reared up on its hind legs, tiny forelegs batting the air, mouth open as if it could not wait to hurl fire. I knew it was a toy made for children, but right off I had thought of Stivers. I could not make up my mind whether to really give it to him, though, because, if you remind people of a dragon, you're probably not going to want to know about it. In the end I decided I did not care. I placed it on his desk, no note. I figured he could just guess who sent it.

Later, though, I wondered if I shouldn't have left a note. Stivers had a lot of girlfriends, I had discovered, and he probably got presents from all of them. I wondered how he hid them from his wife. Maybe he had a special closet. Maybe someday she would open it.

What's all this?

I picked Rose up at five o'clock the next morning under a streetlight at the end of Carol's street. She was sure nobody heard her leave the house. She carried one small suitcase and a raincoat.

We made it halfway to Raleigh under the stars and watched the sun come up in the rearview mirror. We drank coffee and smoked cigarettes, figuring there would be time to quit in Texas. We stopped for breakfast at a McDonald's just outside Raleigh, although we should not have gone in. I told Rose I was fine to go through the drive-through, but she said she was not eating biscuits in any car. So we stopped. That's when my car died.

"Gas?" Rose asked, but the gauge said only half-empty. "Have you checked the oil?"

"It's not the oil, Rose; it's the battery."

"Alma blew her car up once driving it without oil." Rose said. "The engine melted. Dean said it was God telling her she should not drive a car."

"It's the battery, I promise."

We were lucky, at least that's what the girl behind the counter at McDonald's told us, because George Amos's Piedmont Auto was just down the street, although it took them over an hour to send a tow truck. I did not feel lucky. We sat on orange plastic chairs in the customer-service area with old magazines and a television tuned to soap operas. I bought us Cokes and a bag of M&Ms. Rose was nervous like I had never seen her before. She could not sit still, and every so often she would peer through the small glass window at the top of the door.

"I don't even see your car," she said. "You reckon they finished it already and just forgot to tell us?" She was coughing bad, hacking coughs that ended with spurts of gagging. I took away the M&Ms and went to fill a cup with water from the water fountain. When I got back, Rose was studying a map. "Let's go this way," she said, pointing.

I looked. She was tracing her finger along mountain roads in the southwest section of the state, which were narrow, curvy, and difficult to drive. I knew because I, too, had studied the map. "That way will take us right through the mountains, Rose. We don't want to go that way."

"It's shorter, see, Ruthie? This other takes us way north and too far out of the way."

"But it's all freeway, Rose, so it ends up being faster."

She drank the water. "It doesn't look faster."

"You're going to have to trust me, Rose."

She handed me the empty cup. "Let's go there anyway."

It was late afternoon by the time we got back on the road and long past supper time when we came to the Little Swiss Inn in Mount Claire, North Carolina.

Alma. *Are you there, Alma?*

Alma, listen to me.

She's dead.

So I am driving west again. I almost imagine I can still see Lawsonville in my rearview mirror down this straight shot of a road. I never got used to how flat the land is here, like you could stand in one place and see a hundred miles if it wasn't for trees. It makes the sky feel close, like there's a lid over everything. But I cannot see Lawsonville anymore, only tobacco, soybeans, and miles and miles of tall, straight pines scraping against this wide, blue sky.

Rose always told me there are some things you got to do in this world to be a good person. You don't always know what's going to happen; you only know you have to do the right thing. One right thing after the other. Sometimes it works out.

I had wanted to take Rose's ashes to Texas. It was an idea that came to me in the hospital lobby in Mount Claire, where they took Rose after I called the manager of the Little Swiss Inn and told him, "You might want to come over here." I had waited there all night for Carol and Alma, watching the sliding glass doors whoosh open and close from my post of two chairs pushed together. I was braced for whatever Carol had to say. *I'm going to wring your neck,* was what I expected, but it was not that bad. They got there around four in the morning, and maybe now that she was dead, and there was nothing else they could do, they were resigned to it. Rose died of a heart attack. The doctor said it might have happened anyway, even if we had not tried to sneak off to Texas, and besides, the cancer was going to get her soon, the cancer which, yes, had come back, that had been coming back and spreading all this time. To hear this news, a nurse had put us in a small room with white walls, green chairs, one window, and pictures of baby deer on the walls, a room we shared with other knots of worried people. When the doctor left, I took a chair across from Carol so I could look her in the eye.

"How about we cremate her and take her ashes back to Texas."

"We will do no such thing."

"I think it's what she would want, Carol. She was going home to Texas to die. I've been up all night thinking about this, and I am pretty sure of it. It's not her fault she didn't make it. We could scatter her ashes over the beaches of east Texas."

"So people could step on them while they're swimming?"

"We'd figure it out."

"No."

"I'll take them," I said. "You don't even have to go. I can leave right after the funeral."

"Now you listen to me. There aren't going to be any ashes, do you hear? I have not always been the nicest person in my life, but I will never burn up my own mother."

"Carol, she's already dead."

"I want her in the ground in a place I can visit. Texas is not a place I can visit."

Alma put her arm around my shoulder and whispered, "It's a

little thing, Ruth; let her have it." Then she sighed and, looking out the window, said, "I have always loved the mountains. What a beautiful place to die."

So Rose went back to Lawsonville in a hearse. She would have hated that.

The funeral service was outside under a tent with rows of white, cloth-covered chairs placed in a semicircle. The coffin was silver. The day was sunny, and the grass was a color of deep green that could make you think summer never ends. There were more people there than I ever knew, more than came to the Rose Appreciation Day party, more than I had ever seen gathered in one place. I stood in the back with Purdy.

Victor got us a minister from St. Paul's, although I did not know why. Rose never needed one when she was alive, why would she want one now, but I didn't dare tell that to Carol. I could hear her now, *Yes, Ruth. But Rose was not your mother.* I could not bear that. I could not bear it at all, not even if she was right.

Carol stood by the casket in a sea of flowers. She was not crying, although her eyes were red. Other than that she looked okay. Not falling apart or anything like you might think. Alma sat by herself at one end of the front row making it clear she did not exactly welcome company. Jacob was at the other end, also alone. Carol walked over to him. She took him by the hand and led him to the casket, which was closed, and they put their hands on it and talked. I saw Jacob nodding, then I think I saw him smile, and when he looked up, he searched the crowd until he saw me, then he waved. Other people came by, and Carol talked to them as if she were the one giving out comfort and not the other way around, and I was sorry Rose could not see it. Maybe Rose was right. Carol just loved her mother is all. There's worse. Just before the service started, she walked all the way back to where I stood to bring me a single pink carnation.

"There's so many anyway," she said.

Rose was buried next to Raymond in a cemetery behind a Methodist church on the closest thing to a hill as you're going to get in Chocowin County. The best thing about it was you could see the river. Not a lot, just a sparkle in the distance, but you knew it was there. The minister said nice things about Rose, and maybe they were all true, but I was thinking he could have said the very same things about anybody, and they would have been true, too. So I quit listening to the minister and started thinking about my friend. Rose. With the wild, red hair, and the back curved over like the letter "C," who wore funny earrings and pink tennis shoes, who made the best tomato sandwiches ever. Rose. Who once stood on a dead man, who hid from Pancho Villa, who got on a bus in Wilmington and never looked back, whose voice spoke the truth better than anybody. Rose. Who had a friend named Cecil, who had a friend named Victor, who had a friend named Opal, who had a friend named me. When I began to cry, it was Purdy who held my hand.

Good-bye, Rose.

I went back to my job at the *Lawsonville Ledger* with my own metal filing cabinet, my white plastic in and out box, and my drawer full of pencils, pens, and paper clips, but first I asked Purdy for a week. He said I could have longer, but I told him a week's long enough.

I have passed Raleigh. I have passed the McDonald's where my car broke down. I have passed George Amos's Piedmont Auto Shop. I have passed the exit that would take me south to

Mount Claire. I am not going to Mount Claire this time. I am crossing the mountains of western North Carolina on a freeway built through rock, driving fast, driving across an invisible line into Tennessee.

I wish I had told Rose about my mama.

I think Rose would have liked to hear about her. She would have said, *Tell me the stories, Ruth,* stories about Mama and Margaret and William. About Umbrella Rock and Homer Birdsong. About Durwood and Mabel Jones and even my daddy, whom I never knew. But Rose is dead, and all the words I never said are busting out of me now through tears I cannot stop as I drive on a freeway under a sky so high you can't even think about touching it. You can't think there might be an end. It's like she's still with me. Here in the front seat of my car, sipping coffee from a Styrofoam cup. It's all I can do not to say out loud, *Listen to this, Rose. Listen.*

Because I am worth a story. Everybody is. Ask Rose.

The road to Summerville is narrow and winding, a good place to learn to drive is what you hear. *If you can drive the Summerville Road, you can drive anywhere.* I could do it with my eyes closed. It is near sundown. There is kudzu, the smell of honeysuckle, the sound of eager crickets warming up. I turn into a gravel drive.

I see her through the window. She is looking out exactly the way I have pictured a million times, one hand parting the curtain, face set like chiseled stone, like someone who might still want but will not hope. She has heard my car on the gravel. She opens the door and steps onto the porch, but there she stops, one hand on the railing, the other across her chest. It is as far as she will go.

I finish my cigarette and wait for the engine to die. It takes a while. When it quits, I open the door, lean down, and stamp out the cigarette butt on the gravel beneath my feet. I stare at my shoes, the door a shield between me and her. I don't say anything, and neither does she.

But the longer we go on in silence, the more it feels like a dream. You can't go on living like that forever.

I stand up.

"Hello, Mama."

READING GROUP GUIDE

1. What makes the friendship between Rose and Ruth successful? Do you think the difference between their ages makes a difference to their friendship?

2. Of all the characters in the book, which one do you empathize with the most and why?

3. Compare and contrast Rose's relationships with her daughters to Ruth's relationship with her mother.

4. How do Ruth's feelings about her mother change?

5. Discuss the different ways the characters in the book view Rose. What does this say about our society's attitudes toward older people?

6. Why do you think Ruth pushes Rose into another confrontation with Fred Fish? What do they get out of this venture?

7. Why do both Rose and Ruth keep secrets, and what purpose do those secrets serve in their lives?

8. *Some Days There's Pie* is written from Ruth's point of view. What can you learn about her personality from the way she talks?

9. What does Ruth want to accomplish by going home to see her mother?